"I need a beer. Care to join me?"

Hank meant to say no—after all, he still had a full night ahead—but what kind of host would he be to say no? Or, for that matter, what kind of guest?

The bottle was halfway to his lips when Brynn made a small sound. "Crap! I always forget. Would you like a glass?"

"No, thanks. This is fine."

"You're sure? I'm a horrible hostess, sorry. I never remember the gracious touches."

It was so unexpected—the organizational queen, forgetting something—that he felt himself relaxing. Maybe even grinning. "You're feeding me, and you made my kid happy. I can't think of anything more gracious than that."

A slight hint of pink rose in her cheeks, spreading down her neck to the creamy bit of skin visible in the V of her jersey. It was an intriguing sight, for sure. He could swear there was a little freckle at the point of the V. Or maybe it was a fleck of sauce. He couldn't tell. Neither could he pull his gaze away.

Dear Reader,

My mother was one of ten girls, I came from a family of four kids, and I have five or six children of my own, so family is a topic that is near and dear to my heart. Nothing beats a family for intrigue, secrets, politics and shifting alliances, all mixed with need, support and love. There is no stronger system in the world—and no greater source of fodder for a writer.

Mwahahahahaha.

Writing this book took me back to the days of my childhood, when all my best friends were related to me. I remembered sleepovers with cousins. Secrets with siblings. And our family's famous Beach Days, when as many of us as could make it would trek to Rock Point Provincial Park on the shores of Lake Erie for an afternoon of swimming, barbecuing and togetherness. I remember wanting to trade a burger made by my mother for one from my aunt Verna, who made hers exotic by adding an envelope of onion soup mix to the meat. I remember stopping for ice cream on the drive home and having my first taste of mint chocolate. I remember the way the sand stuck to our skin and the slap of the waves as we jumped through them and the green-and-white pattern of the folding chairs my parents would bring with them. Were those days perfect? Anything but. But it is impossible for me to think of my childhood without my family, for they were my world.

I hope that as you read this book, you, too, will remember close ties with loved ones, and that you will become part of my reading family by visiting my website, www.krisfletcher.com. I'll save one of Verna's burgers for you.

Yours,

Kris Fletcher

KRIS FLETCHER

—

Dating a Single Dad

Recycling programs
for this product may
not exist in your area.

ISBN-13: 978-0-373-60861-4

DATING A SINGLE DAD

Printed in U.S.A.

ABOUT THE AUTHOR

Kris Fletcher has never organized a festival or conspired to make someone fall in love, but she is a big fan of dairy products and considered it her duty to learn how to make homemade ice cream as part of the research for this book. Her husband still tears up when he recalls the roasted strawberry-rhubarb with dark chocolate flecks. Oh, the hardship.

A four-time Golden Heart finalist, Kris grew up in southern Ontario, went to school in Nova Scotia, married a man from Maine and now lives in central New York. She shares her very messy home with her husband and an ever-changing number of their kids. Her greatest hope is that dust bunnies never develop intelligence.

Books by Kris Fletcher

HARLEQUIN SUPERROMANCE

1845—A BETTER FATHER
1886—NOW YOU SEE ME

Other titles by this author available in ebook format.

Heartfelt thanks and smooches are gratefully bestowed upon:

My children, especially those still living at home, for understanding that the word "deadline" has many different meanings that Mr. Webster never intended.

My husband, Larry, for being on board with easy meals and a messy house, and for making it possible for me to do this job that I love almost as much as him. And for listening to me that time it really mattered. I'm very glad we get to keep you, hon.

The folks at Express Computer Service, who have saved my computer bacon more times than I can count.

The Barenaked Ladies, for *Boomerang*.

The Purples, for listening to me freak out and reminding me, in the lovingest way possible, that I am a total dork.

My agent, Jessica Faust, for understanding author eccentricities (aka total dorkiness).

My editor, Piya Campana, for not freaking out after reading the early plans and incarnations of this book, even though she had every right to do so.

And my brother Ed for burning my Pop Tarts all those years ago.

CHAPTER ONE

BRYNN CATALANO HANDED her weeping cousin another tissue from the decimated box and wished for a fat little Cupid to descend from the clouds so she could pop him straight in his twisted kisser.

"Taylor..." What was she supposed to say? She had started the visit braced for an afternoon of Taylor, this month's *Brides* magazine and a lively discussion of peplums versus trains. Not that she had any idea what a peplum might be, but hey. Fake it 'til you make it, that's what she always said.

But those plans had gone out the proverbial window when Taylor walked into Brynn's cozy basement apartment, burst into tears and announced that she had to break her engagement because she was in love with her fiancé's brother. Somehow, Brynn doubted that her usual routine of "have a Band-Aid/hug/margarita" would cut it this time.

"Maybe you're just lonely," she said gently. "After all, Ian's been in Tanzania for a long time now."

"Eight months." Taylor wiped her eyes. "But,

Brynn, come on. Real love wouldn't change in that amount of time, even without the Carter factor."

Brynn hooked her little fingers together. This wasn't the time to point out that Taylor had spent a good part of her life complaining about Carter North and his inability to grow up. In fact, just last year, Taylor had said that Carter made the cast of *The Hangover* look like models of maturity.

No. It was better to focus on the real relationship. Not the one that only existed in Taylor's head.

"Listen, hon. You're absolutely right that true love wouldn't disappear in a few months' absence, but that doesn't mean it couldn't, oh, shift. Change. What you're feeling is probably nothing more than… I don't know. Confused hormones. You know. Ian is gone but his brother, who looks and sounds and probably smells like him, is still here. You're just transferring what you feel for Ian onto Carter."

Taylor let her head drop against the back of the sofa, looking cool and blonde and elegant even as she stared blankly at the ceiling.

"I wish I could believe that. But you want the truth? I think it was the other way around. I think… I mean, Carter was an idiot for most of his life, I know. But it's like the seeds of what he is to me now were there all along. I think that what drew me to Ian were the things that I could see in Carter, but they weren't really there yet, you know? Then he came back from law school and everything had settled into place, he was finally who he is supposed to be, but I was already going out with Ian. And then Ian left. And now I see Carter and I think, oh, dear Lord, this is what I was looking for all along...."

The tears began flowing once again. Brynn handed over another tissue.

"It's such a mess, Brynn. I feel like I'm living this giant lie, but I can't do anything about it until he comes home. Every night I pray that I'll wake up in love with Ian, and every day I go to work and see Carter and boom, it hits me all over again."

"Wait, Carter works at Northstar, too?"

A watery smile flitted across Taylor's face. "When they say the dairy is a family business, they aren't kidding. All the brothers work there. Their parents, too, and even their grandmother. The only one who doesn't is Hank."

"Who's he?"

"The youngest. You know. His little girl was supposed to be my flower girl."

"Oh, right. The one whose wife ran off someplace out west." Brynn shook her head free of the extraneous Norths and focused on the only one that mattered at the moment. "Back to you. Does he have any idea how you feel?"

"What? God, no. That's the last thing I need, for Carter to know that I— No. Nothing."

"That's all well and good, but I was talking about Ian."

"Oh." Taylor bit her lip. "I don't think so. I still talk to him as much as ever, and email, and all that. He might have been suspicious when I stopped talking about the wedding, but I said something about waiting until he came home so we could plan it together. That seemed to help."

Considering that Taylor had been planning her wedding since the moment she was able to say the words *I do,* her sudden refusal to discuss it should definitely have been a tip-off.

Brynn needed to think, which meant she needed to move. She pushed herself out of Old Faithful, the battered recliner that had accompanied her on every move she'd ever made, stretched and patted Taylor's shoulder.

"I need a beer. How about you?"

"Do you have any white wine?"

"You've been my cousin my whole life and you have to ask me that?"

Taylor sighed and slumped against the sofa once again. "Fine. At least tell me it's light beer."

It was so easy to tell that Taylor hadn't grown up in a house full of brothers.

"Of course it's light." *Note to self: pour Taylor's drink into a glass.*

Alone in her bright yellow kitchen, Brynn opened the fridge, grabbed a couple of bottles and surveyed the shelves. Taylor was a lightweight, and she'd been crying a lot. She probably needed food. There was that pint of Cherry Garcia… But no. That had met the business end of Brynn's spoon last week.

Another look, another sigh. She knew how to cook a hearty meal with four ingredients and twenty minutes, but she had never mastered the kind of fluffy food that Taylor preferred.

Nor was she loaded with experience to help her cousin. Unlike Taylor, Brynn had never been swimming in admirers. As a teen she'd been needed at home too much to date. Her family obligations had lightened up over the years but it still seemed there were more crises than relationships. And oddly enough, whenever she did dip her toes back into the social pool, there didn't seem to be many guys who could keep up with her no-bullshit approach to life.

So no, she didn't have a lot of personal knowledge of matters of the heart. But she had the desire to help and the ability to make a plan and carry it through. Those, she was sure, were the skills that would go furthest in helping Taylor. They had always worked so far.

Her mind made up, Brynn grabbed a block of cheddar, tossed it on a plate and added a sleeve of crackers. Then, her mother's admonitions in her head, she removed the crackers from the paper, arranged them in a circle around the cheese and balanced a knife on the side.

Martha Stewart was undoubtedly quivering in her hand-tooled Italian leather boots.

She poured Taylor's beer into a mug, shoved her own bottle in one pocket of her sweatpants and the opener in the other, grabbed everything with ease—thanks to a college career spent waiting tables—and sailed back to the sofa. The good news was that Taylor had stopped crying. The bad news was that she still looked as wan and lifeless as if she'd been plucked from the mondo snowbank that loomed outside Brynn's window, pressing against the glass like it was contemplating a career in breaking and entering. Ah, the joys of winter in eastern Ontario.

Spring couldn't come fast enough.

Brynn set the food and drinks on the old trunk that served as her coffee table, opened her beer and indulged in a long, steadying swallow. Then and only then did she trust herself to respond with the brisk compassion she knew was needed.

"Okay. This is a pickle, no doubt about it, but we can fix it."

"I can't think how." Taylor eyed her beer. "Except maybe with mind-altering drugs."

"You only wish. The answer is going to be harder, but trust me, it'll be worth it. All we have to do is make you fall in love with Ian again."

Taylor choked on her drink. Oops. Maybe that hadn't been the best timing.

"Haven't you heard anything I said? I don't love Ian. I probably never did. I'm in love—"

"With Carter. Yes, I know. But, Tay, come on. Don't you think it's suspicious that you never started seeing Carter in this new and dazzling light until Ian was gone?"

Taylor's eyes reddened, but at least she didn't start crying again. Nor did she have an answer.

"You said yourself, you think that the things that attracted you to Ian are the parts of Carter that hadn't bloomed yet. Well, maybe you got it wrong. Maybe the things you liked about Ian are what you were really looking for."

"I don't think that made any sense."

"Of course not. That doesn't matter. Do you trust me?"

Taylor nodded, though without as much vigor as Brynn would have liked.

"Here's what we're going to do. You said you don't want to break up with Ian while he's gone, right?"

"It's not that I don't want to—not that I *do* want to, of course—but I can't do that to him now. He's doing such good work there helping people start their own businesses, but he's all by himself. No family, no real friends. I can't do that to him when he has no one to help him through it."

Personally, Brynn saw that as a sign that deep down, Taylor wanted to stay with him, but this wasn't the moment to mention that.

"Totally understandable. When is he coming home?"

"The middle of May."

"So that gives us four months. I propose we use

that time to get you back on track. You think you aren't in love, but my bet is that you are and it's just…hibernating." She waved a hand toward the snow-covered windows. "We just have to wake you up."

"There's nothing—"

"Taylor Belle Hunter, stop yourself right there. You can't tell me you have absolutely no feelings for Ian."

"Well, of course I do. I might not be in love, but he's a great guy and I still care about him."

"Good to his family?"

"Absolutely."

"Thoughtful and considerate?"

"Definitely."

"Good in bed?"

"Brynn!"

"Sorry. Couldn't help it." She snagged a piece of cheese and popped it in her mouth. "The thing is, he's an awesome guy, you do have positive feelings for him, and they probably run a lot deeper than you think. All we have to do is rekindle what's already there."

"But I—"

"Taylor. What is your plan?"

"Wait until he comes home. Fake my way through a week of hell while he gets back on his feet and the family throws a giant centennial celebration for the dairy. Then tell him the truth, pack my bags and leave town."

"What about Carter?"

Taylor drew in a long breath that turned into a choking kind of sob. Brynn gaped at her.

"You weren't going to tell him?"

"What would that accomplish? I'm doing enough damage as it is. I'm not going to rip the family apart that way."

Brynn sank slowly back into the recliner. She was far too familiar with the hurt that came with families falling apart. Taylor was right.

"What about you?"

Taylor's shrug didn't fool Brynn for a minute. "It's not like I'm the first woman to find herself in love with the wrong man, right?"

Hell and damnation. Brynn hauled herself out of the chair and over to the sofa, where she put an arm around Taylor's shaking shoulders and pulled her close.

"Oh, sweetie," she whispered as she rocked Taylor like a child. "Let me help you. Let me make this right for you."

"I've tried, Brynn. I really have."

"I know you have, honey. I know you don't want anyone to get hurt. But just…let me try. I don't know how yet, but I promise you, I will come up with something. All we have to do is make you want Ian again. That's the key to fixing this mess. To make you love him."

"I don't know, Brynn." Taylor wiped her cheeks.

"You're the queen of organizing and all that, but I don't think even you can manage emotions."

Ha. Taylor had no idea that emotions were Brynn's area of expertise, at least for herself. She had taught herself to ignore fear, fake confidence and feel nothing but a pitying kind of contempt for her own father. Emotions, she knew, had to be controlled, lest they end up controlling you.

But she was willing to concede that it wasn't that cut-and-dried for everyone else.

"Maybe I can't. But honestly, sweetie, what's the worst that could happen? Best-case scenario, you end up happily married to a man you love beyond reason. Worst case…well, I don't think it could get worse than what you already have planned."

Taylor hiccupped before nodding—slowly, cautiously, but a nod nonetheless. "You're right. There's no way it could be worse."

"That's my girl." Brynn gave Taylor's shoulders another squeeze, this time a lot more happily, and pulled a pen and small notebook from her pocket. Now they were getting into the parts she liked— less talk, more action, more chances to make things better for people she loved. "Okay. This would be a lot easier if you lived here in Kingston instead of way the hell up there in Comeback Cove, but we have weekends and—"

She stopped as Taylor made an odd little squeak. "What?"

"I have an idea. To maybe make it so there's not an hour's drive between us."

"You're going to move here?"

Taylor laughed for the first time since walking into the apartment. "No, you goof. But I might be able to juggle things so you can come to Comeback Cove."

"If you're suggesting I quit work and sponge off my brother now that he's living up there, too…"

"No, no. Relax. But isn't your job due to end soon?"

"Probably. That's the thing with temp jobs. They're always ending soon." She winked. "Don't want to wear out my welcome, you know."

"And you know that's why you love them."

True. Let other women search for security and routine. Brynn was all about the next challenge, the next adventure. Or, as was so often the case in her family, the next crisis.

"Do you have your next job lined up yet?"

"Nothing definite." Brynn raised crossed fingers. "But Paige—remember her? My second cousin on the Catalano side. She's pregnant again. I filled in for her first maternity leave and it's ninety percent certain they'll want me to do it again. That's not until late June, though, so I have an opening in my incredibly high-demand schedule. What do you have in mind?"

"I have a meeting tomorrow," Taylor said slowly.

"I think, maybe, I can swing something that will work out to everyone's benefit."

"And you're not going to tell me what you're plotting?"

"Not yet."

Brynn pointed the pen at Taylor. "This would be a lot easier if you didn't look exactly the way you did the time you dragged me down to the graveyard to howl at the old folks walking by. I swear I couldn't sit down for hours after your mom got through with us."

"Oh, relax. I'm trusting you with my heart for the next four months. You can give me a day."

When she put it that way—when she grinned the way she used to, the way, Brynn realized with a shock, she hadn't grinned in months—there was no way to refuse her. Not that Brynn had ever been able to walk away from a family member in need.

She would never wish calamity on her loved ones, but when, life being what it was, it happened—well, it was kind of nice to know that she was the one they trusted to make things better. The one they needed.

"Okay, kiddo. It's a deal. You work on your nefarious plot and I'll search the internet for love potions." She put her pen to the paper. "Operation Sleeping Beauty is officially under way."

HANK NORTH LOOKED around the conference room that overflowed with family members—some laughing, some eating, all of them talking and moving and offering up their opinions—and wondered why he bothered wearing earplugs while working with power tools. There wasn't a chain saw on the planet that could compete with a roomful of Norths.

"For the love of God, people." His grandmother Moxie, usually the only one who could corral this group, sat at the head of the table with proverbial steam coming out of her ears. At the other end, his dad glanced at Moxie, but continued gesturing with a doughnut while arguing with Carter and Cash about the Leafs' lousy attempt at defense during the previous night's hockey game. Hank's mom was singing a song about cows with Hank's daughter, Millie. A laptop beside Taylor sat open in readiness for Ian's Skype call. In short, it was a typical North family gathering—loud, out-of-control and likely to erupt into a complete snort-fest at any moment.

Taylor, though, seemed to be sitting this one out. Usually she would be chatting up Moxie or singing with Millie, but this time she sat in the corner beside Dad with her arms crossed and a funny kind of smile on her face—almost as if she were laughing at some private joke.

Well, at least she was being quiet about it.

Hank pulled his phone from his pocket and checked the time. Ian was due to call in fifteen minutes, and the family had yet to iron out any of the items on Moxie's list. This wasn't gonna be pretty.

A loud *smack* cut through the hubbub, silencing everyone in midsentence—midlyric, in Millie's case—and caused everyone to swivel their heads to where Moxie stood glaring. The shoe in her hand and a dirt mark on the table were all the evidence needed of the source of the noise.

"Now, listen." Moxie pointed the loafer at each of them in turn. "We have a festival coming up in four months and none of you are taking this seriously. For pity's sake, people, we know how to work together. Why are you making this so difficult?"

The silence following her statement would have been encouraging if not for the way Cash nudged Carter and snickered.

"Boys!"

Oh, hell. Now they were in for it. Moxie was about two steps away from a full-fledged snark attack. Hank pushed his chair back a bit, ready to hustle Millie out of the room if needed. She insisted that she was old enough to be part of the meetings now that she had turned seven, but he wasn't sure he was ready for her to see her uncles quivering in fear when Moxie unleashed the Furies.

"You two," Moxie began, only to be interrupted by Taylor pushing up from her chair.

"I'm sorry. Could I have everyone's attention for a minute?"

Well, *that* got people to shut up. Family lore had it that Carter had interrupted Moxie once, back when he was a kid. Millie had asked him about it a couple of years ago. Hank had never known it was possible for a grown man's voice to go that high.

Maybe this meeting was going to be worth the drive into town after all.

Taylor turned the laptop to better face the table before drawing a deep breath and giving everyone a nervous smile. Dad cleared his throat and glanced meaningfully at Moxie, who seemed to be gathering thunderclouds in preparation for hurling. Taylor blinked.

"I'm sorry. I shouldn't have interrupted, but I have an idea that I think could help us. Moxie, could I present it to these folks before Ian signs on and we have to focus on him?"

Ah. Well done. An apology, a reminder of the absent fiancé and the promise of help. Taylor might yet be allowed to live.

Moxie narrowed her eyes. Millie reached for the edge of the baggy white shirt she wore over her jeans and sweater, rubbing the fabric in between the fingers of one hand. Her free thumb popped into her mouth, prompting a nudge from Grandma and a stifled sigh on Hank's part. Taylor rested one hand on the laptop. Her left hand, he noticed, angled so the big family diamond was winking right at Moxie.

Damn. He never knew Taylor had it in her.

At last, Moxie nodded.

"Thanks." Taylor smiled. "Everyone, I think it's no secret that we're in trouble. We want to do this festival. It's the perfect way to thank everyone in Comeback Cove for one hundred years of business. But we're all so busy with our own jobs, running the dairy, and going to school—" she smiled at Millie, who glowed and let the thumb slip from her mouth "—and getting those cabins ready for tourist season, and, well, I think the festival isn't getting the attention it deserves."

Ma nodded. She had said almost the same thing to Hank just last week.

"I admit, I'm not sure why this is so much harder for us than running the dairy. Maybe because everyone has been doing that for so long that we all know our roles, but now…" Taylor shrugged and checked the clock. "Anyway. Here's my point."

"Amen," muttered Cash. Carter elbowed him hard.

Taylor continued as if there had been no interruption. "I think we need help with the festival—someone who can make it her top priority and ride herd on us. Someone who is organized and efficient and capable of keeping a bunch of very opinionated people in line."

Silence descended once more. The other adults in the room looked at Taylor in various degrees of bewilderment, surprise and admiration. Millie had given up on the adult talk and was singing softly to the car that had come with her drive-thru dinner.

Hank tipped his chair back and struggled to keep from laughing out loud as the impact of Taylor's words sank in. He loved his family, he really did, but they weren't accustomed to being told they were messing up. Which, in essence, was what Taylor had just said in her ever-so-diplomatic way.

Moxie spoke first. "Are you telling me, missy, that we need an outsider to take charge of our family dairy's celebration?"

"Yes."

Good for Taylor. She didn't even blink.

"Sounds like you have someone already in mind." Carter's words were tight and clipped.

"As a matter of fact, I do. My cousin Brynn. Here's her résumé." Taylor pulled papers from a folder and passed them to Dad, who took one before handing them to Carter.

Cash whistled. Dad sent him the "shut up" look.

"Taylor. It's an interesting proposal, and I see why you think we need someone to rein us in, but this is how we work. Everything will come together. We don't need—"

"I like it."

Hank let his chair drop to the ground at Moxie's pronouncement. Judging from the way assorted North jaws were sagging all around him, he wasn't the only one taken by surprise.

His mother leaned forward and stared at Moxie. "Mom? Did I hear that right? You, of all people, want to turn this over to someone not family?"

"Hell to the yes." Moxie pulled her shoe off the table at last and tossed it on the carpet with a muffled thud. "Taylor's right, Janice. We all have too much on our plates already. This festival needs to be special. One hundred years in business is something to celebrate, and it should be done right. The way we're carrying on, we're going to come to the weekend of the festival and it'll be just us standing in the park because Cash forgot to advertise it and Carter didn't get the insurance. And Mr. Silent over there will spend the whole time playing invisible, then sign Millie up for a soccer game so he doesn't have to think about it at all."

Hank's cheeks burned. Pegged again.

"I'll give you that." Ma tapped her pencil against the legal pad in front of her. "But Taylor—your cousin?"

Cash rolled his eyes. "Ma. Come on. Don't tell us you're worried about nepotism."

"Of course not! But I...well...this is a very unique project. Taylor, I know you wouldn't recommend her unless you believed her capable, but the fact is, family can... Let's say, you can be surprised by their actions at times."

Oh, hell. That was directed at him, he was sure of it. Ma still wasn't happy about his decision to leave the dairy last year. He shifted in his seat and let his hand settle on Millie's wild mane of hair—a steadying reminder of why he had made his choice.

"You don't need to worry about Brynn. She's the most organized person on the planet. And as you can see from her résumé, she has a wide variety of experiences to bring to Northstar."

"She doesn't stay in one place very long, does she?" Ma squinted at the paper.

"Brynn loves pushing herself. She prefers to take on special projects, short-term positions, maternity-leave replacements—jobs that will let her try new skills in new places. She also knows how to keep people in line, which I think is what we need most."

"There's a challenge if I ever heard one," Cash muttered.

Taylor's smile was the kind that a cat might offer up to a mouse in the seconds before pouncing. "I wouldn't advise it, Cash. I think I might have mentioned my cousin the hockey player, right? The one who was in the NHL and who now lives here in Comeback Cove?"

Hank sat up straighter. The twins exchanged glances—Cash's worried, Carter's intrigued.

"You mean that guy who bought Camp Overlook?" Moxie asked.

"That's her brother," Taylor said. "I have personally seen her guilt, convince and persuade him *and* his teammates into doing what she needed them to do. Even the guys who spoke only Russian or Finnish couldn't get around her."

More looks were exchanged. Chairs shifted. Papers rustled.

"We wouldn't need her for as long as most of her projects," Moxie said. "We're talking three, maybe four months. Is that enough to make it worth her while?"

Taylor glanced at the laptop. Her smile wavered slightly before she met Moxie's gaze.

"The one thing Brynn loves more than a new adventure is her family. Half the reason she takes those short-term jobs is because it gives her more flexibility to help them when needed. Working here would be a new experience and let her be close to both me and her brother. Who, I might mention, would be extremely willing to lend extra support to the festival with Brynn at the helm."

"So you're saying we'd get someone who could whip these sorry asses into shape, take the bulk of the work off our hands and bring in a bona fide celebrity to fancy up the celebration." Moxie folded her hands and sat back. "How much will she cost us?"

"She's not cheap. But I had a thought. Since it's so short-term, maybe we could offer her a reasonable salary and sweeten the deal by providing housing."

For the first time since taking the floor, Taylor looked straight at Hank. It took him a second to grasp her meaning. But as every face in the room turned toward him, the lump of dread building in his gut told him he had interpreted her words correctly.

"The hell I will."

Cash snorted. "And it finally speaks."

"Cash, leave your brother alone." Ma drummed her fingers on the table. "You're right, Taylor. It would make sense to provide housing. But wouldn't she want to stay with you?"

Millie sent her car zooming across the table. "Daddy says Auntie Taylor's place is so small, you have to go outside to wipe your—"

"That's enough, Mills." Time for another talk about boundaries. Judging from the look on his mother's face, Hank was going to be on the receiving end of one himself.

As soon as the laughter had died down, Dad piped up. "It's up to you, Hank."

No way. Hank had spent his entire life playing catch-up—as a sibling, a husband, a father. This time he wasn't going to be rushed into something on someone else's timetable. He was already pushing himself to get the cabins in shape before tourist season kicked in. The last thing he needed was to have to drop everything else to prepare for Wonder Woman.

"I'm not open yet."

"You're not charging her," Taylor pointed out. "It's not like you have to be officially open and ready to roll."

"They all need painting. Most have holes in the roofs, and I'm only halfway through replacing the windows."

"For crying out loud, Hankie," Carter said. "You don't need to have all ten cabins ready. Pick the one that's in the best shape and get it spiffed up. You'll probably have a couple of weeks, right, Taylor?"

She nodded. "And I can help. Either with the painting or with…um…making sure you have the time to get it done." She glanced at Millie, who had returned to driving her car in circles.

"You know," he said mildly, "half the reason I bought the cabins was to have *more* time with certain people who are pretending to not listen. Not less."

Moxie rolled her eyes. "Oh, for the love of biscuits. We're talking two weeks. You live and breathe the child as it is. It'll do her good to have some space, maybe hang out with Taylor for a bit."

He wanted to tell Moxie she was off her rocker, but he couldn't. Because he knew too well that families could become claustrophobic. He didn't want to do that to her.

And even though he wanted—*needed*—a little distance between him and his family, the fact was, he did owe them. That was the other reason he had left the dairy and bought the cabins—to stop being a burden on them. To stand on his own two feet. There was no way in hell he would have made it through the years since Millie's birth and his divorce without his family, but it was time to turn that around.

It would be nice to be the one helping them for a change. He could never repay them completely, but it wouldn't kill him to do this.

He looked at Millie, clad in the old shirt that she had claimed as a lab coat, her hair a halo of kinks he had never learned to tame, pushing her toy car back and forth. Maybe if they let this Brynn into the cabins, it could be good for Mills. A low-pressure way to learn how to deal with the people who would be coming and going all the time once he opened. A test case, as it were.

"This cousin," he said to Taylor. "She's not a diva, is she? Because even if I go full out, the place is going to be rough around the edges for a while. I won't have time to cater to her."

Taylor beamed. "Brynn's idea of a good time is a cold beer and a hockey game on TV. I don't think you have to worry about her."

"Let's do it," Moxie proclaimed, and as if a switch had been flipped, everyone started talking again.

Hank let the voices rush over him and tried to suppress the feeling that Taylor's assurances sounded a lot like something that would have been uttered by the captain of the *Titanic*.

CHAPTER TWO

Two weeks later, Hank stood in the middle of the Wolfe cabin and took in the changes with a critical eye. The missing bits in the fieldstone wall had been replaced, the wood floors were free of sawdust and thanks to a stretch of decent weather, he'd been able to open the windows long enough to clear all scents but a faint hint of fresh-cut wood. Taylor had added some throw rugs, ordered him to buy bed linens in some color he called red, but she insisted was cranberry, and hung curtains at the windows.

All in all, the place didn't look bad. Kind of cozy, actually. And just in time.

Millie rushed in from her observation post on the porch. "She's here!"

"Already?" *Crap.* Taylor had promised she'd be on hand for the move-in. Why did Brynn have to be the punctual cousin?

He reached for his phone, ready to tell Taylor to get it in gear, but Millie grabbed his hand. "Come on. We have to go see her."

"Easy, Mills. Let's not bowl her over in her first thirty seconds, okay?"

Millie huffed out her impatience with his adult ways. "Daddy. This is important. We have to make her like us. She's our first guest. Our test…" Her nose wrinkled as she obviously struggled to remember his description.

"Our test subject? Is that what you're trying to say, my little scientist?"

Her nod sent her glasses sliding down her nose. "Yes. Our first person. So we have to do a really great job with her, so come *on,* Daddy." Tiny hands fastened on his behind and pushed. "Let's go."

"All right, all right. Take it easy." It figured. The one time he would have welcomed some company there was none to be found. He would have to muddle through this on his own. The story of his life.

He shrugged on his jacket, took Millie's hand and headed outside. A little blue hatchback sat at the end of the path he had cleared of snow. Yowzers, he hadn't seen a car stuffed that full since he moved into his first university dorm.

"Hello." He kept his voice hearty and brisk as he approached the car. "Welcome to Northwoods Cabins."

The door creaked open. He spotted reassuringly serviceable boots—no heels, no suede—followed by long jean-clad legs. A head of dark hair followed. At last she emerged, giving him the full picture—one of those Icelandic sweaters the cross-country skiers loved, a hint of curves beneath the intricate design and a smile so dazzling it kind of knocked everything else out of his head.

"Hi!" Her voice was brisk also, a bit lower than he expected and friendly enough to ease Millie's grip on his fingers. "I'm Brynn. I take it my cousin is late, as usual?"

"Sure looks that way." He remembered his manners and stuck out his palm. "Hank North. This is my daughter, Millie."

"Good to meet you." Her hand closed over his. A flash of something—heat?—made him step quickly back, but she had already abandoned him to crouch in front of Millie.

"Hi. I'm Brynn. I know some people say you have to call adults by their last name, but Miss Catalano is just too long for anyone to say, so I'm good with Brynn. Or if your dad has a rule about that, I can be Miss Brynn, but that makes me feel like a teacher—" she glanced up at him, letting loose that smile once more "—so I hope we don't have to use it."

Taylor's words about this woman coercing Russian hockey players to do her bidding took on a terrifying new significance. When she beamed that way, all warm and accepting and as if what she were asking was the most reasonable request ever made in the history of the world, well, it was easy to see how convincing she could be.

Millie pulled her thumb from her mouth. "Hi, Brynn." From the way her eyes were shining, he was pretty sure that "Brynn" had become another way of saying "the most perfect person in the universe."

"Let me guess." Brynn smiled as she tipped her head to one side, studying Millie. "I think you must be in grade...three. Maybe even four."

"Two." Millie's smile dimmed and her little shoulders hunched. Hank frowned. Was it his imagination, or did she do that every time anyone mentioned school lately?

"Only grade two?" Brynn placed a hand on her chest in mock astonishment. "I could have sworn you were older."

That, at least, brought the light back to Millie's eyes.

"So this is the place?" Brynn straightened and looked around. Hank braced himself as her gaze roamed over the snug cabin surrounded by winter-bare trees. She nodded and smiled once more.

"It looks adorable. I can't wait to see the inside." She moved toward the back of the car and popped the hatch. "By the way, Hank, Taylor told me you had to do some quick-time work to get ready for me. Thanks so much. I promise I won't drive you crazy with special requests or anything now that I'm here. My goal in life is to be as low-maintenance as possible."

She probably intended for her words to reassure, but instead they set off a warning bell. In Hank's experience, when someone felt obliged to assure him they would never do something, he could expect the precise opposite.

Millie's first subject might be more of a test than either of them had expected.

Brynn lifted a suitcase from the back. "Millie, could you lead me to my new home?"

They headed down the path, Millie chattering as if she had just been reunited with a long-lost friend, Brynn nodding and asking questions. He grabbed a box from the car and followed. He reached the cabin in time to see Millie grab Brynn's hand and yank her to the center of the room.

"Mills," he called, but he might as well have saved his breath.

"Okay. This is the living room, but it's the kitchen, too, okay? Because see, it's all one big room, but all the parts are in different corners. Aunt Taylor calls it open something." Millie shook her head. "I don't remember. But it sounds good. So here is your couch and here is your table, and here is where you can put your TV if you want one. Daddy says guests don't get TVs. But you're not a regular guest, so I think you will want one, because, you know, that's the only way you can watch *MythBusters*."

"Oh, I watch that on my computer," Brynn said, and Millie froze in place.

"Really?" Her whisper was more reverent than anything he'd ever heard from her in church. "You watch *MythBusters*?"

"All the time. Did you see the one where they

tried walking across banana peels? I laughed so hard."

"I did! I loved that! And when they did the thing about the guys who escaped from—you know, that place, it was Alacrat—"

"You mean Alcatraz?"

Millie's expression shifted from hero worship to complete and total adoration. It was time for him to step in.

"Uh, Brynn? If you get Millie going on this topic, you're never going to have anything resembling a life, if you know what I mean."

She waved his words away. "Oh, please. Like life would be worth living without *MythBusters?*" But she must have caught his underlying meaning, because she pointed to the freestanding island he'd installed the week before. "That looks like a great place to cook."

"Yes. This is your kitchen." Millie puffed up again and led the way, shrugging off her parka as she walked. Hank tensed when Brynn's gaze lingered on the ragged fake lab coat—accessorized today with a ruler and a plastic thermometer peeking from the breast pocket—then let out a slow breath when her lips spread in an indulgent smile.

Shirttails flapping, Millie proceeded to open every drawer and cupboard, offering a running narrative of the things Brynn could either find within them or add to them. He sidled over to Brynn and nodded slightly in Millie's direction.

"Don't feel you have to encourage her, okay?"

"Not a problem. But you're the dad. You call the shots."

It was ridiculous, the way those simple words warmed him. Yeah, he was Millie's father. Biology said so, and the divorce agreement made it clear that he was her primary caregiver. But just because it was on paper, it didn't mean everyone agreed. This was a nice change from what usually happened, when folks would ask him for his opinion, then check with his mother when he wasn't around.

"And now, this way!" Millie flew down the short hallway. Brynn hurried to follow, Hank tagging along with his hands in the pockets of his jeans, praying for Taylor to show up soon.

"There's the bathroom. I guess you know what to do in there."

"Millie!"

"Sorry, Daddy. Okay. This is the extra room. Aunt Taylor said you needed an office so we gave you this cabin 'cause it has an extra bedroom, but she helped us find a chair and table and stuff for you so you can work here. Do you like it?"

Brynn stepped into the room. He watched the way her gaze lingered on the furniture, the slight tilt to her lips as she took in the light from the window falling across the table. It seemed the lady liked what she saw.

Unexpected pride warmed him. He'd been more nervous about her reaction than he'd realized.

"See this?" Millie skipped to the wall where Taylor had instructed Hank to mount a giant whiteboard. "Aunt Taylor said you had to have this really bad. It was important. And it works, too. Me and Daddy played tic-tac-toe on it when he put it up there."

"That was very responsible of you to test it. Did you try out all the stuff?"

Millie sighed. "I wanted to have a sleepover in your bed, but Daddy said that would be wrong."

God, shoot him now.

"Well, that was very kind of you to offer to try it, and very…um…nice of your dad to protect my privacy."

"Yeah, but it really is the best bed. Better than mine. Mine has a dumb old plain top, but yours has this curvy thing, like… Wait, let me show you."

Again, she grabbed Brynn and yanked, this time with a force that pulled a little *yip* from Brynn's mouth as she raced to keep up with the child.

"Millie, don't kill Brynn on her first day here, okay?"

"Right." Brynn's voice was breathless but still tinged with laughter. "Let's wait until I've had a night in this gorgeous— Oh, wow."

They had reached the entry to the main bedroom, where Millie scampered ahead to display the beauty of the cherrywood sleigh bed with all the grace of a pint-size, bespectacled Vanna White.

"See?" She tapped the curve of the footboard. "Isn't it so pretty?"

"It's probably the most amazing bed I will ever sleep in." Brynn smiled at Millie. "It must have been very hard to stay away from it. You get super bonus points for listening to your dad."

"I'm a very good listener."

"I bet you are. Now, I brought my favorite chair with me. Could you help me pick out the perfect place for it?"

"Oh, yes!" Without so much as a glance in his direction, Millie grabbed Brynn's hand and took off down the hall. Voices and hints of laughter floated back to him. For a moment, he let himself enjoy it. He couldn't remember the last time Millie had been so enthusiastic about something that didn't involve a magnifying glass or some kind of chemical reaction. It was good to hear her giggling like a regular little kid. Not that he wanted her to be anyone other than herself, but still.

No, it looked like the biggest challenge facing him now wasn't keeping Ms. Catalano happy, but keeping his daughter from falling head over heels for someone who was going to leave in a few short months.

BRYNN WASN'T AT ALL surprised that Taylor was late to help with the move-in, arriving well after quiet Hank had hustled his adorable daughter back to their place. She'd been prepared for the tardiness.

What did catch her off guard was the thermos of premixed margaritas that Taylor dropped on the counter as soon as she walked in.

"Rough weekend?"

Taylor shook her head. "Rough month, rough day, rough...whatever. Let's just say, it's gonna feel good to help you unpack and exert some brute force on some things for a while."

"Not that I can't sympathize, but you know, I kind of like my stuff. Maybe I'll do the heavy lifting and you take care of the 'getting drunk' part."

"Yay, teamwork." Taylor raised a glass of pale green liquid and downed half of it in one swallow. Brynn took in the shaking of her cousin's hands, the tightness of her movements, and decided that further questioning could wait until the alcohol had kicked in.

"Actually, Hank already dragged in the worst of it. I tried to convince him he didn't have to, but he just shrugged and kept hauling. He even carried Old Faithful in all by himself. Is he always so silent and chivalrous?"

"Quiet, yes. But chivalrous?" She wrinkled her nose. "I've never thought of it, but yeah. I guess he is, in a way."

Brynn had a feeling there was a story behind those words, but she wasn't sure she should hear it. Not when she was going to spend the next few months living in close proximity to the man. Years of short-term jobs had taught her the importance of keeping the work ties loose.

Though when Hank had bent forward to grab a box from the far reaches of the hatchback, she couldn't stop herself from noticing that the stretch of his jeans had highlighted one very fine hind end. One very fine, very single hind end—which happened to belong to a member of the family that now employed her.

Nope. She wasn't asking anybody anything about Hank. Wasn't going to wonder who else in the family had that thick chestnut hair, wasn't going to ponder how he would look without that faint line of stubble along his jawline. Instead, she crooked her finger and led Taylor down the hall to the bedroom and the suitcases that awaited.

"That Millie's a sweetie. Chattered nonstop. How long has she been on the science kick?"

"As long as I can— Oh, damn. You didn't mention your thing about *MythBusters* to her, did you?"

"She brought it up first. I was just being friendly."

"You're never going to get rid of her."

Brynn shrugged and removed a pile of sweaters from the suitcase. "No hardship there. She's a cutie. It's okay with me if she pops in once in a while."

"Oh, Brynn…"

It wasn't Taylor's words that made Brynn look up from the dresser where she was nestling her sweaters. It was the way Taylor hesitated that caught Brynn's heart.

"What is it?"

"It's just that… I really like Millie. The whole family. And it's killing me that I'm going to have to leave them, you know?"

Brynn took an instinctive step, but Taylor shook her head.

"Don't. I'm barely hanging on as it is. I don't want to… Having you here is wonderful, don't get me wrong. But all of a sudden this is real. I'm going to have to go. And I…"

Brynn's throat tightened.

"If this doesn't work, and I do have to leave, will you stay on? Do my job for me until they can hire someone else?"

"Oh, right. Because they would want to keep seeing the person who helped pull the wool over their—"

"Brynn, please. This is important. Will you do it?"

On one hand, Taylor was supposed to be thinking positive thoughts, marshaling her focus on the outcome they wanted. On the other hand, if she was thinking about the job, she wasn't thinking about Carter.

Maybe.

"Sure, hon. If it will make this easier for you, and if they would want me around, then yes. Of course."

"Thanks." After a long moment, Taylor blew out a very loud breath and had another slug of margarita. "Anyway. Enough about me. Be careful with Mills, okay? Her best friend moved over Christmas and she's been having a rough go of it since then. Not that she was ever one of the popular kids, you know?"

"More power to her."

"Well, yeah, you and I can say that now. But when you're little…" Taylor shrugged. "She's not your average second-grader."

"Yeah, you usually don't see little kids running around in lab coats."

"Oh. That." Taylor ran her finger along the edge of her glass. "Don't say anything to her about it, okay? Or to Hank. That shirt was Heather's."

"Who?"

"Millie's mom."

Ooooooh. "I thought Mom's been gone for a while."

"Most of Millie's life, but there are visits. The last one was over Christmas. It takes her a while to get back on track."

Poor little mite. Brynn had found it hard enough to cope with a family breakup when she was a teen-ager. She could only imagine the toll it would take on a little one.

"Well, not to worry. When she comes here, she can revel in total accepting geekery. Or, if she wants to try life on the other side, we can do our nails and watch *Tangled* until we wear out the disc." Brynn closed the drawer and brushed her hands. "Okay, kiddo. You're here, I'm here, there's nobody else around. It's time to commence making you fall in love again."

"This is silly. You know that, right?"

"You agreed, Taylor. It's part of the deal."

"I know." She sighed. "Honestly, I don't have very high hopes. But I promise to give it my best. God knows if there's a way to avoid the hurt that's staring me in the face, I'm all for it."

Well, that was better. Even if Taylor did nothing but follow directions, reluctant or not, Brynn had no doubt that she could make this happen. She'd pulled off harder things in her life than helping a woman fall back in love with a man who used to be the center of her world. Taylor might think it was hopeless, but Brynn was convinced it was a piece of cake. Wedding cake, to be specific.

"Okay. The first step is research. I need to learn all about Ian. More specifically, I need you to tell me everything that ever attracted you to him. What little things does he do to make your heart go pitter-patter? What's the sweetest thing he ever did? How did you first know you were in love with him? Give me ten words to describe him."

"Brynn—"

"Taylor."

"Fine." With a long sigh, Taylor uncurled from the chair, moved to the bed and stretched out full length.

"Hey! I haven't even tested that yet. You do not get to be the one to break in my bed."

"This is serious work, Brynn. Emotionally draining. I need to be supported."

"Support, my ass," Brynn said, but she rooted through the box marked Operation Sleeping Beauty and pulled out a notebook and an ancient tape recorder she had liberated from her mother's basement.

"Is that what I think it is? I haven't seen one of those in years."

"Yes, it is, and you seriously don't want to know how hard it is to find cassette tapes these days. Start talking."

"Fine." Taylor wriggled deeper into the pillows, making Brynn grit her teeth in envy. She'd stayed up way too late packing, and that bed was far too tempting. Though if Taylor was on it, Brynn couldn't sack out and crash, so maybe this was better. "Any particular place you want me to start?"

Brynn glanced down at the notebook full of hastily scribbled ideas. "At the beginning, of course. Your first memory of Ian."

"Um…let me think. That's a tough one."

"Two margaritas shouldn't lead to this level of impairment, Taylor."

"Bite me. I just can't remember a time when he wasn't in my life. I've known him since I was born. My mom and his mom went to high school together."

"So when you say you've known him all your life, you're not exaggerating."

"That's about it."

Well, this might be a bit more difficult than anticipated. How could she help Taylor pinpoint the magic, when the magic had been with her every day?

"So were you in love with him all your life?"

"No."

A simple answer, but there was just enough of a twist to the way Taylor drew the word out, almost dubiously, that made Brynn's ears perk up.

"Elaborate."

"Well, when we were kids, he was kind of on the outskirts of my circle. We saw each other when our folks got together, but there were two elementary schools, so we weren't part of each other's day-to-day lives."

"You wouldn't have been anyway, right? Isn't he a couple of years older than you?"

"Right. He's Greg's age. And since you know how much girls like to hang out with their older brothers when they're growing up…"

Brynn snorted. "Tell me about it. Sam couldn't decide if he was supposed to protect me or sacrifice me to the hockey gods, so he usually did both."

"How did he do that?"

She shrugged. "Put me in goal, shot pucks at me, then swooped in with an ice pack when I got hit."

"Oh, that must have made for a secure childhood."

"It had its moments." At least, until it fell apart. But they weren't supposed to be talking about her.

"Okay. So when did you know that things had shifted with Ian?"

"Um…oh, hell. Promise you won't laugh?"

"I swear."

"Well…I was seventeen. It was his first year of university, and I hadn't seen him since the summer, maybe earlier. He walked into church and he looked so…different. It was like he'd been… You know how, in the movies, the king will pull out his sword and tap the dude on the shoulders and say, 'I dub thee Sir Fancy Pants,' and they stand up and you could swear the guy's standing a little taller? It was like that."

Brynn had to swallow the lump in her throat. "That's beautiful, Taylor."

"Yeah, it was a pretty amazing moment." Her laugh was short. "But, Brynn, I was seventeen. And it turns out that I wasn't the only one who had been glad to see him come home. His old high school girlfriend had finally slept with him just the night before. So all I was seeing was afterglow."

"Must you try to kill any hint of romance that ever existed in the world?"

"Well, no. Because like I said, I was a kid. It was all very romantic and magical, and I fell like that." She snapped her fingers. "The thing is, I don't think I was falling for Ian the person. I was falling for the whole idea of love and romance. He was just the rack that I hung my dreams on. Not like—"

Taylor bit her lip and Brynn knew what she was going to say: *not like with Carter.*

"It wasn't like that with him, was it?"

Taylor shook her head. "But we're not supposed to be talking about him."

Brynn sat on the bed, a small corner of her brain noting how utterly sinkable the mattress was beneath her. She couldn't wait to curl up beneath that fluffy comforter and indulge in an hour of reading when this day was over. "You're right. Talking about Carter won't be helpful." She drew in a deep breath and hoped she wasn't shooting herself in the foot. "But it might be good for me to know what draws you to him. So for the next ten minutes, you can tell me all about him. Anything. How it happened, how you knew things had shifted, the whole works. We're going to lay it all on the table so we can deal with it. And then we're going to stop talking about stupid men and finish off those margaritas and laugh for a while, okay?"

"Sounds like a plan."

"Okay. Ten minutes. Go."

"I won't need that long."

This was interesting. Taylor had always needed at least three sentences to say what Brynn could say in one.

"Go on."

Taylor pulled a pillow onto her lap and hugged it close. "Ian is a wonderful, wonderful guy. Honestly, if anyone were to put him and Carter together and rate them on their amazingness, Ian would probably win, hands down. He's more classically attractive, he's great with kids, he's more outgoing and charismatic. He's got this air about him that makes people just, you know, like him."

"And yet?" Brynn twisted her fingers and waited. Whatever this was, it was key. If she wanted to help her cousin find her happy ending, it was important to have all the facts.

"It's like this. Ian is like a suit you put on for work. You can feel comfortable in it, powerful and happy and all those good things. But at the end of the day, you still want to come home and put on the clothes that call to you. Sweats. Jammies. The ones that are so soft and comfortable that you barely notice them." She looked up. "Ian is the most amazing suit I will ever wear, Brynn. But it's finally becoming clear to me that I'm not a suit person."

Brynn reached for the margaritas. This cake might not be so easy to slice after all.

CHAPTER THREE

ON THE WEDNESDAY MORNING after her arrival, Brynn took a deep breath and walked into Taylor's office in preparation for her first meeting with the entire North clan. She had been in and out of the office over the past couple of days and been introduced to all the players, but this would be her first real test. Her stomach danced a slow jig of anticipation. She'd gone over all the materials given to her by Taylor and had pulled together some ideas that she knew were solid. The hard part would be convincing the family members that she wasn't trying to get rid of their plans, but rather wanted to focus on the best ones.

The *really* hard part would be to get through this meeting without being a total bitch to Carter. Logically, she knew that none of this was his fault, and that he was unaware of Taylor's dilemma. But logic didn't keep her from thinking that everything would be fine if he would just get lost. Or maybe meet someone and run off to Vegas. Or do something so devoid of morals that Taylor would never again look at him with anything other than disgust.

That was Brynn's personal favorite scenario. After all, it had taken just one act of supremely selfish moral cowardice to shred her love for her father. Imagine what such an act could do to a mere crush?

Taylor was alone. She sat behind her desk with a faraway look on her face, barely stirring when Brynn walked in.

"Morning," she said softly. Taylor merely blinked.

"Hello? Taylor?" Brynn waved her hand in front of her cousin's face, grinning at the way Taylor startled. "Welcome back to the land of the living."

"Sorry. I was…"

"Long, long ago, in a galaxy far, far away?"

"Something like that."

The words were light. The misery in Taylor's eyes was not.

"Hey." Brynn glanced into the hall, but seeing no one approaching, she took the chance of slipping around the desk and giving Taylor a light squeeze around the shoulders. "We'll get through this. I won't leave you, I promise."

Taylor smiled faintly and poked at the papers in front of her. "I know. I'm so glad you're here."

"Me, too." Even though she hated the circumstances, she wanted—needed—to be here. *Wait and see* were not words she could live by, at least not when it came to her family. She had to help.

Her father used to tell her that the world would keep spinning if she sat down, but she never quite believed him. Maybe because he usually followed it up with, *Get out of here, Brynn. You're not needed.* And a laugh that never quite struck her as funny.

She shook away the memory and pulled a flash drive from her pocket. "Here you go. The next step in Operation Sleeping Beauty."

Taylor shook her head but smiled as she took it. "What is it, a how-to manual?"

"Music. The songs you associate with him, plus some from when we were silly romantic teens for good measure."

"Thanks." But there was little enthusiasm in Taylor's voice as she dropped the device into her purse.

This wasn't good. Brynn knew her efforts wouldn't be an overnight success, but she had hoped for a slightly more encouraging reaction.

"While we have a minute, I need some more info. Tell me about food."

"Brynn, I really don't think this is going to—"

"Taylor, you promised to give this your all. So all up, kid. What foods?"

"Well…he's a pretty typical guy. Steak. Shrimp. Pasta."

Brynn shook her head. "Deeper. What foods did you prepare for him? Where did you go to eat? Did he ever feed you cotton candy or kiss chocolate off your mouth or anything like that?"

"Isn't this just a little bit kinky?"

"Oh, yeah. I really get off on hearing the details of my cousin's sex life, you betcha." When Taylor blushed, Brynn hurried on. "Look, I know this isn't comfortable for either of us. But food is highly associated with romance, so if I'm going to do my job, I need to know what kinds of things you—"

"Hot chocolate."

"Sorry?"

"Hot chocolate. I'm always cold in the winter and he made it for me."

Brynn stole a piece of paper from Taylor's desk and began scribbling notes. "Homemade or from a mix?"

"Homemade, mostly. With a little almond syrup in it. Half and half." She sighed. "He really does make it better than anyone else."

"Did you have a special mug?"

"Mmm, no. Just whatever was handy."

"Marshmallows or whipped cream?"

"Whipped—" she began, then broke off in another blush. Brynn assessed her over the rims of her half-glasses.

"Seriously?"

Taylor's shrug was as fluid and graceful as everything else she did. "What can I say? He would make a big bowl of whipped cream, and there was always tons left over, and, you know, waste not, want not."

"I think I get the picture." And now she would never be able to get it out of her mind, unfortunately.

"Um…Baileys Irish Cream has some pretty potent associations, too."

"Okay, I think that gives me plenty of material." But Taylor was in her own world again.

"Kung pao chicken. And doughnuts. How did I forget those? Oh, yeah. Ian has a real fondness for doughnuts. But only ones with a hole in the middle, if you get my—"

She stopped abruptly. Brynn looked up from her notes, ready to give thanks to whatever deity had brought this rush of Too Much Information to a halt, but stopped when she saw the look of utter horror on Taylor's face as she stared at the door.

Say it isn't so.

When she turned to follow Taylor's gaze, Brynn saw exactly what she had feared most: the doorway was filled with Norths, covering the whole spectrum of emotions. Moxie sported a sly smile, Carter had his eyes closed as if in agony, and Hank—Hank wasn't looking at Taylor but at Brynn. His face was carefully blank, but there was a glint of intense curiosity in his eyes. It was almost as if he had been waiting for her to chime in with stories of her own creative uses for food.

A small sound from the other side of the desk brought Brynn's attention back to where it was supposed to be: Taylor, the job, making a professional impression on these people who had entrusted her with their celebration.

Silence hung over them. No one seemed capable of speech. Brynn realized that if anyone was going to get them through this, it had to be her.

Long months of caring for her two younger brothers while their mother was sick had taught her that a bright smile and brisk attitude conveyed confidence that usually reassured others, if not herself. She shoved the paper in her pocket and turned to the door. *Big smile. Breezy confidence. Play the part.*

"Mrs. North. Good to see you again. You, too, Carter, Hank. Taylor has told me about your thoughts for the festival, and they sound fabulous. I'm looking forward to bringing them to life. Now, I know you were thinking of horse-and-buggy rides, but did you have any specific…"

She continued chattering while guiding them into the conference room where the rest of the family waited. By the time everyone was seated, Taylor's face was only slightly pink instead of horror-movie white, and Moxie had stopped breaking out in unnerving snickers. Carter still wouldn't look up, but Hank—Hank was watching her again.

Quickly, so fast that she almost thought she imagined it, he winked at her from across the table.

Forget keeping herself from being a bitch to Carter. The real challenge here would be making it through the meeting without sinking through the floor.

Wednesdays were Hank's night off. When he'd bought the cabins and moved himself and Millie out of the home he had shared with his folks and

Moxie, his mother had made him swear on her future grave that he would bring Millie back at least once a week. Usually they grabbed a quick bite together, then he was pushed out the door with orders to see a movie or "be social." Ma said that it was so they could spoil Millie silly without him protesting. He suspected it was really part of her ongoing quest to see him remarried, or at least going out on a regular basis. Subtlety had never been one of her strengths.

As he walked to the sprawling old Victorian and yelled to Millie to slow down before she slipped on the ice, he braced himself for what he was sure was going to be another round of lectures. Tonight's installment, however, was strictly his own fault. He knew he'd made a mistake the moment he let himself wink at Brynn during the meeting.

It wasn't the gesture itself that he regretted. She deserved something after getting them through Awkward Central without anyone wanting to bleach their brains. She'd put on some cute little librarian half-glasses, talking about nothing like her life depended on it, and he saw why Taylor had said she was all about family. She'd been willing to make an idiot of herself if necessary to help her cousin.

Yeah, she had definitely earned a wink. If only he'd been smooth enough to wait until Ma was looking the other way....

Sure enough, no sooner had he and Millie walked

into the house and hung their coats in the hall closet than his mother took him by the arm.

"Moxie, can you amuse Millie for a while, please? Henry and I are going to the laundry room for a little chat."

Ah, hell. She'd called him Henry *and* invoked the laundry room. That was the spot Janice North reserved for the worst transgressions, the ones usually punished by a serious dressing-down and manual labor.

"Moxie, no. Save me. You know what she's like when she gets talking."

Moxie grinned and tugged on the collar of Millie's lab coat. "Come on, sprite. Let's get out of your grandma's way while she knocks some sense into your daddy's head."

"Can I watch?"

Great. Even his kid was abandoning him.

Resigned to his fate, he preceded his mother into the room and boosted himself up to sit on the dryer—an instinct from childhood. It was harder to be spanked if his mother couldn't reach his bottom. "Okay. Let's hear it."

"Henry William North. Before you and Millie moved out, you and I had a little talk, remember?"

"And here it is, your once-a-week dinner as promised."

"There was more to it than that, and you know it. You agreed with me that you were well and truly over the divorce and ready to move on. Start dating. Start having a life again."

Very true. 'Course, he'd had his fingers crossed when he said it, but come on. That was self-preservation.

"You know, Ma, most folks your age are starting to have trouble remembering things. Why is it that your memory is just getting sharper? Are you part of some secret government experiment to steal memory cells from one person and transfer them to another?"

"Be serious for a minute, will you? I know it took a while to get over Heather, and I understand. You had a lot thrown at you very fast, and you needed time. But it's been long enough. You bought the cabins, you and Millie are settled there, you're building the life you wanted all those years ago, back before things got knocked off track."

Hank snorted. Knocked off track? More like *knocked up*.

"In any case, I'm getting worried about you. You haven't shown much interest in a woman in heaven knows how long."

"Hey, hey, hey." He raised his hand. A man could only listen to so much before he had to defend himself. "Not true. In fact, the only reason I saw the last Batman movie was because it had—"

"Anne Hathaway in a catsuit. I know."

"You do?"

"Honestly, Hank. You think your brothers never tell me anything?"

Ian was lucky he was out of the country. Carter and Cash, on the other hand, were dead meat.

"Be that as it may," she said with a pat on his arm, "it's time for you to stop fixating on Catwoman and start looking at the flesh-and-blood women around you."

Wait for it...

"That Brynn... She certainly seems nice."

Could he call them or what? "Drop it, Ma."

"Why? She's smart and funny, and Millie certainly seems to like her."

"Plus, she's living in my backyard, which would make things kind of awkward if it didn't work out, don't you think? Not to mention that she's working for us. Did you even listen to that sexual-harassment training we had to sit through?"

"You're not at the dairy anymore."

And this conversation was a great reminder of another reason why he had left: to be his own boss. To not have his family telling him what to do, in one form or another, 24/7.

"No, Mom. Just...no."

She narrowed her eyes at him before smacking his feet. "Move your legs."

He did it on autopilot, realized how easily he'd slipped, and groaned. Lucky for him there was no punishment on the horizon. Just the squeak of the dryer door as she pulled it open and pulled out a clean undershirt.

"Hank..." She folded the shirt in half, her actions automatic after decades of male laundry. "I know you're reluctant to think about trying again, but life is hard enough as it is, especially when you're a parent. Millie is going to take more from you than you realize. Things are easier when you don't have to go through everything by yourself. And no, I'm not talking about the chores, okay? I'm talking about having someone in your corner. Someone to hold you up. Everyone deserves that, Hank. Even people who had a lousy marriage the first time around. Maybe even more so."

Hell and damnation, how was he supposed to respond to that? Janice North didn't put her heart on the line very often. For her to talk to him so openly, so honestly…she really must be worried.

"Okay, Ma. Total truth here. I wouldn't mind finding someone someday, maybe even get married again. But it has to be on my terms. And my terms include not chasing someone who's only here for a few months."

She tossed the shirt into the hamper and grabbed a fresh one. "You can't let that stop you. I saw the way you looked at her during the meeting today."

Someday, he would learn. "Yes. I like Brynn. The whole, oh, thirty minutes of interaction I've had with her over the past three days have all been pleasant. But as you said yourself, Millie likes her."

"And that's bad?"

"Yeah, it is. Mills already asked me when she could get her ears pierced just like Brynn. She's going to have a hard enough time saying goodbye when the time comes. Can you imagine if she saw me going out with Brynn? Hell, she had me married off to her friend Tish's mom a dozen times before they moved. One dinner with Brynn, and Millie would be planning the wedding. I'm not gonna do that to her."

There. She couldn't argue with that one.

For a moment, it looked like he had won. She folded the shirt silently, let it drop into the hamper, grabbed a handful of socks and spread them across the top of the washer. With expert speed, she began matching them.

"All right, then," she said at last. "Forget Brynn. But you need to make an effort, Hank. It's past time." She swept the paired socks into the hamper and picked up two singletons, one pink and one brown, dangling them in his face. "Because if you don't wake up and get moving, my boy, this is how you and Millie are going to end up."

On Friday night, Hank pulled into the driveway leading to the cabins, killed the engine and tried to muster up the energy to get out of the truck and walk into the house. When he picked Millie up from after-school care she had announced that her backpack wouldn't zip anymore, her shoes were too tight and she needed a white T-shirt for tie-dye day on Monday. His choice had been to try to cram the store run into an already packed weekend, or get it out of the way immediately. He'd opted for door number two. Not a bad choice, but now it was dinnertime, they were both tired and grumpy and he'd forgotten to pull something out of the freezer that morning.

Great. Another Friday night of Kraft Dinner and ketchup with a side of guilt.

Compounding his frustration was the fact that, while Millie was more than happy to tell him about the items she needed, she had spent the entire shopping trip tap-dancing around any discussion of school itself. He knew better than to ask a simple *What did you do today?* He drew instead on his mother's ancient lines: *Did you read any good books? Who did you play with at recess? What did you draw in art?*

Nothing.

Well, not a total nothing. She gave an animated reenactment of Curious George's antics. But all other questions were met with shrugs, silence or sudden declarations that she wanted a telescope.

His mother said that Millie had too many other interests to think about school when she wasn't there. Her report cards said she was attentive and contributed to classroom discussions. But his gut told him something was wrong.

"Hey, Mills. I was thinking—do you want to have a friend over this weekend?" Maybe she was just lonely, what with her best friend moving away. Maybe he could juggle the jobs, let Millie have an hour or two, maybe do some eavesdropping in case she let something slip with a classmate. "We could get a pizza and you could invite—I don't know. Who do you like to play—"

"Daddy! Is there another car at Brynn's place?"

He peered through the dying bits of daylight, unsure if this was a true question or an attempt at distraction. But sure enough, there was a second shape in front of the Wolfe cabin.

"Guess she has company. But about this week—"

"Oh! Maybe it's Casey! She told me Casey was coming!"

"Who is Casey, and when were you talking to Brynn about him? Her? Whatever." More important, might this Casey be a potential playmate?

"You know. Casey is her little boy. Not *her* little boy, but her… What's that word? Not like uncle, or cousin, but…"

"Nephew?"

"Yes! That's it! He's her nephew. And he lives at a camp but he likes to play with her, and she was going to see him a whole lot while she's living here, because the camp is… I don't remember. Somewhere close."

"And when did you get all this information?"

But his words were lost in a burst of movement as Millie opened her door, scrambled out of the truck and took off.

"Brynn!" She raced down the path between the trees. "Hey, Brynn! Can I come see Casey, please?"

"Millie," he called helplessly. So much for that attempt at conversation. With a curse he slammed his way out of the truck and followed his daughter.

Millie barely avoided smacking into the man walking away from the cabin. "Whoa, kiddo." The man laughed and stepped off the path. "Careful. You don't want to slip."

Millie nodded and scooted around him, aiming for Brynn, who was standing in the doorway with a kid in her arms. Millie crashed into her legs, causing Brynn to stoop and hug Millie to her. Hank groaned. He was never going to get her home now.

The man who had almost been Millie's punching bag caught Hank's eye. "Let me guess. That's Millie, and you're Hank." He extended his hand. "Sam Catalano, Brynn's brother. Good to meet you."

Hank nodded and stuck out his hand, wishing he'd thought to pull on his gloves. His hands were probably like ice. Of course, if this guy was the hockey player, he was probably used to that. "Sorry about my daughter's manners. She's on a quest to set a new speed record from my place to here."

"She's off to a great start." He grinned. "So, has my sister made your life a living hell yet?"

"Yeah, I've had to call the cops three times for her wild parties."

"Excuse me?" Brynn said. "Hank, it was only one party. And Sam, remember, your night out with your wife depends on me babysitting, so you should watch your mouth, mister."

"Oh, hell, she's right. I'd better get out of here before I say something wrong and piss her off. Nice meeting you, Hank."

"You, too," Hank said, but his attention was already on the scene in front of him. Brynn's nephew was squealing on her hip and Millie was chattering at top volume, yet Brynn still radiated calm while smiling at him. Nothing extraordinary. Just two adults sharing a moment in the midst of some kiddie insanity. But something about it felt so warm, so welcoming, that he was hit by the most ridiculous sense of longing he'd had in ages. It was almost like he was seeing the Ghost of Should-Have-Beens.

But that was ridiculous. And probably due to the amazing smells tickling his nose as he drew near.

"Hi, there." He pointed toward Millie, but spoke to Brynn. "Sorry. She saw the car out front and figured that was her own personal invitation."

"Well, of course it is. I told Millie to pop in anytime, and I meant it. That is, assuming it's okay with you," she added quickly.

"Please, Daddy? Please? Can I have a visit, oh, please, oh, please, oh, please?"

He wanted to say yes. Millie needed friends, true. But they should be her age, and local. Permanent. He couldn't let her start thinking that everyone who stayed in the cabins was there purely for her enjoyment. She had to learn—they *both* had to learn—how to be friendly and helpful while maintaining the boundaries they needed to make this work for everyone involved.

"Mills," he said gently. "We have to have dinner."

"Why don't you join us?" Brynn nodded at the toddler clinging to her like a monkey. "It's just me and Casey, and I'm sure he would rather play with another kid than with his decrepit old auntie."

She didn't look decrepit, not that he could say that to her face. In a Leafs jersey that hung midthigh and something that looked like the leggings Millie wore beneath her lab coat, Brynn looked casual and relaxed and limber.

Dangerously limber.

"That's a great offer, but—"

"Oh, Daddy, please!"

"Mills, come on. You have homework, and I'm in the middle of some things, and we have—um—plans."

Brynn shook her head. "But you have to eat anyway, right? And seriously, you'd be doing me a favor. I learned how to cook by feeding hungry males, and I still don't know how to make anything less than army quantities. If you don't stay I'll be eating spaghetti and meatballs for the next two weeks."

Ah, hell. They *did* have to eat. If he didn't have to spend time cooking, he might be able to work ahead a bit, freeing up that hour or so he wanted to give to Millie and a playmate. And since he would be helping Brynn...

"Okay." He raised a hand to stifle Millie's squeals. "But I wasn't kidding—we have to be rude and scoot fairly quickly. Duty calls, and all that crap."

Brynn gave him the kind of assessing look that made him feel distinctly uneasy, as if she had other plans that couldn't be revealed yet, but she nodded quickly and stepped back to allow him entry. "You're right. That's horrifically rude. You'll have to apologize by coming again another time when you can stay longer."

Millie clapped her hands. "Oh, yes! We can do that. Right, Daddy?"

"We'll talk," was all he said as he stepped inside and shrugged free of his jacket, hanging it from the wall pegs already sporting a bright red parka and a tiny blue snowsuit. He looked from the suit to Millie and shook his head.

"Hard to believe she was ever that small."

"And Casey's a big guy. Right, squirt?"

Casey nodded slowly. Big blue eyes checked Hank out from head to toe. Apparently satisfied, he patted Brynn's cheek.

"Casey blocks. Pease."

"Good manners, bud. Millie, there's a bunch of toys in the bedroom. Could you take Casey in there and show him around?"

The smile on Millie's face was bright enough to ease his worries, at least for the moment. "Oh, yes! Come on, Casey!" She held out her hand. Miracle of miracles, Casey grabbed hold and followed her down the hall while Millie talked about the rooms, the work and whether they might be able to make something explode that night.

As her voice faded, Hank realized that, thanks to his own weakness, he was now alone with Brynn and would have to make conversation. Dammit. Ian could talk about anything, Carter and Cash put Millie to shame, but the small-talk gene had skipped him.

Still, he needed to say something.

"This, uh, really is nice of you," Hank said as Brynn headed back to the kitchen area.

"My pleasure. And, like I said, army quantities." She lifted the lid of a slow cooker and gave a stir. He caught sight of deep red sauce, inhaled the warmth and felt like he'd walked into a sixties sitcom. "Without help, I'd be eating this three meals a day for a week. No hardship, but my jeans wouldn't be too happy about it."

He couldn't help it. That was a comment that begged a man to check out the curve of her hips. She might not be wearing jeans at the moment, but he remembered the way they'd fit her on move-in day, the way they had hugged as she lifted and hauled, and he had to agree that any action that spoiled that view would indeed be a sin.

"So are you settling in okay? Have everything you need?" He glanced around the space, which already felt cozier. "You're kind of our test case for this cabin-rental thing, so if I messed up anything, let me know. Don't be shy."

Oh, that was rich—*him* telling *her* to not be shy. Pot, meet kettle.

She laughed as she opened the refrigerator. "My brothers would tell you that shyness is the least of my issues. Everything is great so far. This place really is adorable—not just my cabin, but all of it. How long have you been here?"

"A few months. My sort-of uncle Lou finally admitted he couldn't keep up with things anymore and let me buy it off him."

"So it's been in the family a while."

"Yeah."

"That's so cool. We moved a lot when I was little, and my brothers were more into taking things apart and destroying them than preserving them." She pulled grated cheese and salad ingredients from the shelves and handed them to him. He took them automatically. "It's nice to see things being passed down through a family. Traditions, heirlooms. Things that last."

He couldn't hold back the snort. "The only things that were lasting around here were the river, the rocks and the foundations. Lou should have admitted defeat years ago. I still don't know if I'll have everything up and running by May."

"Given what I've seen of your work thus far, I have no doubt that you'll do just fine."

"Thanks."

"Total truth." She held out a bottle. "I need a beer. Care to join me?"

He meant to say no—after all, he still had a full night ahead—but what kind of host would he be to refuse? Or, for that matter, what kind of guest?

The bottle was halfway to his lips when she made a small sound.

"Crap! I always forget. Would you like a glass?"

"No, thanks. This is fine."

"You're sure? I'm a horrible hostess—sorry. I never remember the gracious touches when I'm off-duty."

It was so unexpected—the organizational queen forgetting something—that he felt himself relaxing. Maybe even grinning. "You're feeding me and you made my kid happy. I can't think of anything more gracious than that."

A slight hint of pink rose in her cheeks, spreading down her neck to the creamy bit of skin visible in the vee of her jersey. It was an intriguing sight, for sure. He could swear there was a little freckle at the point of the vee. Or maybe it was a fleck of sauce. He couldn't tell. Neither could he pull his gaze away. Because even though he couldn't see it, he was suddenly very aware that the opening of the jersey was a few tiny millimeters above the sweet line of cleavage, a part of the female anatomy he had always found highly alluring.

She turned slightly to grab a bubbling pot from the stove, breaking his concentration and making him realize, with embarrassment, that he'd been staring a bit too intently for a little too long at a particularly dangerous zone.

And he'd been worried about Millie overstepping *her* bounds.

"Did your brother play for the Leafs?" Okay, lame line, but it sort of excused his blatant perusal.

The slight quirk to her eyebrows told him how much she bought it. But instead of giving him the lecture he deserved, she simply dumped pasta into the colander in the sink.

"No," she said. "He was all over the place for a while, but didn't really hit his stride until he landed in Detroit."

"So you wear that to harass him?"

She turned back, her face twisted in a mix of humor and chagrin. "I wear it for me. Because try as I might, I can't stop rooting for them."

A feeling he knew well. "A sucker for the underdog, huh?"

"It's pathetic. If they're playing lousy and I try to cheer for another team, I feel like a traitor, but if they actually do a good job, I can't walk away because this might be the year they turn it around."

"I'm sorry."

She laughed and gave the colander a shake before swishing her hands at him, a motion he recognized as a request to step back. "Sometimes I think about forming a support group—Diehard Leafs Fans

Anonymous—but then I wonder if anyone would be willing to admit to it."

"Well, winters can get pretty long around here. Time it right and it could be the biggest excitement to hit town in years."

She laughed again, dumped the drained pasta back into the pot and added a heaping ladle of the sauce. The smell of all that beef and garlic was getting to him. It was the only way to account for the slight light-headedness that was taking him over. It had to be the food. Maybe the beer on a mostly empty stomach.

God help him if it was the woman.

CHAPTER FOUR

BRYNN HAD ALWAYS felt that Sunday afternoons in winter were meant for curling up with a good book and a bottomless cup of peppermint tea, but she could count on one hand the number of times that life had decided she'd earned that reward. Which was undoubtedly why she was spending this particular Sunday talking about work and men—not necessarily in that order—with Taylor.

"I stopped at the park on my way over," she said as Taylor frowned at the pile of Ian's clothes spread across her bed. "Something about it doesn't feel right to me."

"What do you mean?"

"I know it's the center of town and everything, but I don't think it's right for the festival. This is all about the dairy. It should be held someplace with a Northstar connection."

Taylor shrugged and plucked a sweater from the stack. "Well, we could hold it in the parking lot beside the offices, but I think the park has nicer ambiance."

"There has to be something." Brynn frowned at

the collection of clothes and grabbed an old sweatshirt emblazoned with a Northstar Dairy crest. "Here. Wear this."

"Not that. It won't make me think of Ian."

"Why not? It's his, it's got his smell on it—"

"And it's for the dairy, which is where I work with Carter."

Oh. Good point.

"Anyway," Brynn continued, "if you have any legitimate suggestions for another venue, I'm all ears."

"I'll think about it, but Brynn, we have the permits already and the flyers and ads are almost ready to print. Changing now would be a pain in the patoot."

"So? I'm the queen of pain." She grabbed a navy fleece that sported the word *Coach* in gold letters. "How about this one?"

Taylor glanced at it, appeared to think, then shook her head.

"Why not?"

"Ian used to coach peewee hockey. But his assistant was—"

"Don't say it." Those damned North brothers were freakin' inseparable. Hank seemed to be the only one who didn't share their pack mentality.

Brynn ran her finger over the lettering on the fleece and remembered, just for a second, that moment when she caught Hank checking her out. She wasn't used to quiet men. In her experience, all males were a walking assortment of bad jokes, clumsy—if sweet—gestures and copious amounts of gas, so it had almost been a relief when she caught him staring at her boobs. Nice to know he was capable of the Neanderthalesque qualities she associated with most men. And, if she were being totally honest, it was nice to know that he had been trying to scope out what was beneath her loose jersey.

Not that she planned to act on his apparent interest. She had two jobs here, and neither would be made easier by indulging in *anything* with a member of the family that was involved in both those endeavors.

Still, she hadn't quite been able to stop herself from brushing her arm against his shoulder when she passed him the salad, sending the loveliest vibrations running through her....

With a start, she realized that Taylor was talking. "...Moxie dropping hints about weddings."

"Oh. Wow." Hoping to hell she'd given an appropriate response, she plucked blindly from the pile, emerging with a cranberry-colored sweater so soft it begged to be fondled. "How about this one?"

Taylor's nose wrinkled and she backed away. "Crap! How did that get in there?"

"What?" Brynn rubbed the luxurious softness between her fingers. "Is it poison?"

"Bad memories. Turns out I'm allergic to cashmere." She shuddered. "A very nice night ended up being a whole lot less pleasant."

"Damn. The color would be great on you."

"Yeah, but it would clash horribly with the hives." Taylor ran a hand over the pile of clothes on the bed, patting them almost wistfully. "Brynn, I don't know if this is going to work. It's getting so I can hardly be in the same room as Carter without falling apart, and since I see him all day, you can imagine how well that's going. I think he knows something is wrong."

"Of course he does. Your fiancé is away and has been gone for months. That's all he knows."

"I don't know.... Sometimes I get this feeling that he's watching me. Not in a creepy way, but like…like the way I know I look at him when no one else is around."

Brynn's hands froze despite the fleece surrounding them. "You think he might— Oh, Taylor. No. Don't say you think he feels it, too."

"I hope to God I'm wrong. But it's… I don't know. Maybe I'm reading things into it that are totally wrong. You know, projecting my own secret wishes and all that Psych 101 crap."

"Look. You have that social marketing conference coming up in spring, remember? He's not going. That will give you days and days away from him, and when you come back, it will be just a few more weeks until Ian comes home. Once he's here, you'll remember how much you love him and everything will be wonderful again."

Taylor shook her head. "I hope you're right," she said softly. Then she looked at the fleece in Brynn's hands and smiled sadly. "Not that one, either."

Brynn didn't dare ask.

"Carter has the same one. Their mom gave them all matching fleeces for Christmas last year." She ran her hand over the fabric. "It's what he was wearing when I realized I wanted him instead of Ian."

HANK PULLED INTO his parking space at Northstar Dairy, killed the engine on his old pickup and let out a sigh that was equal parts frustration and anticipation.

"Stupid damned meetings."

The frustration was easy to figure out. Hauling Millie out of bed, having to abandon the wiring job he'd been working on when he realized he was going to be late, driving through February snow... The morning had been a perfect storm of irritation, and it was only a little past ten.

But he would rather focus on his annoyance than on the little jolts running through him at the thought of watching Brynn marshal them through another session. Or, more accurately, the thought of watching her in her business clothes while remembering how she had looked with her jersey dipping and the spaghetti steam making her hair curl around her face. He'd been trying to push the picture from his memory since Friday night. Thus far it had insisted on staying there, which annoyed him all the more.

And now he had to sit through a meeting with his mother doing her best eagle imitation. Son of a—

A muffled bang to his right caught his attention. Carter was climbing out of his Saab. Huh. Carter was never late.

Hank grabbed his gloves and his files, opened his door and winced as a metallic *skreeeek* cut through the snowy silence. Oops. He had planned to take care of the door last night. And the night before, come to think of it.

Sure enough, the noise was enough to draw Carter's attention.

"You ever gonna give up that bucket of bolts and drive something that can be seen in public?"

Hank shrugged. "Look who's talking—a man who drives a compensation-mobile. At least my truck has character."

Carter snorted. "Sure it does. A character that's begging for a serial killer to come and put it out of its misery."

Hank fell into step beside Carter, both of them bending slightly forward against the bitter wind swirling snowflakes around their heads.

"I can't believe they had school today. Millie was pissed."

"Can't say I blame her."

Saying that Millie had been reluctant to get on

the bus that morning was like saying that snow was a little cold. It had been getting progressively more difficult to drag her out of bed each day. Her teacher assured him that all the kids were tired. His mother reminded him that when he was a kid, she had to wake him by firing stuffed animals from the other side of the room, because he woke up smacking at anything he could reach. All of which reassured him until the next time he saw the dread on Millie's face as she mounted the steps of the big yellow bus, and his gut told him there was more at play here than simple fatigue or loneliness.

Especially today, when, at the last minute, she had yanked off her lab coat and tossed it on the floor. He should have counted it a victory. He'd been telling her to leave it at home for weeks now. But the vicious way she had tugged at it left him suspicious that his suggestions had nothing to do with her last-minute abandonment.

He would talk to her again tonight. Maybe this time, he'd find the magic words to get her to open up.

"Hello? Earth to Hank?"

He looked up in surprise. Carter's fist hovered in front of his face, undoubtedly ready to do the old knock-knock on the forehead.

"Sorry. I was distracted."

"No shit, Sherlock. I asked you the same question three times. You sure you're awake?"

"Right. Because if this was a dream, of course I'd plop us in the middle of a blizzard."

The doors to the office building were dead ahead, shining like the pearly gates. He couldn't wait to slip inside their warmth. Just a few steps to go.

"So what were you asking?"

"Forget it."

"Look, I'm sorry, okay? I've got a lot on my mind these days."

By way of apology, he held the door for Carter.

"Age before beauty," he quipped. A guy had to take his fun where he could find it.

"So." Carter stamped snow from his feet. "How is it having Brynn in the cabin?"

"Fine."

"Just fine? I thought I'd get more of a reaction than that."

"Why?"

Carter shrugged. "Because, blind one, she's a good-looking woman."

Hank stopped midstomp. "Did Ma put you up to this?"

"To what?"

Pointing out Brynn's assets and proximity. Pushing me to start dating. Reminding me that I'm turning into a grumpy old man and I'm not even thirty.

"Nothing."

"God, aren't you all sunshine and flowers this morning."

Hank waved to the receptionist and hustled down

the hall toward the conference room. "You earned it fair and square when you burned the last Pop-Tart."

"What the— That was twenty years ago, Hankie."

"Yeah, but you did it on purpose because we were out of your blueberry ones, so you didn't want me to have any, either. And they were strawberry-frosted, man. With sprinkles. Best Pop-Tarts ever."

"You know, most people let go of the past at some point."

"Lucky I don't have that problem."

Carter snorted and shook his head. "You keep telling yourself that, bro."

Hank pulled open the door to the conference room and deliberately walked in ahead of Carter this time. He subjected everyone to the kind of look he would give Millie when she pushed him beyond his limits and dropped into his seat without once making eye contact with Brynn.

All he could say was that it was a damned good thing he loved his family.

BRYNN WATCHED THE assorted Norths carefully as they straggled into the room, trying to gauge the emotional climate of the group before she started. She could and had handled hostile, indifferent and present-in-body-only groups in the past, but each situation required a different approach. Last week the Norths had been mostly curious. This week would be the real test of how they felt about working with her.

As expected, Moxie arrived first. She nodded at Brynn, took her seat at the head of the table and launched into a loud recap of that week's *Dancing with the Stars*. Janice and Cash entered next, deep in a discussion of schedules. They barely glanced at her, but a wave and a quick smile let her know that they were on board. Mr. North—"Call me Robert"—trailed behind with his typical bemused look, as if he had been dragged from his research and had yet to reenter the real world, but he was the first to actually talk to her, asking how she was doing and if she needed anything. She had a feeling his genes were the ones that had asserted themselves when it came time to mold Hank's personality.

Taylor scuttled in on the dot of ten. The worry lines on her forehead gave Brynn pause, but her cousin tugged on the collar of the shirt peeking out from beneath her argyle sweater and winked. Brynn recognized both items as ones that belonged to Ian and her happy meter zipped up a couple of notches.

Carter and Hank walked in together, five minutes late. Correction: Carter walked in, paused to survey the room and slipped into the empty chair beside Moxie. Brynn breathed a small sigh of relief. She had feared he would take the seat next to Taylor.

Hank stalked into the room with a chip on his shoulder so huge, she could almost see an indentation mark.

Oh, hell. He was not going to be happy by the time this meeting was over.

"Sorry," Carter said. "Someone went into the ditch right in front of me. I had to give him a push."

Moxie waved a hand, which Brynn interpreted as something along the lines of a papal dispensation. Taylor shot him a quick smile that made Brynn's stomach clench, then reached up and rubbed her collar. Whew.

All eyes turned to Hank. He met them without blinking.

"I was late. So fire me."

Moxie sighed. Janice gave him the kind of stern, one-fingered point that Brynn recognized as a universal gesture of motherly reprimanding. Cash rolled his eyes.

"Shall we begin with a rousing chorus of 'If You're Happy and You Know It'?" The words were out of Brynn's mouth before she realized it, the rote reply born of years jollying her brothers through marauding catastrophes. Just in time, she stopped herself from wincing over the blunder. Better to have everyone think she'd said it on purpose.

Fake it 'til you make it.

Hank stared at her like he couldn't believe what she had said. The disbelief slowly faded into something resembling respect mixed with humor, laced with chagrin. Underlying it all was a hint of something else, something that brought a flush to her cheeks.

He quickly resumed the bland-indifference act, but now she saw it for what it was.

Hank was trying to fake out someone, and it wasn't her. She probably shouldn't be curious. And he definitely wasn't going to like what she was about to propose.

But she had to admit that things had just become a lot more interesting.

"Let's hear how everyone has progressed this week. Mrs. North?"

"Dammit, girl. I told you to call me Moxie."

Reports were given. Items were checked off the agenda. Brynn filled them in on her progress, noting with satisfaction the looks of approval being sent her way. There were few things she loved more than attacking a to-do list and bringing order out of chaos. Another week and she would have this group purring like a finely tuned kitten.

There was just one bump in the road to navigate first.

"Okay folks, we're making excellent progress. There's one last item I want to raise. You might not agree with me. That's fine. But I feel very strongly that the festival should not be held in the village park, charming as it is, but someplace with stronger ties to the family." She offered her best smile, feigning a confidence she sure as hell didn't feel as she looked straight over her glasses at Hank. "I propose that the festival be held at the Northwoods Cabins."

The color drained from his face. So did any traces of warmth.

"Are you out of your ever-loving mind?"

"Quite probably," she said with all the cheer she could carry off. "But it's still on the table."

"What, uh, what brought you to this conclusion?" Janice glanced at Hank.

Brynn ticked off the points on her fingers. "A stronger family connection. A gorgeous location, filled with trees and the river and plenty of places to park. The cabins would make perfect staging areas for the activities—there can be a kids' cabin with face-painting and games, a craft cabin for the milk-bag crocheting, a history cabin, et cetera. If it rains we won't need a tent because the activities are already inside. We can do the closing fireworks over the river and use the central area for the stage and picnic tables." She smiled again. "Plus, it would be a fabulous grand opening for the cabin business."

"I don't need—" Hank stopped, seeming to struggle to collect himself before continuing. "Look. It sounds really great, I know, but I— No. Just no."

"It sounds pretty good to me, Hank." Moxie sent him the evil eye. "What's your problem?"

"Other than the fact that Millie and I have to live there while all these strangers traipse through our front yard?"

"You mean the way they'll be doing once you

are officially in business?" Robert's quiet comment brought a halt to the whispers and mutters that had begun.

Hank looked slightly taken aback, but only for a moment.

"That will be different."

"How?" Janice spoke with the authority that only a mother could muster. "I think this would be an excellent way to get you accustomed to the comings and goings."

"I don't—" He stopped again. Brynn waited. She could convince him to do this, but it had to come from him.

Moxie spoke up. "Henry, when your great-uncle built that house and those cabins, he was as proud of them as he could be. He used to have the whole family out there every year for Halloween. He'd fill the woods with ghosts and pumpkins, have a bonfire, make it a party place. We loved going there." She shook her head. "Then your uncle Lou took over and it all went to hell. Used to break my heart to see how he let it go to pot. Me, I'm mighty proud to see you bringing it back to life. Lou would have been too dumb and lazy to grab this chance. You're not either of those. So for the love of Pete, boy, don't pretend you are."

Hank closed his eyes. Brynn saw the lines in his face, saw the way his fingers tightened on his pen, and felt a flash of guilt. Was she asking too much?

"Fine." He pointed the pen at Moxie. "I'll do it.

But you have to swear you'll have everything and everyone out of there within two days of it being over. I have folks checking in Thursday night and I'll need time to get ready."

"I'll help with that." Brynn spoke quickly. "I'd be happy to do it. And anything else you might need."

He arched an eyebrow in her direction. "Gee, thanks, Brynn. But I think you've done plenty already."

SATURDAY MORNING FOUND Hank exactly where he'd been for days: in the Carleton cottage, pounding the hell out of floorboards that needed replacing and sending dark thoughts in the direction of the Wolfe cabin, home of the woman who had made it necessary for him to speed up his timetable by a full week. More, really, since folks would need to get into the cabins ahead of time to set up.

His schedule was a mess. His mood had been launched into permanently foul. He was juggling catch-up and Millie care. And, because life wasn't exciting enough, his daughter seemed determined to do everything in her power to make his job even more time-consuming.

Like taking off when his back was turned.

"Millie?" He poked his head into every room of the cottage, even though he'd checked each space twice already. It wasn't like there were many places to hide. Remembering one of her favorite tricks from toddlerhood, Hank opened all the cupboards, hoping to hell he'd hear her familiar giggle with each creak of the hinges.

No go. She wasn't in the cottage. And since she would have told him if she were simply running home to grab a new toy, he had a pretty good idea where to find her.

He shoved his hands in his pockets as he tramped through the piles of rapidly melting snow toward Brynn's. He'd been avoiding her since Wednesday's meeting, not certain he could look at her without his blood boiling. Or, worse, without wanting to take her up on her offer of help. Not because he needed it. Or because he wanted to spend time with her. Just because...well, because she should see, firsthand, the extra work she was causing him.

Yeah, that was it.

He rapped sharply on the door, ready to dispense dire warnings and punishments to his offspring and anyone else who might deserve it. All of the words died on his tongue the minute Brynn opened the door.

She was in a bathrobe. Not a serviceable terry-cloth robe, but a thin one made of something purple and shiny, dotted with red lips, that hugged and clung in so many places that she might as well have been naked. She must have been dripping wet when she yanked it on.

And, God help him, he wanted to yank it off her, right then and there.

He felt like someone had kidnapped all his

senses, stripped them of every other memory or association and replaced them all with Brynn. He saw nothing but her curves and the damp patches on her chest where her hair dripped on her robe. He smelled nothing but a slight hint of orange. He felt only the heat surrounding her, tasted nothing but his own sudden lust and heard nothing but—

But his daughter's muffled squeak.

Millie. Crap, for a minute there he'd forgotten his own kid.

He shook himself like the dog he was and scraped up something that resembled a brain cell. "Hi. Sorry to interrupt—" that was a lie if ever he'd told one "—but I couldn't find Millie."

"Funny thing, that." She stepped back and walked into the room, which he took as an invitation to follow her. Not that he had much choice in the matter. She was the Death Star and he was caught in the tractor beam that was the picture of everything he imagined beneath that purple haze. "It just so happens that I found a Millie. I was about to text you and ask if you were looking for her."

He glanced at his daughter, huddled on the corner of the sofa, looking like she couldn't decide if she wanted to burst into tears or celebrate her rebellion. All of a sudden he dreaded her adolescence in a way he never had before.

"Mills? What's going on?"

She stuck out her bottom lip. "I wanted to play with Brynn."

"I know, but you can't take off like that, kiddo. Do you have any idea how scared I was when I couldn't find you?"

Yeah, you were terrified until you caught one gander at Brynn in her robe and your brain took a hike south. Real Father-of-the-Year material there, North.

"I'm sorry," she said, but he could tell she was mostly sorry she'd been caught.

"Sorry alone doesn't cut it, Mills. You need to…" What? He had no idea where to start. He couldn't tell if he was simply out of his league, or if his thought patterns had been scrambled even worse when Brynn sat on the edge of the couch and her robe parted, giving him a glimpse of knee and calf and, holy shit, was that her thigh?

She pinched her robe closed and sat straighter, the picture of primness. "You only missed her by a little while, at least as far as I can tell. She wasn't here when I got in the— I mean, she's only been here a few minutes."

Wait a minute. Something wasn't being said here, probably because Brynn didn't want to get Millie in any more trouble than she already was. But parenting was a job that quickly taught a man how to read between the lines.

"Don't tell me she let herself in while you were in the shower."

Brynn bit her lip, sighed and nodded. "I'm afraid so." Her cheeks flamed almost as red as the lips decorating her robe. "And, I'd better tell you up front, I wasn't expecting company when I walked out of the bathroom, so Millie might have received a bit of an anatomy lesson."

He closed his eyes, but it was too late. His brain was doing an excellent job of filling in the blanks. Worse was the fact that he was suddenly and intensely jealous of his misbehaving daughter.

"Millie," he said. "Did you let yourself into Brynn's cabin?"

"I knocked first."

"Oh, good to know you remembered something. So you knocked and then waltzed on in?"

"No, Daddy. I knocked again. A lot. But I was cold and she didn't open the door and I knew she was home because her car was right there, so I opened up the door and I waited." She glanced down, eyes hidden behind her glasses. "But then I had to pee."

If he got through the next ten minutes of his life, he could get through almost anything.

"Please tell me you didn't march into Brynn's bathroom while she was in the shower."

"You know, maybe I'll put on some clothes while you guys talk about this." Brynn rose but Hank slowed her flight.

"Hang on. We'll get out of here. Millie, you need to apologize. Now."

Her eyes filled with tears. "I really had to go, Daddy."

"Mills, it's more than that. Tell Brynn you're

sorry you let yourself into her place and invaded her privacy. Now."

She crossed her arms over her chest. Tears ran down her cheeks. But she said nothing.

He glanced at Brynn, who was watching them with a mix of compassion and embarrassment that struck him as so endearing that he was brain-dead once again. Or maybe that was because the top of the robe had gaped a bit when she stood, and now he could see a lot farther down. The top of the sweet hollow between her breasts was plainly visible.

Forget Millie. He was the one who needed to get out of there fast.

"Mills. Say you're sorry and let's go."

"But I'm not." The words were barely more than a whisper, clogged with tears and thick with emotion, but they came through loud and clear.

"Amelia Jacobs North—"

"I told you I was bored, Daddy." Her voice cracked. "But you didn't talk to me. You just kept working. So I left. Because I wanted someone to play with me."

"It's not Brynn's—" he began, but a movement from the other side of the room caught his attention. Brynn was waving in a universal time-out motion.

"Could I talk to you for a moment?" She jerked her head toward the back of the cabin. "In private?"

He probably should make Millie speak before he left her, but on the other hand, this way she'd have more time to feel guilty. Stewing in her own juices, as his mother would say.

'Course, he couldn't remember a single time when that had worked on him, but maybe it was different for girls.

He was so filled with irritation at his daughter that he barely registered the fact that Brynn had led him down the short hall. They stood in the small alcove between two doors. One stood open. The one to the bedroom, of course, with the giant sleigh bed draped with clothing—probably the things she'd planned to don when she came out of the shower. He caught a glimpse of jeans, something blue and sparkly and a bit of blue lace that he knew had to be a bra.

He closed his eyes, but that which had been seen could never be unseen.

She tugged the door closed, her cheeks pink once again, but her gaze was steady as she looked at him.

"I might be way out of line here, but I have a proposition for you."

He couldn't help it. She said *proposition,* and his mind jumped to the precise place it had no business going. Lucky for him, Brynn seemed to have a lot more class than he did. She continued talking as if she hadn't said some of the most provocative words he'd heard in years.

"I know you're insanely busy, mostly because of me. I meant it when I said I'd like to help. Since I'm right here, and Millie seems to like me—which is totally mutual, by the way—well, instead of repeating this scenario, why don't we set up something official. Have scheduled times when she can hang here with me so you can work without interruption."

Her words worked the miracle he'd thought impossible as his interest went from sixty to zero in no time flat.

"No."

"Why not?"

He would have barked out something about not needing help, being fine, coping on his own—but she wasn't accusing, he could see. She was genuinely curious.

That was a new one. His family brushed off his need to do things himself as Youngest Child Syndrome. To have someone actually want to know his reasons—well, it made a difference. Almost as much as the fact that she had crossed her arms and now her breasts were pushed higher and there was more cleavage visible at the opening of her robe and if he didn't look away in the next three seconds he was going to do something really insane instead of merely stupid.

"When I said that you're our test case, I wasn't kidding. Millie needs to learn boundaries. That won't happen if she's visiting you all the time. You might have no problem with it, but the next person to stay here might not be as understanding."

"I get that. I do, and I think it's very wise of you to take it into consideration. But—"

"Brynn, this setup is awkward enough already, what with you living here and working for my family." *Not to mention the fact that I have now seen you far closer to naked than I ever should have, or that my mother would be delighted if she knew about it.* "I think we need to keep the lines as clear as we can. No more dinners or unexpected visits. If she wants to pop in once a week or so, that's great, but she needs to set it up first. Otherwise I'm never going to be able to keep her away from the cabins. You can imagine the problems that could create."

"But I'm right here, and it's really no bother, and it makes so much—"

"Brynn." It came out a little harder than he intended, but maybe that way she would listen. It wasn't like she was used to people refusing her. "I'll manage."

She seemed ready to argue, but after a moment she bit her lip and nodded. "Of course. You're right."

Yep. He was right, and he was doing the right thing. No need to feel like he'd just taken slippers from a helpful puppy and tossed them across the room.

He shoved his hands in his pockets. "For the record, I understand why you want to have the festival here. I'm not thrilled, but I'll live. And…yeah, I guess it will be a good kickoff for the place."

Her smile looked only 50 percent fake instead of the 90 or so he probably deserved. "Okay."

"Okay," he agreed. "I'll take my kid and get out of your way."

She nodded. He gathered up Millie, who stared at the floor while offering the world's least sincere apology, and a minute later they were headed back to the job—though he detoured to grab his laptop and a Disney movie. He didn't want to reward Millie, but neither could he really blame her.

Just the same, it was probably very wise for both him and his daughter to stay as far from Brynn as was humanly possible.

CHAPTER FIVE

BRYNN CLOSED THE DOOR behind Hank and Millie, stomped to the bedroom and let loose with a Tae Bo kick that would put the guy on the DVD to shame. Then she fell to the bed, grabbed the pillow and shrieked out a string of words that made no sense whatsoever, but absolutely fit her mood.

"Mother-loving candy maggot freakomatic numskull!"

Where the hell was her brain? She knew he'd been checking her out again. Actually, she'd sensed that more than seen it, because she had been too busy scoping him out herself. She'd been damp and flushed and naked beneath her robe and instead of feeling shy, it made her bolder. She had been irresistibly aware of the skin peeking through the rips in his jeans and the holes in his chamois shirt. There had been one spot above his navel, just the right size to hook a finger through. She'd stared at it and wondered what would happen if she were to snag it with her pinkie and yank. Hard. Hard enough to pull him closer, hard enough to shred that fabric and reveal the muscles hiding beneath his shirt, exposing his skin to the cold air and then pressing her own still-hot-from-the-shower body against him.

And then—because fantasizing about knocking him into the dying snowbank hadn't been enough—she had dragged him down the hall and thrown out words like *proposition* with that overly tempting bed just three steps away. She'd pulled him into that tiny space where a deep breath meant they would be almost touching, and she'd caught him peeking at her clothes—*oh, like you* really *forgot your bra was lying on the bed, Catalano?*—and her hormones had jumped to a level that usually required candlelight, wine and some serious adventures in foreplay. If it had been up to her body she would have cued up an endless loop of *MythBusters* for Millie, then dragged her daddy into the bedroom to create a few explosions of their own.

Thank heaven he'd frozen her out when she offered child care. Not that she enjoyed being made to feel like a kid who couldn't get a clue. Far from it.

Get out of here, Brynn. You're not needed.

She shook her father's voice out of her head. Hank's refusal hadn't been condescending or patronizing—just brusque enough to slap some common sense back into her.

Well, at least back into her brain. Her body still hadn't gotten the message—probably because it had been busy ogling his biceps.

She needed a distraction. A punitive, unpleasant,

totally gag-worthy one that she could remember the next time she was breathing in the sawdust scent of Hank North. One that would help her remember that she was here to make things *less* complicated, not more.

She grabbed her phone and sent Taylor a text.

Shopping?

As she'd expected, the response was swift and affirmative. She closed her phone with a determined nod.

So she was hot for Hank North. Now that she was painfully aware of that fact, she could work around it. Accept the facts and respect his boundaries and move on. It was only a couple of months. She could last that long.

In the meantime, there would be shopping, God help her, then ice cream and a long talk about the ways to put distance between a screwed-up female and a totally unsuitable man.

And Taylor would never know that the lecture would be aimed at Brynn even more than at her.

THREE NIGHTS AFTER Millie pulled her disappearing act, Hank was finally starting to breathe easy again. They had hashed things out, drawn some lines. Much as he'd hated to do it, he'd had to remind her that not all their future guests would be like Brynn. Some wouldn't want a little girl intruding on their privacy. Others might be very eager to welcome her for all the wrong reasons. Millie had to learn the boundaries and rules now, for the sake of both their future guests and her own safety.

So they had talked. They set up a schedule for Daddy's work, and the rewards Millie could earn by letting him get his chores done. They decided what Millie should do if she wanted to visit Brynn— because he wasn't fool enough to believe that he could keep her away completely—and sent Brynn an email with the plan. Her response had been crisp and agreeable, professional and responsible. All was as it should be.

Best of all, he'd seen Brynn only once since the day of the bathrobe, and she'd been on her way to her car, bundled and shapeless. There had been nothing to remind him, nothing to tempt him.

He could do this.

He was on his back beneath the kitchen sink in the Grindstone cabin, trying to determine the source of a particularly persistent leak and cutting out damaged wood, when Millie wandered over from her corner.

"Daddy?"

"Hmm?"

"I'm hungry. And my movie is done."

Crap. They'd made a deal. He was only supposed to work for the length of one movie. If he didn't stop now, it was going to cost him an extra story at bedtime.

"Okay, Mills. I need three minutes to finish up and get my stuff together. You pack up your things, I'll do mine, and—" he glanced longingly at the pipes "—we'll head home."

"Okay."

But as he pulled himself out from beneath the sink, she lingered.

"Daddy?"

"Yeah, babe?"

"When I get bigger, will I get…you know…bigger?"

He sat up with a groan and rubbed his back. There were days when he completely understood why Uncle Lou had given up on these cabins. "Well, yeah. That's usually the way it works. You get taller and everything gets bigger and—"

"No, Daddy. I mean, like, here."

As soon as he looked, he wished to hell he hadn't. Because Millie, his beautiful, tiny daughter, was holding her hands in front of her lab-coated chest in the approximate position of breasts.

Hell and damnation.

He'd always known that they would have to have these talks. They'd already discussed, many times, why Daddy stood up to go to the bathroom while she sat down, why Daddy had parts that Millie didn't have. And he'd always managed to swallow his discomfort to tell her that when she got older, her body would change and she would have breasts like all the women around her, like her grandmother and teachers and mother.

But none of those lessons must have carried the weight of spying a nude, generously endowed Brynn. Which made sense. Because thinking of what Millie might have seen had certainly been affecting him in powerful ways, as well.

He had learned long ago that awkward talks were better handled while the hands were busy. So he tossed wrenches into his open toolbox and focused on keeping his voice casual. "Yep. When you get to be a teenager, your breasts will get bigger. That's part of growing up."

"Oh."

Her silence drew his gaze. She was drawing small finger circles on the shirt pockets.

"I only have little tiny points here."

"Yeah, I know. That's what you're supposed to have now."

"Brynn's were bigger."

He gulped and focused on the damp rags he was pulling from beneath the sink. "That's 'cause she's all grown up. A woman." All woman, all enticing, all *totally off-limits, North.*

"She has boobies."

Holy— "Where did you learn that word?"

She stuck her thumb in her mouth.

"It's not a very polite word. Try not to say it again. And take your thumb out of your mouth."

The thumb slipped free, but she continued to rub

the shirt fabric between her fingers. "Okay. But when I grow up, I will have them."

He drew in a long breath. "Yeah. That's right."

"What if I don't want them?"

He barely held back the snort as he tossed the last rag into the bucket. "Sorry, kid. You don't get to choose. Like Grandma says, you get what you get and you like it."

"But they're so weird! They were pointy and jiggly, and the ends were all brown and—"

"Whoa, whoa, Mills, stop!" Sweet Jesus, he was doomed. "Listen, kiddo." He grabbed the saw from beneath the sink. "You shouldn't have gone into her cabin, and you shouldn't have gone into her bathroom and you shouldn't have seen her in the shower. But since you did, you really shouldn't talk about what she looks like to other people, okay? That's invading her privacy." *And driving your father bat-shit crazy.*

"Oh. I'm sorry."

Her little head bent. One finger ran slowly over the edge of the toolbox.

Ah, crap.

His heart ached at the sight of her, quiet and forlorn. His Millie always seemed slightly out of step with the world. Not lagging behind, as he often felt, but definitely marching to a different beat. Long-term, he knew, this could be a good thing. She would have a much stronger sense of who she was once she got older and all the other kids were just waking up to the fact that there was a world beyond glitter and SpongeBob. But right now…

Maybe this was the time to find out why she had stopped wearing her lab coat to school.

He set the saw down to kiss the top of her head.

"Mills. It's okay to ask things, and you can ask me anything, anytime. Never worry about that. But other people don't need these kinds of questions. And even when you're asking, or wondering, let's keep the focus on you, not what other people might, you know, look like. Okay?"

"I can really ask you anything?"

"Anything, babe." *And then we're gonna turn the tables for a few minutes.*

"Okay." She lifted her face to his, her eyes wide and trusting. "Am I gonna get hair down on my privacy like Brynn, too?"

He was so frickin' doomed.

"Yes, you will. I'll be right back."

The thud of his work boots echoed through the cottage, shaking the small space. A moment later he was alone in the bathroom, splashing icy water on his face in a vain attempt to shock some sense back into himself. He gasped and blinked and back-handed the drops from his cheeks, then stared at himself in the mirror.

"Millie," he said out loud. He needed to focus on Millie. Talk to her. Find out what was happening with her. Bring the spotlight back where it belonged, not on…on…

Okay. So Millie had seen something and she had questions. That was normal. And good, really, that she was okay with asking him these things. Right?

He'd long since stopped missing Heather, assuming he ever had—fury tended to cloud the emotions—but damn. These were the times when he wouldn't mind sharing the parenthood gig. Maybe he could try talking to her about this. She'd been a lot more open lately, less defensive than she used to be.

Of course, that didn't mean she would appreciate hearing that he'd let their daughter see another woman naked.

Brynn. Naked.

His brain hazed over. Blood rushed south. His mouth went dry as he let himself imagine, just for a second, how it would feel to run his hand over Brynn's curves, to lick that spot where neck met shoulder, to stretch her hands over her head and taste one of those breasts and—

A scream tore through the cabin.

"Daddy! Daddy, Daddy, owwwwwww!"

He was out of the bathroom before the panic had fully registered, pounding down the hall that seemed to triple in length while Millie's cries bounced off the walls.

"Millie? Millie, what hap—"

He rounded the corner and froze. Millie crouched on the floor and cradled her hand, blood oozing from between her fingers, her face a terrifying shade of white while her mouth hung open in fear. At her feet lay the saw he'd been using. The saw he'd abandoned in his hurry to get away from the questions and images, the saw he'd left within reach of his curious child.

"Okay, baby. Hang on. Hang on." He pried her good hand away, wordless prayers flooding his brain as he coaxed open her fist. "Let Daddy see what you did. Let me have a—"

Sweet Jesus. She'd sliced her palm. Bad. There was too much blood for him to get a good look but he didn't need to see any more.

"Daddy, Daddy, Daddy, it hurts!"

"Shh, baby. I know. We'd better take you to the doctor."

He pressed a corner of the shirt against the wound, cringing at the red wicking up into the fabric, then scooped her up, threw his coat over her back and headed into the icy night. Millie never stopped crying. Every sob, every hiccup, was like a scrape on his soul.

He ran up the path as fast as he could, cursing the darkness that made him second-guess each step. Nothing would be helped if he fell flat on his ass and they both ended up injured.

"It *hurts!*"

"I know, honey. Hang in there, okay?"

"But Daddy, it *hurts!*"

He moved a little faster, as much as he dared, but it still wasn't enough. He needed light. He needed his keys. He needed to get something clean on Millie's hand and put pressure on it and call the doc and drive and—

A light winked at him from between the trees. Brynn's door opened.

"Hank? Is everything okay?"

He looked down at his sobbing child and admitted the truth.

"I need help."

A FEW HOURS LATER Brynn held the door for Hank as he carried an exhausted Millie into the house. Brynn moved as quickly as she could, considering she'd never been inside, switching on lights and pulling back the covers on the twin bed in the small room crammed with stuffed animals, junior telescopes and an oversize stuffed Minion from the *Despicable Me* movies. She slipped out of the room as he got Millie settled and made her way to the kitchen. The polite thing might be to excuse herself and get out of the way, but the hell with that. First she would feed Hank. Then they were going to have a talk.

After a run back to her place and a few moments to acclimate herself in Hank's cluttered kitchen, she had corn bread on a plate, chili in the microwave and water heating for the tea she so desperately needed. She grabbed a bucket from beneath the sink, filled it with cold water and set the bloodied lab coat soaking. By the time the microwave beeped, she had cleared school papers from one side of the tiny round table and had bowls ready and waiting.

Less than two minutes later, Hank stumbled into the room.

"Brynn?" He ran a hand over his chin, blinked in her direction. "What's this?"

"Dinner." She glanced at the clock. "Okay, maybe it's closer to a midnight snack, but whatever. I haven't eaten, I'm pretty sure you haven't and I don't know about you, but I'm hungry. So. Food."

He looked like he was on the verge of protesting, even though she could tell he was half-dead. Time to dig deep into her experience wrangling reluctant males.

"It's chili. I made it last night. And I know we talked about boundaries, but sometimes you just have to be a decent human being. Now sit down and eat."

He reared back the tiniest bit. For a second she was sure she'd reverted too much into bossy-older-sister mode. Then a small smile tugged at the corner of his mouth and he dropped into his chair with a gracelessness that spoke volumes about how much he needed someone else to lend a hand for a moment.

"Lucky for you I'm too tired to fight." He spooned up some chili. "And too hungry to last long if I did happen to be stupid enough to— Oh, God, this is good."

She shrugged as she seated herself across from him and popped a spoonful of beans into her mouth. "Like I said, lots of brothers. I don't cook a ton, but I know how to do filling, cheap and satisfying. Have some corn bread. You need it."

He nodded, shoveled in more chili and helped himself to the bread. She poured tea, added cream and waited. It didn't take long.

"Have I mentioned that you were a godsend tonight?"

"About a dozen times."

The crookedness of his grin was far too endearing. "Sorry. You'd think the blood came from my brain instead of Millie's hand."

"You're her father. You're allowed to lose the ability to think rationally when your kid is hurt." She drew in a deep breath, bracing herself. "But now she's fine, and the worst is past and you've had some food. It's time to talk."

He hesitated a beat before breaking a piece of corn bread. "My mother used to do that."

"What, say that it's time to talk?"

"No. Make sure we were okay, get us fed and relaxed and breathing again and then pounce. I'd forgotten how well it worked."

"Glad you figured it out. Now you're prepared." She cradled her mug in her hands, strengthening herself with the warmth as she leaned forward. "I understand your reasons for putting some walls between Millie and the people who will be in the cabins. But—"

"But you think I'm being a horse's ass."

Her lips twitched. "Thank you for not making me slam it through your skull."

He dipped his spoon into the chili again, slower this time. She wasn't sure if it was because he wasn't as hungry, or if it had to do with her words, but years of harassing her brothers had taught her that sometimes, silence was the best policy.

At last he sighed and looked at her, fatigue and confusion lining his face. "How am I supposed to tell her that it's okay with you but not others?"

"The way you said it just now. 'Brynn is going to be here longer, and she's working with Daddy, so this time, it's fine. But we will have different rules for other people.'"

"Isn't that too confusing?"

She sat back. "Seriously, Hank? You think a kid that smart doesn't know that there are different rules at home and at school and at Grandma's?"

The mulish twist to his mouth faded almost as fast as it had appeared. "Yeah. You have a point."

Good. He was beginning to see the light.

"Hank," she said gently, "I'm very glad that I was here tonight, but personally, I would rather not have a repeat of this evening anytime soon. I bet you and Millie could live without that, too."

He looked at her with eyes that were the definition of *overwhelmed*. "You don't pull your punches, do you?"

"Not over things that matter."

He leaned back in his chair and hooked an elbow over the back. "Why are you so hell-bent on doing this?"

"I'm here. I like Millie. I like you. And sometimes, like I said, you just need to be a decent human being."

He sighed. "It feels like I'm taking advantage of you."

There was more to it than that, she was sure. Probably a smidge of ego and a hint of Superman complex and some of that need to prove himself that she had seen in her baby brother, Lukie, since he was born. The last thing he needed was to feel like he would be indebted to her.

She chose her words carefully. "I have this suspicion that you wouldn't have been out there sawing things at six o'clock at night if I hadn't pushed to have the festival here. So maybe I need to do this for me as much as for you."

He ran his last bit of corn bread around the edge of the bowl, popped it in his mouth and sighed again, though this time with resignation. "We'll need ground rules."

She refrained, barely, from giving a little cheer. "Absolutely. You're the dad, you call the shots. Tell me what's important and I'll go from there."

"Okay. First rule—we wait until the morning to talk about the details."

"That's one I'm more than happy to work with." She lifted her teacup as she stood. "In fact, now that we're in agreement, I'm going back to my place to get some sleep."

He shuffled to his feet, fatigue dropping off him. She had the most unwelcome desire to grab him by the elbow, march him down to his room and tuck him into bed before he fell over. And then she could curl up beside him and—

Where on earth had that come from? Sure, she had indulged in a few minutes—okay, more than a few—of lusting after Hank, but that was just biology and proximity and a really great-fitting pair of jeans. Lust, she could live with. Wanting to take care of him, to do more than lend a hand and share some extra food, that was a whole other ball of snow. It wasn't like he was family.

He followed her to the door, reaching past her to open it as she shoved her arms inside her coat. He swayed a little and bumped up against her shoulder. She looked up, surprised, and lost her breath. For she'd been totally blowing smoke when she said she could handle plain, old-fashioned lust.

Hank's face was mere inches from her own. His eyes had gone wide and were as filled with surprise as she was sure hers were. And the tiredness that had slowed his movements seconds earlier had fled, pushed aside by something far more insistent.

Kiss him.

The thought shivered through her, magnified tenfold when she saw that he was searching her face, his gaze lingering on her eyes, her cheeks, her lips.

She tipped her face up. Then, quick as a light being turned off, sanity returned.

She jerked back, cheeks burning, and raced for the cold and the night and the safety of outside. "Good night," she said quickly. "I hope Millie has an easy night."

She slipped into the dark, picking her way down the path between their cabins. When she reached her door she looked back. He was in his doorway. Watching to see that she made it home safely? She smiled despite her confusion, waved and let herself in.

He was just being a nice guy. She was reading too much in to this.

She almost believed herself.

Until she turned off the light and peeked out the window, where he still stood silhouetted against his door. As if he were trying to figure out what had happened.

As if he were as reluctant to see her go as she had been to leave.

HANK BLEW OFF the festival committee meeting the next morning so Millie could sleep. He called Brynn to let her know of his plan and asked her to tell everyone what had happened. It wasn't until he hung up that he realized he'd made a critical error in talking to her first instead of his mother. Ma was bound to read something into this.

That moment in the doorway the night before, with Brynn so close and tempting… Thank God she had backed away before he did anything. It was going to be hard enough to convince his mother that the only reason he had asked Brynn to deliver his news was because she had been part of the whole episode. It didn't mean anything. As for that fleeting moment… Hey. He'd been exhausted, she had helped without making him feel incompetent, they had been almost touching and, yeah, she was pretty and he hadn't seen any action in longer than he cared to admit. But no lines had been crossed. No relationships had shifted, other than her taking on child-care duties. There was nothing to make his mother suspicious.

Thank God.

All thoughts of Brynn and his mother were knocked out of his head when Millie crept out of her room with her bandaged hand pressed to her chest and tear tracks on her cheek.

"Daddy, when will my hand stop hurting?"

He dosed her with medicine, made her favorite mini-chocolate-chip pancakes and let her eat cuddled up to him in front of the TV. Maybe Sponge-Bob could cackle away the pain. But when the episode ended, the tears started rolling again.

"I don't like this," she wailed into his chest. "I don't wanna be hurt!"

He rubbed her back. She needed to cry it out, his mother would say. Once she got rid of the leftover fear, she would be better.

Ma never had a good answer for how he was supposed to deal with the parental guilt that lingered after the child moved on.

The sobs were interrupted by a sudden gasp as Millie jerked upright, her face filled with almost as much horror as it had been when she realized what "getting stitches" really entailed.

"My lab coat! I left it at the hospital!"

"No, you didn't, babe. We brought it home."

"I need it."

Crap. He should have washed it as soon as he noticed it in the bucket this morning. "Sorry, Mills. It's dirty."

"I don't care. I need it."

"I know, but it's wet. Brynn soaked it last night. To get the blood out."

Fresh tears filled her eyes. "But I *need* it!"

He was about to suggest they grab one of his shirts to use as a substitute when he figured out what she was really saying.

"Do you want to Skype with Mom?"

Thumb in mouth, she nodded. He kicked himself for not thinking of it earlier.

"Okay. You go to the bathroom while I get things set up."

She nodded again and scampered off his lap. He grabbed the laptop and called Heather on his cell.

"Hank?" Her voice registered the mix of surprise and worry that always accompanied unexpected contact. "Is something wrong?"

"Hey, Heather. Everything's okay now, but Mills had some excitement last night." As quickly as possible, he gave her the details of the evening's adventures, conveniently glossing over the part about him leaving her alone with the saw in the first place because he'd been fantasizing about his tenant/semi-employee.

"Oh, my God, the poor doll. How is she today?"

"She'll be okay, but she's hurting and a little shook up. She wants to talk to you. Is now a good time?"

"Of course."

Thank God. Heather might have decided that parenting was best done from the other side of the freakin' country, but over the past year or so she'd become much better at calling and emailing and doing as much as possible to be part of Millie's day-to-day life. So much so, in fact, that he felt compelled to offer an explanation for the delay in keeping her up to date.

"I, uh, thought about telling you last night, but I was pretty beat by the time we got home." *Plus, I was busy being fed and enticed by my forbidden semi-employee/tenant.* "Then this morning I didn't want to scare you by calling too early."

"Not a problem," she said. "I understand."

That was another recent development—her willingness to give him the benefit of the doubt. No, not doubt. Trust. It was like Heather had decided to trust him more lately. There was a time when she would raise holy hell if she wasn't consulted on everything, from which day camp Millie should attend to what she should wear on the first day of school. Pretty rich considering she was the one who left, but, thank God, lately that had eased.

Millie bounded back into the room, already looking more cheerful than she had a few minutes earlier. Within a couple of minutes she sat hunched over the laptop, holding her hand to the camera so her mother could see her bandages.

Hank usually tried to fade into the background during their calls, but this time he stayed beside Mills in case things took a turn for the worse. Sure enough, after the first few minutes of putting up a brave front, the tears started flowing again. Not just from Millie, either.

For a second the old hurt flared. *If you hadn't left, you'd be here hugging her instead of crying over the computer. If you hadn't left, I wouldn't have been juggling this myself in the first place. If you hadn't left, I wouldn't have needed a semi-stranger to help me get her to the doctor last night, wouldn't be depending on her to lend a hand now so I can—*

But no. He wasn't going down that road. The past was past, what was done was done and all that mattered was making sure Millie knew that both her parents loved her. Judging from the way she and Heather were pressing their hands against the screens, that message was coming across loud and clear.

"And, Mommy, I can't wear my lab coat! 'Cause I got blood all over it and I thought I left it at the hospital, but Brynn put it in a bucket and it's all wet!"

Heather wiped tears from beneath her eyes and offered a watery smile. "Oh, honey. I'm sorry. But Daddy will get it ready for you as quick as he can. You know that. And—" Suspicion crept across her face. "Wait. Who's Brynn?"

Oh, *crap.*

He leaned sideways to face the camera. "She, uh, she's running the big festival for the dairy. She's been staying in one of the cabins."

"Yes?"

There was a boatload of emotion in that one simple syllable. Too late, he realized that it could sound like he was about to confess a romantic involvement. The whole damned world seemed determined to throw Brynn at him.

Best to nip this one in bud right away.

"Mills, did you show Mom that pot you made at school? Why don't you go get it so you can show her?"

Suitably distracted, Millie hightailed it down

the hall. As soon as she was out of earshot, Hank dove in.

"Brynn gave me a hand last night—you know, helping along the drive, that kind of thing—and she volunteered to look after Millie for a while at nights so I can get more done around here. Mills doesn't know that yet, but she likes Brynn, so it seemed like an easy, convenient solution."

"Oh."

There was such doubt in Heather's voice that he instinctively tensed, bracing himself against her objections.

"Well," she said after a lengthy pause. "That... Okay, I guess I can see... She's good with Mills?"

"Very."

"And you've checked her out?"

Oh, hell, yeah. But that was going to stop. Immediately. "She's Taylor's cousin. We have work references, obviously, but I can get personal ones if you want. She's good with Mills."

"I guess it makes sense, then."

She looked like she wanted to say something more, and he sat up straighter, ready for whatever it might be. But after a second she merely pushed her hair back and sighed. "Okay."

He felt like he'd dodged a bullet, and just in time as Millie reappeared with a lopsided clay pot in her hands.

"Right. So, here's Millie again. I'll get out of the way and—"

"Wait. Hank?"

He braced himself.

"Thanks. For calling, and taking care of her and…and everything."

He muttered something to cover his surprise and handed the laptop back to Millie.

Something was up with Heather. He hoped it was that she had settled down and relaxed, but he couldn't be sure. It made him twitch.

So did his mother's interference.

So did Brynn's very presence.

If Millie grew up to be like the other women in his life, he was in for a hell of a ride.

CHAPTER SIX

FITTING MILLIE INTO her schedule worked so well that Brynn was almost afraid to say anything, for fear she'd jinx it. But it was true. She put in a full day of festival work—most of which flew by, because she absolutely loved it—grabbed a bite to eat, usually alone, sometimes with Taylor at a place that held special memories of Ian, then took on Millie duty for an hour or so. Usually, by the time Hank got there, she and Millie were scrambling to finish whatever they had been working on.

The only fly in the ointment was that she was in Hank's house. Rather, his home. There were bits of him everywhere she looked, from the jacket that stayed on the back of the rocking chair to the shaving cream in the bathroom to the balled-up socks circling the laundry hamper. It was too easy to picture him walking past on his way to the shower, tossing the socks like a basketball, doing a little cheer when they landed true. Too, too easy to imagine him naked from the waist up, pajama pants riding low on his hips, barefoot and rumpled and ready to be rumpled up some more.

All in all, it was almost a relief when Saturday night rolled around and she and Taylor headed to Sam's place for a wild night of harassing Sam, commiserating with his wife, Libby, and cuddling Casey. For a couple of hours she got to forget about misfiring hormones—both hers and Taylor's—and reveled in the kind of laughter that could only be found among family.

Except she couldn't. Because every time Sam leaned over to give Libby a kiss, she remembered standing in the doorway with Hank swaying beside her, drinking her in despite his exhaustion. Every time she and Casey knocked down a block tower she remembered Millie helping him do the same thing at her cabin, remembered teasing Hank in her tiny kitchen and wishing he would kind of fall into her. Every time Sam sat back and laughed— so carefree, so casual, his eyes never leaving Libby as she swatted and scolded and snickered—Brynn found herself wondering how he had done it. They both had grown up in the same screwed-up home, had both been abandoned by their father when life went to hell. Yet here he was. Settled. A damned fine father. Crazy in love.

It had taken a long and sometimes messed-up road, but Sam truly had it together. In fact, now that she thought about it, she couldn't remember the last time he had needed anything more from her than an address or a night of babysitting.

It was a surprisingly unsettling realization.

Of course, being older, he had never needed her the way Lukie and Trent had, but still. There had been many a night in those first scary weeks after life went to hell when he would call—"Just checking in"—and they would talk for ages. She knew, as no one else had, how much it had ripped him apart to be away when so much was happening at home. She was the only one who suspected how lonely he was back then, how desperately he poured himself into hockey in the hope of helping the family by snaring a pro contract. And in the dark days after Casey's mother died when Sam thought he might lose his son, Brynn had been the first one he called, the one he had trusted with both his child and his fears.

She was beyond delighted that he had found Libby. She couldn't be happier for them, couldn't have chosen anyone more perfect for Sam if she had tried, as indeed she had a time or two.

She had just never expected to sit in her brother's house and feel a little bit like a guest.

She was so caught up in her thoughts, fighting off her sudden melancholy, that it wasn't until it was almost time to leave that she realized Taylor had not been her usual chipper self that evening. Of course, she was always a little subdued these days, but this night was worse than usual.

Oh, crap. She'd been so fixated on her own needs that she'd completely forgotten why she was in Comeback Cove in the first place.

She waited until they were walking to their cars and the crisp night offered a bit of privacy before saying, "So, kiddo, I get the feeling there's been a new development in your love story."

Taylor stopped in the middle of the gravel path, hesitated, then shoved her hands in her pockets.

"I should have brought gloves. I knew I would be freezing, but it was so much milder today that I thought…"

"Tay, if you don't want to talk—"

"I had a dream last night, okay?"

"Uh-huh."

Taylor's head tipped back as if she were searching the sky. "It, um, was a dream I really shouldn't have had."

"Ah."

A moment later came the deep and ragged breath Brynn had been expecting.

"It was such a good dream, Brynn."

Squeeze eyes closed, do not let yourself imagine… "You know, there's a reason God gave us double-A batteries, Tay."

"What do— Oh! Geez, Brynn, not *that* kind of dream!" Taylor gaped at her before hustling down the path. "Give me some credit," she called over her shoulder. "I wouldn't tell you about those."

"Sorry. But it was a logical assumption." Made all the more logical because of Brynn's own troubles sleeping recently. Her body had decided that the closing of her eyes was the signal to roll out some vivid suggestions as to ways she and Hank might have helped each other fall asleep after Millie's visit to the E.R.

"Well, it was nothing like that."

"So tell me about it."

"I don't remember much. I was in a house. Maybe mine. It wasn't any place I recognized, but it had this homey feel to it, you know? I was in there doing something, I don't know what, but then Carter walked in. And oh, Brynn, I was so happy. There was no guilt, no worries, just…just togetherness, and knowing it was right."

"And then he scooped you up and carried you off to the bedroom?"

Taylor's mouth set in a line. "I told you, it wasn't like that. It was…deeper."

Brynn's heart sank as she reached her little hatchback. Taylor was talking like this a lot lately, insisting that her attraction to Carter was more than physical. Unease flickered through Brynn's veins. She knew how to deal with lust, with temptation, with attraction. But what if Taylor was right? What if she was really in love with Carter?

"We need to fix this."

"I know." Taylor sagged against the car door, her face a picture of misery. "I spent the morning practicing my affirmations. I read through the stories with Ian and I wrote a couple more. I've been keeping him firmly in my head, and, Brynn, honest, when I'm awake, I feel like it's working. I like talking to him again—well, at least until he asks about setting a date—and I don't walk around feeling like I'm going to burst into tears all the time. I can even be in the same room as Carter and not feel like I'm going to fall apart. Those things are all helping, really helping, and I am so glad you thought of them."

"There's a hell of a *but* coming next, isn't there?"

"But…the dreams are getting stronger. Almost like my subconscious is trying to tell me I'm wasting my time."

This was getting worse by the minute. It was time to step up the intervention…. But how?

"Look, Tay. I have a suggestion. You leave pretty soon for the conference, right?"

"Right."

"So from now until then, and even during the conference, immerse yourself in as much Ian as you can manage. Douse yourself in his aftershave before you go to bed. Sleep in his pajamas. Eat foods that make you think of him, watch movies you watched with him, wear his underwear if you have to. Write his name over and over. Write letters to him."

"But I email and—"

"I don't care. These are for you, not him. Write him letters filled with all those things you're putting in your memory book. Remind yourself over and over of how much he meant to you. Do a poster filled with pictures of the two of you together, the way you want it to be in the future."

Between the moonlight and the streetlights Sam had added to the parking area, there was just enough illumination for Brynn to see the way Taylor's face sagged momentarily before she dredged up a smile.

"Okay. You're right. I need to try harder, right?"

"Right," Brynn echoed, hoping she sounded more confident than she felt. Because after a night of watching the real thing in action, courtesy of Sam and Libby, she couldn't help but compare and wonder if the real thing should require this much effort.

On the other hand…

She patted Taylor's arm. "Remember how happy Sam and Libby are. Keep replaying everything that happened tonight, but put you and Ian into the picture. Keep smiling."

"Fake it 'til I make it, huh?"

"That's right," Brynn said, wishing it didn't feel so wrong this time.

She got into her car and sent up a prayer that Taylor was wrong, that this was nothing more than a combination of absence mixed with abstinence. Lust, Brynn could handle.

That stupid flying Cupid was another horror story.

TUESDAY AFTERNOON, WHEN Hank was about ten minutes away from finishing the painting he needed to do before he had to clean up and get Millie, his phone rang. He cursed, pulled it from his pocket and frowned when he read the name.

"Hey, Heather."

"Hi. Sorry to bother you, but I want to talk to you without Millie around. Is this a bad time?"

He glanced at the windowsill in progress. Maybe he could work one-handed while talking. That would cut at least a few minutes from the task.

"I can manage," he said. "But I'm painting. So if I sound distracted—"

"Don't take it personally. Got it." She laughed lightly. "Listen, I'm being sent to the Ottawa office again, starting in a couple of weeks. For three months this time."

So that was why he'd had the feeling something was up the last time they talked.

He had no idea what to say. This would be the third time this had happened in two years. Much as he knew it was good for Mills and her mother to be in the same time zone, his brain couldn't help but hopscotch to the point four months from now. Heather would fly back to the west coast and he would be here, watching Millie cling to a threadbare old shirt after her mother said goodbye.

Again.

His hand tightened on the phone. He wanted to tell her to forget it, that her constant comings and goings were doing more damage than good. He wanted to tell her to find a new job that wouldn't keep sending her out here. He wanted to ask if she was coming back because Millie needed her, or because she needed Millie.

Oddly enough, it was none of those words that sprang to his tongue, but something entirely unexpected.

Sometimes, you just need to be a decent human being.

"Uh…wow. She's gonna be psyched."

That was as much as he could manage at the moment, but Heather seemed to understand. "I know this is hard on you, and on her. But I'm hoping… There have been some changes here. I'm hoping, if I do a good job, this will turn into something permanent."

His paintbrush hit the floor. "You mean like moving back here?"

"God, I hope so." There was no mistaking the fervor in her voice. "I don't want to change anything with you and her—really, I'm not planning to change the custody agreement or anything—but I'm praying I can make this happen. I don't want to mess things up, but I want to be there with her, too. To do Wednesdays and alternate weekends, to go to her parent-teacher conferences, to see her up onstage at the Christmas concert."

Heather. Coming back again. Maybe for good.

His nod felt slowed by fatigue and surprise and that ever-present sensation of being one step behind. All he could do was stammer out something about getting back to her. He said goodbye, shoved his phone back in his pocket and stared at the white paint dotting the floor where he had dropped the brush.

"Son of a…"

He didn't know what to make of this. His head knew it was better for Millie to have both parents close by, but his heart was running an endless loop of scenes from the last times Millie had said good-bye to Heather.

But if she moved back…

He swiped at the paint and scratched at the bits that had dried already and told himself to breathe, that they would get through this, that nothing good could come of panicking.

And that there was absolutely no reason to freak out because in those first knocked-on-his-ass moments, the voice of sanity in his head had been not his own, not his mother's or Moxie's—but Brynn's.

HIS HEAD WAS STILL whirling that night when he crawled back to the house after his second go-round in the cabins. He was tired beyond belief, aching in places he never knew could ache, covered in paint and sick to death of his own company and thoughts. All he wanted was to jump in the shower, read Millie a chapter of *Harry Potter* and hit the hay. He knew he should spend some time working on the Northwoods calendar or looking through Millie's backpack or checking out her teacher's website, but all that was going to have to wait.

He walked in from the cold night to a house over-flowing with laughter, music and the sight of his daughter prancing around in the most ridiculous pair of sunglasses he had ever seen.

"Sequined shades?" He looked at Brynn. "When did you turn my daughter into a diva?"

"Daddy, it was so much fun! We did an exara-ment."

"Experiment." Brynn rested her hand on Millie's head and smiled.

"Right. To see if you could do anything to onions so they wouldn't make you cry. We put one in the freezer and lit candles and cut them under water. Brynn did that one. But they all made my eyes run anyway, so Brynn said I should wear these. She got them at a party and she never wears them, so I can keep them!"

Her utter joy pulled a smile from beneath his layers of worry and fatigue. He dropped into the kitchen chair and pulled her close, listening to her excited recitation of the evening's events while his gaze lingered on Brynn. She wasn't doing anything unusual—wiping down the counter, rinsing off a knife, adding little clarifications to Millie's tale in such a way that it made sense to him without ever intruding on the story. Yet when she reached for her jacket and bent to pull on her boots, a pang of longing arced through him.

Don't go.

He wanted her to stay. Not in a "hey, girl, want to

have some fun?" way, but because she made things better. Lighter. Almost magical.

Holy— *Magical?* He shook his head. Must be more exhausted than he'd realized.

"Okay, I'm off." Boots in place, she stood and smiled. "Give me a hug, Mills. And, Hank, I'll see you at the meeting in the morning, right?"

Hell and damnation. He'd managed to put that out of his mind. "Uh—right. Though I might as well warn you now, I haven't done anything about the band."

"Not to worry. You're getting our site ready. I don't expect anything else of you. Besides, Moxie and I talked today and we have an idea for a kick-off that will blow the lid off this town, so that will take up a lot of the meeting."

Why did the thought of Brynn and Moxie plotting together make him want to notify the authorities?

Millie pulled back from the hug she'd been bestowing on Brynn's legs and pushed her glasses higher on her nose. "What are you going to do? Tell me!"

"Oh, I shouldn't say anything. It's a secret."

"But I am in the family, too, and I don't get to go to meetings now because you do them when I'm in school. So you should tell me." Her eyes took on a sly gleam. "Or I could skip school and come. I could wait to hear the secret if you let me skip."

"I bet you could," Hank said dryly. He still hadn't

been able to wring anything out of her about her reluctance to get on that bus every day. "Points for trying, Mills, but it's not happening. Brynn, could you please tell her your big news so I don't have to spend my next waking hours explaining why school is important? I can put my fingers in my ears if you need me to."

"Well, as long as you promise not to tell…"

Millie made a zipping motion across her mouth. "Zip it, lock it, put it in my pocket."

"Okay. We decided to kick off the festival with a family dance."

Oh, hell.

"Something fun," Brynn said. She was so focused on Millie that she hadn't noticed he wasn't smiling. Good. That gave him a minute to play catch-up. "Maybe that 'Celebration' song. Or 'We Are Family.' Moxie wants that one. We'll have all of you Norths up there, dressed in outfits from the different eras of the dairy—a flapper, a fifties greaser, a hippie. You'll do an easy, fun dance like folks do at weddings and flash mobs. Moxie thought it would be a hoot."

"Sounds great." He bent to untie his work boots so he wouldn't have to see the disappointment on her face. "But leave me out."

"Sorry?"

He tugged at a stubborn knot, still not looking at her. "This festival is cutting into my schedule enough as it is. I don't have time for rehearsals and—and everything." Not to mention the fact that the last time he had danced in public had been what most folks would call an epic failure. "My folks will do it, and everyone else. Millie can be in it, too. But count me out."

"But, Daddy, it will be fun."

Not for him, it wouldn't.

"Look, Brynn," he said, "you go right ahead and plan what you want, okay? I'll do my part. I'll run cables and rewire the whole damned campground and turn myself inside out to make things work. But that's my limit, and I'm kind of tired of people jerking me around. So plan what you want, but leave me the hell out of it. Got it?"

Millie, wide-eyed and silent, stuck her thumb in her mouth. Brynn inhaled sharply but glanced at the child and pasted on a smile that went straight to his guilt meter and elevated it another notch.

"Of course. I— Sorry." Her expression softened as she bent to hug Millie. "Sleep sweet, kiddo. I'll see you tomorrow."

Millie glanced over her shoulder at him and gripped Brynn a little tighter. "G'night, Brynn."

She slipped out the door quickly, lightly. Just as well. He didn't need her to linger, didn't want to have to explain things that were best left in the bad-memory bin.

Magic. Right.

HANK SLEPT LIKE SHIT and stayed silent throughout the meeting. He was pretty sure that if he said anything it would come out wrong and make an unpleasant situation even worse.

Not that anyone would know there was a problem from watching Brynn. She was cheerful and professional as always, smiling over her half-glasses, making appropriate jokes and keeping even Moxie in line. Taylor had been right about her. Brynn was a force of *über*-nature.

But this time, she wasn't going to win.

The minute the meeting was declared finished and the rest of his traitorous family had embraced the dance idea with open arms, he was out of the conference room. Down the hall he went with a fleeting wave to the receptionist as he plowed through the double doors toward sunshine and freedom. He was about three steps from the truck when his phone rang.

Son of a—

He slowed long enough to dig it from his pocket. He knew it was Brynn, it *had* to be her, but if he didn't check then this would be the time it was the school.

It wasn't the school. But neither was it Brynn.

"Hey, Ma." He grabbed the handle. "Is this important? I'm kind of in a—"

A soft hand landed on his shoulder. Before he could protest or spin around, the matching hand plucked his phone from his grasp.

"Got him, Janice." Brynn didn't smile as she walked in front of him, speaking into his phone. His stomach clenched. "Thanks for your help."

She handed the phone back to him. He had never personally identified with Russian or Finnish hockey players before, but suddenly he was feeling great empathy for the ones who had tried to outwit Ms. Catalano.

Still, he wasn't going down without a fight.

"Slick move. But I don't care what you do, I'm not dancing at the festival or any other—"

"Millie told me something last night. About school."

Oh. Well, now he felt like the world's biggest idiot. Luckily, that wasn't a new experience for him.

"What about it?"

The breeze caught a bit of hair that must have escaped her ponytail and blew it across her face. He shoved his hands in his pockets while she pushed it back in place.

"There's a girl in her class. Noelle. Apparently, she's decided that Millie is her personal punching bag and is making her life miserable."

He'd always thought that "seeing red" was just an expression. Turns out it was an extremely apt one.

"What's she doing to her?"

"Millie says that Noelle teases her in front of the other kids, and calls her a baby when she sucks her thumb. Things like that. The kicker was yesterday at lunch—a bunch of them asked her to play with them at recess, but then when she ran to meet up with them this Noelle stood in front of them and said, 'Why don't you go home and wash your dirty shirt, baby?' and they all ran off laughing."

He breathed in sharp and fast around teeth clenched so tight he found it hard to draw in oxygen. He hadn't been able to get the bloodstains out of the lab coat, but Millie had insisted she didn't care, had wrapped it even tighter around her since her injury. "Shit."

"Yeah, that was my reaction, too. But don't worry. I didn't say it in front of her."

"She's heard worse than that on the school bus." He rubbed his hand over his face, sought some measure of control that would let him go forward in a calm, adult manner. It wasn't easy. His baby was hurting and he hadn't been able to prevent it.

His baby was hurting and she had told someone else about it first.

Shit, shit, shit.

He pushed his own pain into a corner where he could examine it later, when he had a bit more reason at his command. "Was she upset? When she told you, I mean."

"She wasn't happy, but she wasn't crying, either. I think she was equal parts hurt and perplexed. Though maybe it's just easier to focus on *why* someone would do something like that. You know. Stay one step removed."

"Yeah, well, she's not the only one who's thrown

by it." He shook his head and rested his hand against the truck. "First grade and they're pulling this crap already?"

"My bet is that Noelle isn't the oldest in her family. Kids learn all kinds of things at the feet of their siblings."

Yeah, he knew that one all too well.

That loose bit of hair was dancing in front of her face again, fluttering around her mouth where it seemed to stick for a second. He hunched his shoulders against the wind and curled his hands tight in the depths of his pockets until she swiped it back into position.

Silence fell between them. She seemed to expect a response, but damned if he could figure out what to say. His focus was divided between thoughts of Millie at recess, questions as to why Millie had gone to Brynn instead of him and if that bit of hair was now coated with Brynn's cinnamon-colored lipstick.

"Anyway," she said after a moment, "sorry to be the bearer of bad news, but I figured you should know."

He nodded and was about to let her walk away when he realized there was more to ask. "Brynn?"

"Yes?"

"What did you say to her? To Millie?"

"Oh." The wind kicked up again. Her hand went to the side of her head. "I told her that it sucks and it happens to everyone, but if it bothered her, maybe she could make the lab coat a just-for-home thing again. And if Noelle said anything more else, Millie could just walk away."

Brynn, suggesting someone walk away from a problem? Not the answer he would have expected. Or the one he would have given.

"I told her the main thing was to make sure Noelle didn't see that she'd hurt her."

Okay. Now it made sense.

"And then I told her she needed to talk to you."

"Which she didn't do, as you can probably tell." Not that he was upset by this. Not at all. But at least Brynn had tried.

"My bet is that once she got it off her chest, it didn't bother her as much."

Maybe.

"I didn't want to go into it more than that. But if she mentions it tonight, is there anything in particular you'd like me to say?"

"I can think of a few things. But most of them would probably get her suspended." He smiled a bit. "I'm more of a stand-your-ground kind of guy when it comes to that stuff, but I'm not sure of the best way to phrase it for a kid. Let me get back to you."

She nodded. "Sure. You need to talk to the teacher and all that."

Ah, hell. He hated talking to teachers. He always felt like they were assessing him as a parent, as a single father. Except, of course, for the ones that tried to hit on him. He'd never known how many lonely single women were in the world until Millie started junior kindergarten.

"Yeah. I'll do that."

She nodded again. "Okay. I guess I'll see you later, then."

"Right. Tonight."

She was almost gone before he realized that he needed to get his head out of his ass, and soon.

"Brynn."

She turned back to him with an unreadable expression.

"Thanks. I'm kind of—I don't know. Blown away by this. But thanks for letting me know, and for, you know. Being someone Millie can trust." He breathed in, forced himself to say what needed to be said. "And I'm sorry I was such a jerk last night."

She moved closer. Waiting, he knew. Waiting for him to give her the explanation she deserved, if not for his refusal to participate in the dance, then at least for his rudeness. He debated making some kind of easy excuse—lousy day, tired, coming down with a cold—but to his surprise, he didn't want to do that.

He wanted to tell her the truth.

His brain fired off a thousand reasons why that was a stupid idea, starting with her being his sort-of employee and ending with the fact that she was already too damned wise for her own good. But then he looked at her. Really looked, and saw things he had never expected to see in her face. Hurt. Hope. Uncertainty.

Had he ever seen Brynn look uncertain?

"My ex called me yesterday and told me she's being transferred to Ottawa for a couple months. Maybe permanently."

Brynn's mouth sagged open the tiniest bit. "Oh."

"She wants to be closer to Millie," he clarified, because for some reason it was important that she understand Heather wasn't coming back to him. "It threw me for a loop and I took it out on you. That was stupid. I'm sorry."

"I… Wow. Okay. I see how that could do a number on you."

"This has happened before. Not the permanent part, but her being in Ottawa. It's good for Mills, but at the same time it's hard."

"I can believe it."

"I haven't told Millie yet, so don't say anything, okay?"

"Not a word." She shook her head as if to emphasize her point. The strand of hair came loose again, beckoning him, and this time, he didn't think. His hand lifted before he realized it. He pushed the runaway bits behind her ear quickly, lightly. The way he would for Millie.

Except his hand seemed to be stuck to the soft curve of Brynn's cheek, the sweet strength of her jaw. His thumb was drawing a slow line down, slipping across warm skin, gliding toward lips that had parted with a soft intake of breath and then remained open. Like an invitation he couldn't refuse any longer.

"God, Brynn."

He stepped forward, she moved and, sweet heaven, he was kissing her. His hands cradled her face, her hair teased his fingertips and her mouth—oh, her mouth—was open to him, tugging his closer, making him wonder and want and *feel* for the first time in longer than he could remember.

She made a small sound, somewhere between a question and a whimper, and moved closer. Her hands flattened against his chest and slipped up as he let his hands slide down, his palms learning the length of her neck and the strength of her shoulders and the curve of her lower back as he tugged her closer, pulled her against him and swayed as her curves molded perfectly—

Until the loud *beep* of a car horn slammed some sense into him, making him wrench himself away from her.

Holy— He'd been *kissing* her. Kissing and feeling and, shit, maybe even groping. In broad daylight. In a parking lot within full view of the street—thus explaining the horn—but, worse, of anyone at the dairy whose window happened to overlook the lot. Like Moxie's. Or his mother's.

"I—"

She leveled a finger in his direction. "So help

me, if you say you're sorry, I…" She gave herself a shake.

He didn't know what to say. Sanity was making its slow way back to him, pointing and laughing at the many ways he'd made a royal mess of things, but, God help him, he had kissed her. She had kissed him back. Sweet heaven, how she had kissed him back.

She took a step back and swallowed. She seemed as rattled as he was. Sure, she covered it better, but he couldn't help but feel a jolt of male pride that he, Hank North, had been the one to shake up Brynn Catalano.

"We will talk about…about this." Her hands flew to her head, scooping her runaway hair back from her face, making him long to feel those curls surrounding his fingers once again. "Just…don't you dare apologize."

He was still too stunned by what had happened to say anything insightful or coherent so he settled for a quick nod, and briskly said, "Right. Whatever."

She took a couple of steps back. She bit her lip and his fingers inadvertently went to his own mouth in search of the last remnants of her taste, her heat.

At last she turned, head down against the breeze, and hurried back inside. He yanked on the truck door and pulled himself inside the cab, where he sat and stared at the parking lot and tried to figure out what the hell had just happened.

Only two things were clear. The first was that he was an idiot.

The second was that at the moment, he was too damned happy to care.

CHAPTER SEVEN

BRYNN'S FIRST TASK after hurrying back inside the dairy offices was to do a slow walk along all the corridors on the parking-lot side of the building. Her ears were perked up for laughter, whispers or conversations that came to an abrupt halt with her approach—anything that would indicate that someone had been glancing out the window at the precise moment when Hank—*oh, my God*—had kissed her. Or when she—*oh, my God, oh, my God*—had kind of tried to crawl inside his coat while kissing him back.

Luck seemed to be on their side. She didn't see or hear anything that made her think anyone had seen or heard them. Which meant the only one she would have to panic about facing again was Hank himself.

Hank, whom she had threatened with dire consequences if he dared apologize. Well, tried to threaten. Stupid, damned, misbehaving brain cells.

Her patrol of the halls complete, she found a deserted ladies' room where she locked herself in a stall and sat down to make sense of the thoughts bubbling through her brain.

Nobody saw us. Why do women always hide in the bathroom when they need to think? I shouldn't have kissed him back. I hope no one comes in here. What will I say to him tonight? Oh, my God, what if someone saw us? Damn, he's a good kisser. I wonder what else he— Oh, no. No. That's not happening. Moxie would be— No, there's no way to predict what Moxie would say. Should I tell Taylor? Damn, I want to kiss him again.

She sat and breathed in and out, slow and steady, letting the thoughts pour out uncensored. In the worst days of her youth when her mom was in the hospital and her so-called dad was AWOL and her brothers were scared and crying, she had figured out that it was useless to bottle up her own runaway imagination. Better to get it all out. Then and only then could she move forward with the bright smile they needed.

For a minute or two, maybe more, she let the thoughts flow unchecked. Then, with her head emptied of all the competing worries and memories, she was able to focus. Get herself back under control. She pulled a notepad and pen from her purse and listed the items to be considered. Somehow, when she did this, things never seemed quite as overwhelming.

- Talk to Taylor about Hank's past, but make sure she doesn't suspect anything.

- Decide what to say if anyone should mention the kiss.
- Decide what you want to happen next.
- Decide what to say to Hank tonight.

She chewed on the end of her pen and considered her points. The second one was the easiest. If anyone should say anything, she decided, she would shrug, act like it was no big deal and then ask if they were planning to watch the game that night. Hockey was the one topic that could always distract a Canadian from any other subject.

Decide what you want to happen next…. That would have to wait. First, she needed time for her body to stop sending out little messages of joy every time she remembered those moments. She could almost hear her various bits and pieces whispering their approval. *Please, Brynn, can we have some more?*

Her body might have a pretty strong agenda, but she was still the one in charge around here. No decisions could be made until she had more time and a lot more information. And since she couldn't plan what to say to Hank until she had made a decision, she needed to start with the first item on her list.

She tapped out a quick text to Taylor. Meet me for lunch?

Sure. Indian?

When had Taylor developed a taste for Indian food? Sounds good.

After setting the details, she snapped her phone closed with a nod. She immediately popped it open again and sent another message, to pregnant cousin Paige, inquiring both as to how things were going and if any maternity-leave decisions had been finalized. That should help her subconscious remember that her focus belonged on her family, not on Hank North. No matter how great a kisser he might be.

She might have lost her head out there in the parking lot, but she was back in charge now.

Everything was under control.

THIRTY MINUTES LATER, she breezed into Comeback Cove's one and only Indian buffet and slid into the booth across from Taylor.

"You beat me!"

Taylor's smile was so wide, she looked almost like her old self. "I swore I'd get here first this time, so I left fifteen minutes before I thought I should, just to be sure."

"A change. I like it. And a new cuisine, too."

"Oh. Well, just doing my part. This is one of Ian's favorite places."

"Really? Good girl!"

"I deserve more than a 'good girl.' The only thing I can really eat is the chicken tikka and the *pakora*. Oh, and the rice." This smile wasn't quite as glowing, but the determination shone through. "The main thing is, it's bringing back memories, and they're good, and that gives me hope."

"That's awesome, Tay." *I wanted to pull Hank into his truck and fog up the windows.*

Brynn blinked. Where the hell had that come from? She'd thought the hormones had been wrestled into submission on the drive over.

Huh. This was what happened when she went too long between men. Her body went into sex-zombie mode, but instead of moaning for brains, it shambled off in search of nooky.

But she could handle this. She was in control. And she had a job to do.

As soon as they had filled their plates and settled back into the red vinyl booth, she took a healthy sip of her mango *lassi* and eased sideways into her topic. "Hank is point-blank refusing to be part of the dance, and I have a feeling there's more to it than self-consciousness."

"Congenital grumpiness?"

She wanted to agree but couldn't. Hank was grumpy, yes, but not all the time. Not when he was teasing Millie, not when he was eating chili after a long night in the emergency room and sure as hell not when he was kissing her knees out from beneath her in the parking lot. In fact, if she had to define his temperament, she would be more likely to say he was…shy? Socially rusty, for sure. But capable of immense warmth.

"I don't know. I told him about it last night, and he said he was too busy. But he seemed kind of— I don't know. Embarrassed? Defensive?" Which could have been explained by Heather's bombshell, true. But since she was mostly using this topic as a way to slide into her true questions, she could fudge things a bit.

"Oh, crap." Taylor sat back, her fork stabbing the air. "How could I forget? The hockey dance."

"The what?"

"It was in high school. Hank was in grade nine, I think—yes, because I was at the dance with Brian Quinlan, and he was my grade-eleven guy."

"I don't remember you talking about that one."

Taylor patted her hand. "When I was in grade eleven, you would have been in grade ten. You were kind of busy that year."

Oh. Right. Sometimes Brynn forgot that most people hadn't spent their high school years in such a blur that they hadn't had time to formulate anything more than a few memories. Not that she would have wanted to hold tight to much about those years, but it would be nice if, once in a while, she could conjure up a story to share with Trent and Luke.

"Anyway, every year there was a big dance before the first hockey game of the year. It was the social highlight of the fall. Hank went, and he... well... The only way to describe it was that it was like watching a grasshopper do gymnastics."

Brynn winced. "Ouch."

"Yeah. I don't know what happened, because, you know, he played trombone in the school band so he knows music and rhythm and stuff. But that night he was all over the floor. I think he must have just seen *Boogie Nights* and was trying to use some of the moves from that."

"Well, that must have sucked for him."

"Worse. It followed him around all year. Every time there was a dance his picture would pop up on some of the posters. There was something in the talent show… It went on and on."

Brynn pushed a piece of chicken with her fork. "And Comeback Cove being the kind of place it is, I imagine there's a lot of folks still living here who remember this."

"Probably not as many as he thinks. I mean, I had forgotten about it. But in his shoes, I don't think I would be in any hurry to strut my stuff in front of a hometown crowd."

"All the more reason why he should do it."

A plan was taking shape in her head. A plan that she was pretty sure Hank wouldn't like, but one he couldn't refuse, because it would help Millie.

But while that plan percolated, she had some other investigating to do. After some more distraction, of course.

She asked Taylor about Ian, about her mom, about work. Carter's name never came up, and Brynn had enough presence of mind to take note of that fact. It was too soon to celebrate, but Taylor was committed to the plan at this point, and that, she knew, was half the battle.

It wasn't until they were spooning up thin, sweet

rice pudding that Brynn let herself ask the question that had brought her to lunch in the first place.

"So…Millie's mom. Where is she?"

"Somewhere on Vancouver Island. Nanaimo, maybe. Why?"

Brynn shrugged. "No real reason. It's just I've seen a lot of pictures of her while I've been hanging out with Millie, and I was curious."

"About where she lives?"

"No, dipstick. About what happened."

"Why? Do you have the hots for Hank?"

The best defense is a good offense. "Oh, yeah. I fantasize about him constantly. Can barely get my work done, I'm so busy imagining the day he'll notice me."

Taylor snickered. "Okay, okay. I get the point."

Oh, good. Her scheme had worked. Nothing would be gained by gushing to Taylor that Hank's years playing the trombone had left him with some majorly amazing lip muscles. But at the same time…

No.

"Look, we both know I'm a nosy bitch. But Millie talks about her mom, and there's pictures and notes and things from Heather everywhere. It all seems very…I don't know…civilized and friendly. Which is wonderful. You know I'm all for fathers who put the kid first."

"But you don't know why two people who seem to be so friendly got divorced in the first place."

"Like I said, nosy."

"Well, in this case, you're going to have to stay curious, because the honest truth is, I don't know."

"Oh, come on. No one ever really knows what goes on in a marriage, true, but there's always speculation when it ends."

"Well, yeah, of course." Taylor shrugged. "But really, it wasn't hard to predict. Heather got pregnant while they were still in university. They got married, Millie came along, Hank finished school and worked at the dairy while Heather finished her degree. Then she up and left."

"Just like that?"

"Just like that. It was before I was with Ian, so I don't know many details. Apparently, Hank came home one Friday night, Heather told him she couldn't do this anymore and boom. Exit stage right." Taylor sipped her Diet Coke.

Ouch. "So Millie was, what, two?"

"Around that, yeah."

Brynn ran her spoon idly through the bits of pudding left in her bowl, watching the lines appear in the creamy whiteness and then fill back in. Here and gone, here and then gone. Just like Heather.

Walking away from marriage, Brynn could understand. Walking away from a child—no.

Lukie had been not quite five when their father left. Watching her baby brother sobbing in fear had been enough to destroy any last bits of love Brynn might have felt for their disappearing father. She couldn't imagine being on the receiving end of the kind of treatment Heather had dished out and still being willing to leave the photos on display, facilitate the phone calls, do everything possible to ensure that the bond between mother and child wasn't permanently severed.

But that was exactly what Hank had done.

Brynn was pretty sure that a man who could do that, a man with that kind of history, wasn't the kind to kiss a woman on a whim. There would have been a lot of thought beforehand. A lot of deliberation. She had told him not to apologize, and she'd meant it. She didn't want him to regret those moments when they had pushed each other to forget the wind and the onlookers and the consequences.

But there was no way that she could give a man like Hank what she feared he was seeking....

Forever.

CHAPTER EIGHT

Hank was certain that he messed up every single thing he touched for the rest of the day, right down to putting too much milk in the Kraft Dinner and then accidentally popping Millie in the nose when he spun around in an attempt to drain it. It was no better in the buildings. He had planned to look at the wiring in the Grindstone cabin, but he was so distracted by the memory of Brynn pressing against him, kissing him back with a hunger he hadn't anticipated, that he knew he shouldn't be allowed near anything with potentially lethal consequences.

No, this was definitely a hammering-and-painting kind of night—or so he thought until he cut his last piece of plywood too small, knocked over a can of stain and got sawdust in his eye. By the time he conceded defeat and headed back to the house, he had decided that even without another reason, he had to stay away from Brynn for the health and safety of himself and everyone around him.

He kept his focus on Millie when he walked back into the house, just as he had done when Brynn had first arrived that night. But even so he knew where Brynn stood, what she was looking at, what she was planning. It was no surprise to come out of Millie's room after tucking her into bed and find Brynn sitting on the sofa, tapping on her laptop. It was probably what he would have done if their positions had been reversed.

Not that he was going to let himself think about positions....

He dropped into his favorite overstuffed chair—mostly because there was a coffee table between it and the sofa—and clasped his hands together.

"So," he began, "we need to stay quiet, but—"

Brynn raised one finger, hit a couple more keys and glanced up at him.

"Almost done."

After a minute she hit one last button, pulled off her glasses and closed the laptop.

"Sorry. I had this great concept for the newspaper ad and I wanted to get it down before I lost it."

"Not a problem."

"Do you think Millie can hear us?"

"I put some music on and closed her door as much as she would let me, and she usually passes out pretty fast. But we'd better keep it down. If she knows you're still here she'll never get to sleep."

Of course, that was all the encouragement his imagination needed to toss out suggestions as to things he and Brynn could do that would be a lot quieter than talking. His only consolation was that, judging from the pink in her cheeks, her thoughts had taken the same direction.

That was fine. There was nothing that said they couldn't be traveling down the same road. The important part was to make sure their paths stayed parallel instead of intersecting.

"So about this morning," he began, but she shook her head.

"Not to worry. I know it caught you by surprise as much as it did me. We're two adults who are together a lot and who, if I might be so bold, have both been without adult companionship for a while. It makes perfect sense that there should be some sort of attraction between us. But we're both smart enough to know that there would be no point in taking it any further, because it would be too damned complicated and I will be out of here before you know it. So. It was a heck of a—a moment, but now it's behind us and we need to talk about the things that really matter." She breathed in deep. "Like, you owe it to your daughter to be part of the family dance at the festival."

He was pretty sure that his mouth was hanging open, and definitely certain that the past minute was the closest he would ever come to a hurricane in his life.

Brynn continued rattling off her obviously rehearsed speech as if he hadn't made a sound. Come to think of it, he hadn't. His pleas for mercy were all in his head.

"Now. I know about high school and all that nonsense. But really, Hank, you need to—"

"Whoa, whoa, whoa. Hold on." He raised his hands as if he could stop the flow of words by force. "What do you mean, no adult companionship for a while?"

"I— Oh, come on, Hank. You're not going to distract me. Millie is being bullied at school and you have the perfect chance to show her how to stand up to that kind of behavior. You owe it to her to—"

"You mean you're going to pretend it never happened?"

Her expression lost some of its zeal. "Of course not. Nothing is ever accomplished by ignoring the truth. I've just found in life that it's better to…to accept what's happened and move on."

"Move on."

"Right. Which is exactly what will happen when you take part in the dance. You'll put those last fears and memories behind you and provide Millie with a positive role model that will help her stand up to—"

"What did you have to put behind you, Brynn?"

She stopped. Blinked. "Pardon me?"

"You heard me." He leaned forward, noting the way she pulled back, the sudden wariness in her eyes. "It's pretty obvious that you're speaking from experience. So, since it's also pretty obvious that you have uncovered all my secrets, it's my turn to do some snooping. What have you had to put behind you so you could move on?"

This time, he knew that her flush had nothing to do with awareness. "None of this is relevant right now. You're trying to get me off-topic."

"Could be. Or I might be a little ticked off that you seem to know everything about me and my past but I know next to nothing about you." His voice softened. "Or maybe I'm asking because I think you're a hell of a woman and I want to know what made you who you are."

He knew that was a mistake as soon as he said it. He was supposed to be distancing himself from her, not delving into her past. Nothing would be served by learning more, finding points of commonality, being tugged closer.

Except he really wanted to know.

"I— Fine." She sat up a little straighter. "If it will make it easier for you to focus, then fine. When I was sixteen, my mother was diagnosed with terminal cancer. The terminal part turned out to be wrong, thank God, but my father decided that a dying wife and four kids were too much for him to handle. So he left."

Holy— He hadn't felt this kind of a kick to the gut since the night Heather handed him a crying toddler and picked up her suitcase. "Son of a—"

"Yeah. That was about it."

"So those jokes you made about learning to cook

to feed your brothers—they weren't really jokes. You were the one who kept them going."

"Sam and I, yes. It was really harder for him, I think, because it was his first year of university. He wanted to be home, to help, but we agreed that the best thing he could do was to focus on the game and hope for a pro contract. As it turned out, that's what happened."

"So you were running the household by yourself."

He knew her well enough to realize that her casual shrug wasn't an attempt to minimize what she had done in the past. She simply didn't want it to take over the present.

Her suggestion that Millie walk away from Noelle suddenly made a lot more sense.

"I did what had to be done. It wasn't like he was much of a father in the first place, though I didn't understand that until later. Mom pulled off a miracle, Sam's team won the Stanley Cup, Trent joined the military and Lukie started university last year. Happy endings all around."

Did she realize she hadn't included herself in that list?

"So that's my story. It sucked and then it got better and now it's time to move on. The first dance rehearsal is tomorrow night, in the lobby at the office. You and Millie should be there by seven."

His knee-jerk reaction was *no way*. Not because it was a school night, which should have been his reason, but because he was in no hurry to don the spiked hair and ripped jeans of his youth to relive one of the most cringe-inducing episodes of his school career.

Which meant that—crap—she was absolutely right. He had to do it.

He could tell Millie to stand up for herself until he was as blue as a Smurf, but that was just talk. If he really wanted to help his little girl, he needed to walk the walk. Stand his ground. Look like an idiot for the greater good, and do it with a smile.

God, Millie was gonna owe him for this one.

He sighed and leaned back in the chair. "You know I'm not doing this because you decided I should."

"Of course not. I can't make anyone do anything they don't want to do." A shadow crossed her face, so fast he wasn't sure if he had seen it or imagined it. "All I can do is help people see things in a different light. What happens next is entirely up to them."

"You honestly believe that line?"

"It's always worked before."

"I might have to start taking notes. Some of your tactics might come in handy once Millie gets older."

"You make me sound so mercenary."

He couldn't help it: his gaze went straight to her mouth, to those lips that were burned into his awareness. "I don't think *mercenary* is the word I would use."

She stilled.

"Hank." Her usual confidence was nowhere in sight as she traced the seam of her leggings. "I wasn't kidding before. Another time, another place…"

"You took the words out of my mouth." And the breath from his lungs, but nothing would be served by mentioning that.

"I guess I should head back. Unless there's anything else to discuss."

The only things he could think of were all in direct violation of everything they had just agreed on, so he settled for a simple nod.

"Then I'll get out of your way." She flashed her smile, gathered her laptop, unfolded herself from the sofa.

"Brynn. You want to ride with me and Mills tomorrow?"

"Sure."

It didn't mean anything, he told himself as he walked her to the door. Millie would be with them. There was nothing that said they couldn't be friends, and carpooling was nothing more than that—a friend thing. Totally innocent. Totally within the boundaries of being safe and permitted.

And if, secretly, he knew he was totally blowing smoke out his ass, well—that was for him to know and no one to find out.

FATHER OF THE YEAR that he felt like sometimes, Hank almost forgot Millie's dentist appointment the next morning. Consequently there was a hustle to rearrange his plans, a rush to call the school and a race to get to the office on time. Then, when she was finally in the chair, things really went downhill.

He staggered back to the truck with his head full of warnings and consequences. The drive to school was spent trying to come up with a strategy. Once Millie had been delivered to her classroom, he climbed back in the cab, slumped behind the wheel and let out the string of curses he'd been holding in since the dentist looked up from Millie's mouth and asked, "Is she still sucking her thumb?"

Decay. Speech problems. Braces. All because he'd been too much of a softie to make her stop.

Well, those days were over. Millie wasn't happy, but he and Google were about to spend some quality time researching the most effective ways to put an end to this. If he didn't find anything helpful there, he would bite the bullet and call Moxie. God knew she would have suggestions.

And maybe Brynn—

He shook his head. He couldn't let himself become dependent on her. A little blurring of the lines, okay. But he would be the world's biggest idiot if he let himself see her as anything other than exactly what she was—a very smart, very attractive woman who was here to do a job and then leave.

I've just found, in life, that it's better to...to accept what's happened and move on.

She'd been talking about herself when she said that. But the words had kept sounding in his head through the night. Not about Brynn, and not about Millie or even the stupid dance he'd been conned into doing. But about someone else. Someone who was soon going to be a lot more involved in Millie's day-to-day, maybe for the rest of her life.

Heather was trying. Which meant he should try, too.

His mind made up, he grabbed his phone.

"Hey, Heather, it's me. Don't worry, nothing's wrong. But I wanted to bring you up to date on a couple of things."

Slowly, picking his words very carefully, he told her about the dentist's concerns and the troubles with Noelle. She listened and commiserated and even had a couple of half-decent suggestions. By the time he said goodbye, he almost felt like this could work. Like maybe, even though he and Heather would never be together again, they and Millie could create a new kind of family.

Maybe, just maybe, it was time to move on.

IN ALL THE WORRY of convincing Hank to take part in the dance, Brynn had managed to overlook one teeny tiny little problem. She didn't know how to dance.

Oh, she could fake it pretty reasonably at weddings. She could do the Macarena with the best of them, and she had long ago mastered the Electric

Slide, the Cupid Shuffle and the YMCA. But actual dancing, all the ballet terms and official moves and graceful motions—no.

Online research had taught her how to chart the song. Like a first-grader learning to print, she had sketched out page after page of lineups in a lucky blue notebook. Her final routine drew heavily from those group dances she knew, generously salted with moves copied from YouTube videos. She had practiced it over and over by herself until the steps were deep in her muscle memory, so ingrained that she could start the song at any point and immediately jump into the proper step, turn or kick.

Her brain told her that the Norths would be too focused on learning the steps to spare a thought for her lack of knowledge, but she knew. Feigning ability in an area where she had training or related experience was no problem. Faking a skill that wasn't part of her usual toolbox left her feeling the slightest bit like a fraud.

A fraud wearing a blouse that—as she realized when she ran into the bathroom off the Northstar lobby—was an invitation to disaster.

She scowled at her reflection. Two minutes before departure time, after spilling milk on her plain black tee, she had grabbed this top. It was a simple white peasant number embroidered with red and blue flowers around the neckline. Modest, short-sleeved and lightweight. Plus, it was elasticized at the waist, affording easy movement without hugging or revealing.

But she hadn't worn it since last summer and had forgotten that the scoop neck had started to sag, revealing a hint more cleavage than she had anticipated. The shoulders were a tiny bit too big, giving them the tendency to slip off her shoulder. And the fabric was just sheer enough that if she wore the wrong color bra, the outline could be detected.

Because, of course, when she made her last-minute change before leaving tonight, she had forgotten that the girls were clad in hot pink satin.

Forget confident, competent professional. After a half hour of dancing in this outfit, she was going to look like a milkmaid in heat.

There was nothing to do about it now. She had to go out there, fake her way through this and try to forget that Hank would be one of the ones whose eyes would be glued to her every move. But only her feet, right?

"Right," she told her reflection, fully expecting it to burst into laughter at her pathetic attempt at rationalization.

She gave her neckline one final tug, let loose with one of her favorite Russian swear words—sometimes it was very handy to have a brother who played hockey—and pushed herself out the door.

Showtime.

HALF AN HOUR into the first rehearsal, Hank made two decisions. The first was that if he were going to put himself through this—onstage, no less, in front of a town full of people who would be only too happy to remember his last public attempt at dancing—Millie was going to owe him a nursing home approximately equivalent to the Taj Mahal.

The second was that bright pink had become his new favorite color.

Not that he was trying to look. Hell, no. At first all his energy went to following the steps. Brynn kept up a rousing line of chatter, praising, teasing, cajoling. Cash stumbled a lot, Carter was frustratingly good and Moxie strutted like someone forty years younger. Millie's cheeks glowed and her thumb was nowhere near her mouth, so he called that a double win. His own movements were stiff and jerky at first, but if he focused very hard on what would come next, he could push the thoughts of public humiliation to the background.

Too bad he couldn't do the same with thoughts of Brynn.

She faced the wall of windows as she demonstrated the steps for them, so she couldn't see that he was drinking in her every move. At first he told himself it was necessary. Hey, it wasn't like he had a lot of practice with this stuff. But as time went by and even his mother was staring at Brynn, he decided it was okay to look. So look he did. He couldn't kiss, couldn't touch, couldn't do any of the hundreds of other things he longed to do, but dammit, he could look.

So while he stumbled along, his eyes feasted. Her feet were smaller than he'd realized until he watched them point, tap and scuff. Her leggings ended just above her ankle, revealing the bottom edge of what he was pretty sure was a tattoo. Maybe someday he could cradle her foot on his lap and push up the edge of those leggings while pulling down her sock. He could run his finger over the edges of whatever design she had inked there, tapping and sliding and tracing until his palm flattened over it and slipped higher, sliding over her skin, and—

No.

Her calves seemed more muscular than he'd thought, though given the number of times he'd spotted her heading out for a morning run or jumping from rock to rock with Millie, he shouldn't have been surprised. Her blouse came to midthigh but didn't conceal the swing of her hips as she stepped and turned.

Maybe they could do a conga line. He could be behind her. His hands would close over those swaying hips and he would be able to feel the muscles ripple beneath them slower, then faster, sideways, then back and forth—

No!

He dragged his gaze higher. Her back. He could look at her back. Sure, hers led to curves and valleys that called to him, but her back itself was safe. Maybe even a little too wide across the shoulders if he were being totally objective. Yes. He could look at her back as much as he wanted.

Until the dance went on and the body heat went up and her blouse began to stick to her skin. And the outline of her bra—so flimsy, so forbidden, so magnetic—grew ever more impossible to ignore. When her blouse slipped off her shoulder, exposing another strip of mesmerizing pink, he stumbled straight into Millie and almost knocked her to the floor.

And he'd thought that making himself dance again would be the definition of torture.

At last the hour was up and Brynn called a halt. The music ended and was replaced by laughter and groans echoing through the lobby. Millie ran to her grandpa. Carter and Cash swarmed Moxie. Taylor handed Brynn a water bottle. She took it with a smile, tipped it up and drank. His eyes traced the exposed skin of her neck. His hands relived the heat they had found there. Her hair flowed back. His fingers curled as if they were once again cradling her head and filling himself with her want, her *need,* that had matched his. His breath caught and his mouth went dry and he knew he had to find some reason, some excuse, to touch her again. Her hand, her arm, maybe the small of her back as he helped her into the truck.

Then she turned back to them and he spun away—
And caught his mother watching him with a look of total satisfaction on her face.

BRYNN CLIMBED INTO the Tundra while Hank got Millie settled into the second seat. Despite her fears, the evening had gone off well, at least from what she had seen. No one had laughed at her, no one had caught the moments when she screwed up, no one had been unkind enough to mention that by the end of the evening she might as well have been wearing searchlights on her breasts. Taylor had never mentioned Carter or gone near him. Yep. Total success.

Except that with every step and every twist, she had practically felt Hank watching her. And instead of doing the smart thing and ignoring it, or trying to discourage it, she had, well, reveled in it.

There was no other way to describe it. She had sensed his gaze following her moves and she'd put a little more oomph in her hips, a little more shimmy in her shoulders and little more breath in her laughter. It was wrong and stupid and precisely what she wasn't supposed to be doing, but, God help her, she had done it anyway. She had been aware of his gaze and even more aware of her body, of the need prickling along her arms and legs and everywhere in between, and somewhere during the night, the brazen milkmaid she'd been imitating set up shop inside her.

Which would have been okay if she could have jumped in her sane and sensible little hatchback and scooted home through the cool night. But no. She had thought she had this all under control and agreed to ride with him. So now here she was, beside him in a truck that all but oozed masculinity, breathing in the slight tang of him, knowing that she was the reason he was so sweaty. Knowing, too, that if not for Millie chattering behind them, she would be plotting ways to put that already sweaty body through some more dips and turns.

"So the dentist said I hafta stop. But I like my thumb. I need it. How do I sleep if I don't have my thumb, Brynn?"

She muttered something soothing and stared out the window. There were reasons she couldn't get mixed up with Hank. Good reasons. She just wished she could hear them over the chorus of *want, want, want* pounding through her head.

Other than Millie, no one spoke. She didn't know about Hank, but she was scared to say anything. She probably should congratulate him on taking the first step, thank him for trusting her to not make a fool of him, but she had the horrible feeling that if she said his name it was going to come out floating on a wave of pheromones that she was incapable of controlling.

Control. Stay in control.

At last they turned off the road and bumped up

the rutted path to the cabins. Each pothole, no matter how gently Hank eased over it, sent new ripples of alertness running through her. How was she supposed to forget about her body's wishes when every jolt sent her swaying toward Hank's shoulder and left her various bits and pieces saying, "Hey, remember us? We're here, and damn, we're hungry!"

"Ow! Daddy, those bumps made me bite my tongue!"

You're not the only one, Mills.

At last the car jerked to a halt.

"Can I open the door, please, Daddy?" Millie scrambled free of her booster and leaned over the seat, dangling between them. "I hafta pee."

"Sure." Hank handed her the keys. "I'll be right there."

"No! I want to do it myself. You stay here and watch me. You, too, Brynn. I can do it!"

Shit. Brynn undid her seat belt in preparation for a fast escape.

"'Kay, Mills. But hurry up, okay?"

Millie kissed Hank's cheek and scrambled out of the truck, slamming the door behind her, plunging the cab into shadows. Brynn held her breath. Surely she had at least one brain cell that hadn't been hijacked by the knowledge that it was dark, they were alone and they weren't likely to be interrupted for at least two or three minutes.

She slid a bit closer to her door, trying to block the little voice whispering in the back of her mind, reminding her that two or three minutes could make a hell of a difference in a person's state of mind. Or body. Or even both.

The door to the house flew open. The kitchen light clicked on. Millie dropped her coat to the floor and disappeared inside.

"I guess it's safe," Hank said.

Brynn knew what he meant. Millie was in the house and he could join her without intruding on her independence. They should get out of the truck and go their separate ways. She knew it.

Yet somehow her body interpreted his words as meaning that it was now safe to dive-bomb him.

She sprang across the seat. Judging from the speed with which his arms closed around her, she wasn't the only one who had been primed to move. She pushed him back against the door and twisted sideways and almost climbed on top of him as she searched for his mouth, tasting the leather of his jacket and the salt of his skin and then, sweet heaven, the heat of his lips against hers. One of his hands slid under her coat and the other cupped her bottom. He tugged, she wriggled and in a moment she was straddling him, kissing him and wanting him more with every slam of her heart.

"Brynn. Jesus, Brynn, we—"

She didn't want to hear it. Didn't want to acknowledge anything but the heat and the need. She pushed against him. He pulled her tighter, pressing against her in all the hungry places. His hand went to her shoulder and she tried to shake her head, to tell him no, but still he pushed. She opened her mouth to protest but then he nuzzled her breast and his hips hit a different angle and the light washed over her and—

The light?

Shit! *Millie!*

Brynn blinked against the sudden brightness and stared stupidly at the child standing in the now open rear door. Her brain whirled, her body howled and beneath her, she felt Hank stop, drop and roll back against the seat.

"What's taking you so long?" Millie asked.

Brynn took a deep breath and prayed that the oxygen she was inhaling would be loaded with mind-clearing substances. If they were very, very lucky, Millie would stay there on the running board and never once clue in to the fact that her daddy was currently beneath a very disheveled Brynn.

"Hey, Mills. Your dad said something about running down to the Grindstone cabin—I think he said he left his wallet there today. And wouldn't you know it, I knocked my purse over and all my stuff went flying. My, um, my lipstick rolled over here and I had to dive for it. Give me a minute and I'll be right there. Are you scared in the house all alone?"

She edged herself upright as she spoke, doing her best to tug her clothes into position while easing around the steering wheel and chattering in hopes of distracting the child.

"Okay, I have everything now. You go on inside so you don't get cold. I'll be right behind you, and Daddy will be back in two shakes of a lamb's tail."

"Okay."

Brynn pulled away from Hank while Millie ran inside once again. Disentangling was a lot more complicated than getting tangled up had been. Also a lot less fun.

Light fingers brushed her cheek. "Are you okay?" he asked softly.

Not nearly as okay as she would like to be.

"I'll be fine." The words came automatically, years of habit rising when needed.

"You can go straight to your place," he said. "I'll tell her I caught up with you and sent you home."

"It's okay. I can—"

"Brynn." The urgency was back, thickening his voice and sending sparks skittering beneath her skin once more. "If you step into my house tonight, I will lock you in my bedroom until Millie is asleep and then I will finish everything we started here. And even though that sounds like the best idea I've had in my whole freakin' life, we both know that—"

"It would be stupid. Right."

"Not stupid." He sighed. "But not in anyone's best interests, either."

She nodded and reached for the handle. She felt

she should say something, do something, but for the life of her, she wasn't sure what.

And for the first time ever, she knew there was no way she could fake her way through.

CHAPTER NINE

AFTER A NIGHT spent alternating between fury and frustration, with a healthy side of guilt just to add excitement, Brynn dragged herself into the office with the biggest coffee and the most decadent doughnut to be found this side of Toronto. She set her haul on the desk with a defiant air, fully prepared for Taylor to make a crack about a rough night.

"Morning." She refused to even pretend to describe it as "good."

Taylor made a small sound somewhere between a grunt and a whimper. Brynn looked at her, fast, but Taylor was firmly focused on whatever was on her computer screen, so Brynn opted to let it go. She busied herself with arranging her food substitutes and opening her laptop. She kind of hoped that Taylor's reading material would take a long time. She wasn't sure if she was ready to put on the bright and cheery act quite yet.

"Come to me, my sweet." She cradled the coffee as if it were a hummingbird egg, delicate and precious. Ah, God. There was nothing like that first perfect sip of heat and sugar and—

"Ian wants to set a date."

Oh, hell.

Brynn closed her eyes, allowed herself one more moment of just her and the beauty that was caffeine, then took a deep breath and pushed her worries to the back of her brain. So she was messed up over Hank. That was nothing compared to what Taylor was going through.

"Tell me."

Family first, Brynn.

Taylor sniffled, stood and shot a pointed look at Brynn's doughnut. Good thing she'd opted for lemon-filled instead of one with a hole. Then, after carefully closing the door, Taylor pulled her chair up close.

"We were talking last night, and I— Oh, Brynn, it's so hard. I really do like him. If I hadn't been stupid enough to think I was in love, we might have been such awesome friends. Because he's funny and he's got these insights and…"

The temptation to interrupt and get the conversation back on track was strong, but Brynn tamped it down. Taylor was so busy listing Ian's good points that she was doing Brynn's job for her. Shutting down the flow would be counterproductive. Instead Brynn settled for nodding, making sympathetic noises and doing her best to banish the memory of Hank's lips at the side of her neck. He'd had just enough stubble on his jaw to scrape her skin. She hadn't noticed it at the time, but this morning, one look in the mirror had made her grateful she'd brought a couple of high-necked sweaters with her. A quick wardrobe change and the proof of her mistake was hidden from the world.

But she knew. And her usual pattern of accepting and moving on wasn't doing a thing for her today.

"...I convinced him that we really needed to wait until he came home to make any decisions, but, Brynn, this is so damned hard." Taylor's eyes filled with tears.

Oops. Shouldn't have let her go on this long.

"Stop." Brynn made herself speak far more brusquely than her heart would have chosen, but sympathy wouldn't help at this point. "You're not going to start crying. You can't. You have a meeting in twenty minutes, and Carter is going to be there. You will not give any hints whatsoever that you are anything but a competent, happily engaged professional. Got it?"

Taylor's eyes were far too wide and glittering for Brynn, and her chin had that wobbly look that spelled danger, but she blinked furiously and nodded.

"Good. Did you listen to yourself just now? To that list of Ian's good qualities?"

"I never said he was a lousy person. He's a great guy. If I had any brains, I would be head over heels for him. But I'm—"

"Not trying." Brynn made a point of sniffing the

air. "Why don't I smell his aftershave? You know you're supposed to wear it."

"Oops." Taylor opened the bottom drawer of her desk, pulled out a bottle and dabbed obediently.

"Now. Eyes closed. Deep breath. Remember inhaling this when Ian wore it. Remember how it smelled on you after you held him. Remember... remember his hand at the small of your back. His other hand is holding the back of your head and his fingers are pushed up in your hair. They're so strong.... Remember how it felt to walk into this office and be all prim and proper on the outside, when inside, all you could remember were the things you had done with him the night before, the things no one else knew about—"

Oh, *crap.*

Somewhere along the line she'd closed her own eyes. She opened them fast, but standard-issue beige walls and neutral desks couldn't blot out the bright colors blooming in her memory—the red of Hank's shirt beneath her palm, the hint of darkness along his jawline, the deep brown of his eyes when he opened them after kissing her senseless. All she could remember was that perfect moment, that fast heartbeat, when nothing mattered but want and need and promise.

Oh, shit, she was in trouble.

Taylor, good girl that she was when she wasn't committing emotional adultery, sat in her chair with a faraway expression on her face. She hadn't seemed to notice Brynn's lapse. Hallelujah. It gave Brynn a moment to slug down more coffee in the hopes of searing the truth into her head.

After a long moment of silence, Taylor breathed in again, slow and deep. When she opened her eyes she seemed more relaxed, and her smile wasn't quite as heartbreaking.

"Thanks," she said simply. "That, um. Wow. It helped. A lot."

No, no, no. "Really?"

Taylor laughed. "You shouldn't sound so surprised. Whatever happened to projecting confidence in your ability?"

Brynn raised her cup as if in a salute. "Bite me, goof. You've never seemed so receptive before."

Taylor shrugged, feigning casual, but there was no hiding the way she averted her eyes. Or the pink creeping up her neck.

"You painted a pretty vivid picture there. Made it a lot easier for me to pull up some…some good memories."

Oh, hell. Did that mean that Brynn was going to have to relive Hank's kisses every time she was trying to help Taylor? Was she doomed to weeks of self-torture in order to maintain her cousin's engagement and protect Northstar?

Brynn had the sudden, horrible feeling that something that had already been complicated had just become a hell of a lot more so.

HANK SPENT THE next two weeks walking around with the proverbial angel and devil on his shoulders.

Avoiding Brynn was impossible. Between the nights when she looked after Millie and the weekly festival meetings and dance rehearsals, she was always there. Even when she wasn't in his face she was in his head. He turned on the TV, the Leafs appeared and all he could see was her in her jersey. He walked into his bathroom, her perfume lingered in the air. He took Millie out for dinner and ordered chili and realized that it wasn't nearly as good as Brynn's.

And every time he hopped into the truck, he remembered the way she had clutched him, the heat and weight of her over him, the fierce desperation in her kisses. Every drive became an exercise in torture and a nonstop recitation of the reasons why getting involved with her would be a bad choice. Unfortunately, the more he listened to himself ticking off reasons, the more he was able to rationalize them away.

She was going to be leaving. Well, he wasn't looking for anything permanent, anyway.

He didn't want Millie getting too attached and getting hurt, especially with another Heather arrival and departure on the horizon. Still true. But he doubted she could adore Brynn any more than she already did, so the farewell was going to be painful no matter what. Besides which, Heather seemed pretty positive that this transfer was going to be long-term, that any return to Vancouver Island would last only as long as it would take her to settle her affairs there. Not to mention that he was now going to have some child-free time on alternate weekends, time when he could do anything he wanted and no one would be the wiser....

She was his sort-of employee. Except not really. He wasn't at the dairy anymore, and she refused to take money for child care.

And then there was the fact that he had promised his mother he would start dating again. Sure, her focus was on getting him married off and acquiring more grandchildren, neither of which seemed likely with Brynn. But he'd been out of the dating pool a long time. Wouldn't it be good to ease himself back in with someone he already liked? Someone who already knew he could be grumpy and busy and sure as hell seemed to like him anyway?

Needless to say, he didn't offer any more rides to or from rehearsals. Neither did she.

But after driving himself around the bend and back with trying to figure out what he should or shouldn't do, he decided there was one thing he could do. Something to repay Brynn for the help with Millie. And, if it meant she might end up sticking around a bit longer, well...

To do it right, though, he needed help. The thought stuck in his craw until he rationalized that it was okay to ask for assistance when he wasn't the one who would be benefitting. It was a slightly self-serving kind of logic, but since he was planning to tap a lawyer for aid, he figured it was appropriate.

He waited until the next Friday, knowing full well that Carter was always in the Comeback Cove office then and that he kept the afternoons clear for catch-up work. Hank walked into the office at noon, his arms filled with strategic gifts which he dropped on Carter's desk before taking a seat.

Carter did the eyebrow-arch thing that Hank suspected was one of the first lessons they taught in law school. "What's this?"

"This," Hank said, hefting the bag that was filling the room with the aroma of meatballs in sauce, "is lunch. This bottle of rye is a bribe. And this visit is your chance to finally redeem yourself for the Great Pop-Tart Disaster of our childhood."

Carter stared at him for a moment before nodding. "Close the door."

Hank held in his grin until he was up and facing away from his brother.

Talk was light while they ate—the usual catching up, a few Millie stories, some conjecture as to whether or not their mother would be planning a giant welcome-home party for Ian. Hank made it through the meatball subs without once mentioning Brynn. He figured he deserved a reward for that, so he broke out the dessert he'd hidden in the bag.

"Whoa. Doughnuts, too?"

Hank set the six-pack in front of Carter, who

opened it with a whistle. "Honey dip, maple glaze, walnut crunch—all my favorites."

Hank nodded.

Carter sat back, drumming his fingers on the desk. "I have to tell you, Hank, you have me worried. These are major-league bribes. Well beyond traffic tickets. Your divorce is final, your truck can't go fast enough to get a speeding ticket and you already bought the cabins. So who did you kill?"

"I need some help."

"No shit, Sherlock. We've known that for years." Carter grabbed the walnut crunch. Of course he picked that one. He knew damned well that Hank had a soft spot for walnut crunch.

"I want you to suggest something to Moxie. It has to be done in such a way that she'll never guess I was behind it." He swallowed. "Her or Mom."

Carter stopped chewing for a second, a smirk appearing on his lips. "Well, well, well. Hiding things from Ma and Moxie? That's world-class." He took another bite. "So you and Brynn finally got a clue?"

"What? No, shit, it's nothing like—"

"I thought you seemed less grouchy lately. Figured you started taking some new vitamins or something. I never thought you might have a helper adjusting your attitude. Does Ma know? No, wait. She doesn't. If she did, she'd be bugging you instead of riding my ass about asking Jenny in Accounting to Sunday dinner."

"You know, I'm only paying in food and booze.

There's no billable hours involved here. You don't need to keep flapping your mouth to make this take longer."

"Good point." Carter raised the doughnut in Hank's direction. "Talk to me."

"It's pretty simple. And yeah, it does involve Brynn, though not the way you think. But since that's the way Ma thinks, too, I have to be kind of, you know, subtle."

"Spit it out, Hankie."

"I think she's smart and a good worker. I want someone to drop a bug in Moxie's ear about finding a permanent job for her."

"You want us to offer her a job."

"Yeah."

"Because she's smart and hardworking."

"That's what I said, isn't it?"

Carter grinned. "I knew you had the hots for her. Cash said no way, but I told him, hell, yeah." He let out a hoot of laughter. "Wait 'til he hears this!"

Dammit! Why had he thought he could pull this off? "It's not like that, and if you say one word—"

"Not even the one you want me to whisper in Moxie's ear?"

Ah, hell. "She's been a real help with Millie," he said stiffly. "I thought I could do something nice for her without it turning into a federal case. Guess I was wrong."

"Well, little brother, if you want to do something nice—purely for altruistic reasons—then I guess I can do the same. It so happens that Moxie and I were already discussing something along those lines. Unfortunately for you, though, the lady seems to prefer job-hopping. Free as a bird, and all that jazz. I wouldn't get my hopes up. Other parts, maybe, but not my hopes." He reached for the bottle. "But I'm keeping the bribe anyway."

"That's for your silence."

"Oh, for God's sake, Hankie. I don't know how to tell you this, but everyone knows you've got it bad for her. We go to those rehearsals and you're either making sure you don't look at her—not a good plan when you're learning a dance, I might point out—or drooling so bad that the rest of us have to steer around the puddles. I gotta say, though, you have good taste. A little above your gene pool, maybe, but she's a good one."

"You know what? This was a stupid idea. You don't want to listen to me, you just want to hear yourself talk. I'm out of here." He stood and grabbed for the doughnut box, but Carter was too fast for him, seizing him by the wrist.

"Hank, listen to me. Believe it or not, I'm glad you're showing some interest in a woman again, okay? You've been turning into someone we don't know. It's nice to see the old you coming back."

It would be easier to appreciate his family's concern if it didn't come with a side order of implications.

"Well, that's very nice of you all to spend your

time speculating about me, but you can stop now. Nothing is happening between me and Brynn." At least, nothing he would mention to any of them. "And even if I were interested she swims in a different gene pool, as you so kindly pointed out. You think I'm stupid enough to fall for someone when there's no chance of it ever amounting to anything?"

The change in Carter was so fast, it was like he was inflatable and someone had pulled the plug. He set down the last of his pastry, folded his hands together and bowed his head.

"Yeah." The word was muffled and raw. "Yeah. That would be a really stupid thing to do."

Hank's worries for himself faded as he took in the lines in Carter's face, the bleak cast to his voice.

"You, uh, you have a problem, Car?"

Carter continued to stare at his hands for a long moment before drawing in a sharp breath and lifting his head.

"What? No, no. I'm… You know. Memory Lane. You just caught me by surprise."

Bullshit.

BRYNN SAT CROSS-LEGGED on Taylor's bed Thursday night, mainlining bean dip and calling instructions as Taylor buzzed around the tiny room, adding and removing things from the suitcase at the other end of the bed.

"There are always boring sessions at these conferences. Use them. Did you upload the Ian playlist to your iPod?"

"Weeks ago."

"Did you pack it?"

"It's in my carry-on."

"Good girl. Do you have some of his aftershave?"

Taylor added a pile of bras to the suitcase. "No, but there's a drugstore beside the conference hotel. I'll buy aftershave, cashews and that disgusting beef jerky that I refuse to eat, but which will perfume my room with its gross scent."

"Excellent." Brynn frowned at the bowl. Empty. "Is there more dip?"

"No, you piglet, you plowed through it all." Taylor whizzed into the room, grabbed the empty bowl and headed to the dimple in the wall that passed for a kitchen. Brynn shrugged and followed.

"I need ice cream." She opened the freezer and peered past bags of green beans and boxes of assorted chicken products. "Ew, you really eat those fake burritos?"

"No. They're part of the Ian plan. And there's no ice cream, so get your nose out of there."

"How about beer? You have any beer?"

Her rapid opening of the refrigerator door was followed just as quickly by Taylor reaching behind and slamming it.

"What's with you today? You're acting like a teenage boy who hasn't eaten in three hours."

"I'm hungry, that's all." Not a lie. But even Ben and Jerry couldn't help with this kind of hunger.

She and Hank hadn't discussed the incident in the truck. They hadn't said much of anything to each other, actually, other than the essentials—*remind Millie to keep her thumb out of her mouth; I'll be a bit late tonight; there's a drip on my porch roof.* But it was Hank's most recent bulletin that had her scrounging for satisfaction in the cupboards.

"We won't need you Friday," he had told her a couple of nights ago. "Heather is in Ottawa and she's taking Mills for the weekend."

Millie would be gone. Hank would be alone. It would be just the two of them and all those empty cabins. Cabins, she had come to realize, that Hank had named after islands of the St. Lawrence.

Islands were well and good, but at the moment, Brynn was contemplating bridges. Maybe even a ferry. Anything that might connect those isolated land masses, if only for a while.

"I have a hard time believing you're that hungry," Taylor said, cutting into Brynn's mental wanderings. "No. Wait. That, I can believe. It's *what* you're eating that's got me worried. I can't remember the last time I saw you eat this much junk, and I don't have time to go all Dr. Phil on you. Why don't you tell me what's happening so I can pack and you can stop doing your imitation of John Belushi in the cafeteria in *Animal House?*"

Oops. The focus was supposed to be on Taylor, not Brynn. Diversion time.

"Hey, you're the one who had this food in her cupboards."

"I had the pita chips. You brought the dip. And the chocolate. And the red licorice, though I'm not giving you grief about that because I'm taking it on the plane."

"That's right. Steal my stuff and then insult me. Did you pack Ian's shirt to sleep in?"

"Yes."

There was an interesting twist to Taylor's voice that pulled Brynn away from her own idiotic melancholy. "Yes?"

"Of course."

"Why are you refusing to look at me when you assure me that you're following instructions?"

Taylor stared at the floor.

"Taylor?"

"Fine." She flounced past the bathroom to the corner of the room affectionately known as the bedroom. "Okay. The truth is, you keep saying I have to keep Ian in mind whatever I'm doing. Wearing his shirts was a nice thought, but the fact is that when we shared a bed, I was usually—"

"Naked?"

The lovely pink coloring Taylor's cheeks was all the answer Brynn needed.

"Every night, Tay? You dog!"

But her hoot of laughter couldn't negate her brief

stab of jealousy. Lucky for her, Taylor cut through her self-absorption with a quick shake of the head.

"No, not every night. Just when I stayed over."

"But I thought you two were practically living together before he left. You certainly have enough of his stuff lying around."

"Right. He was pretty casual about all that. But we weren't— I liked having my own space. I was there a lot, sure, and he was here. At least two or three times a week. We talked about me moving into his place, but I didn't want to give Grandma a heart attack."

"And you only got engaged a few weeks before he left, right? After he had already arranged for the house sitters?"

"Right. So moving in together—it didn't seem like the right time, you know? I kind of wondered…"

Her voice trailed off. Brynn braced herself for what she was sure was coming—that Taylor thought her hesitation about living with Ian was a further sign that she wasn't truly in love with him. Even Brynn was having a hard time rationalizing the fact that two newly engaged people weren't jumping each other's bones nonstop, especially when one of them was about to depart for umpteen months.

But before the panic could spread from her stomach to the rest of her, Taylor continued.

"Anyway, none of that matters. All I need to

focus on is what I'm feeling now. There's been kind of a change the last couple of weeks. It's getting easier to bring all those feelings and memories back to life."

The last couple of weeks. Ever since Brynn had started consciously drawing on her brief but searing interactions with Hank to fuel her pep talks and visualizations with Taylor.

"In fact," Taylor went on with a happy smile, "the other night when he called, I almost pulled out a calendar to start looking at dates."

"Really? Tay, that is awesome!"

"Isn't it?" Taylor dropped on the bed and took Brynn's hand. "Honestly, I think this conference is coming at the perfect time. I'll be away from…from everyone else, and surround myself with Ian, and by the time I come home, I think, maybe—" she bounced a little on the bed "—maybe there might be a happy ending here after all."

Brynn pulled Taylor close for a long, rocking hug. "Oh, sweetie. Not a happy ending. A happy *beginning*."

Taylor grinned. "Talk about efficient. Only you, Brynn, could engineer things to work yourself out of two jobs at once."

"Well, you know what they say. If you're going to do something, you might as well…" Brynn paused, gripped by a fleeting pang of something she couldn't quite identify. Loss? Sorrow? But that was ridiculous. She was doing what she'd set out to do. She should be feeling joy and relief and pride in both herself and Taylor.

"You might as well do it right."

Which was exactly what she was doing. No matter how many unexpected pangs left her wondering if something was actually very wrong.

ON FRIDAY NIGHT, Hank steered the truck into the parking lot of the Foodland on the outskirts of Ottawa where he and Heather had agreed to meet, turned off the engine and took a deep breath.

It didn't help.

"Where is she? Daddy, is she here?" Millie freed herself from her booster and slithered over the seat. For a moment she was a tangle of legs and shoes and hair. Then she righted herself, grabbed the dash and peered through the rain-spattered windshield around the deserted corner of the lot.

"I don't see her, Mills." He wasn't sure if that was good or bad. He didn't want Millie to have to wait, but the thought of letting her go still hit him in the gut.

"Send her a text, okay? 'Cause she might be on the other side or something."

Highly unlikely, since Heather had named the spot, but it was an easy enough way to keep Millie happy. No sooner had he sent it than a small red Nissan pulled off the street and aimed for them.

"Is that her? Is it— I can't see, Daddy. Is it— It's her!" Millie vaulted toward the door. Hank snagged her around the waist a mere second before she would have launched herself from the truck.

"Mills, I know you're excited, but wait until the car stops, okay?"

"But I have to see her!" Nonetheless, the squirming ceased, at least for a moment. But the instant the Nissan came to a halt beside them, Millie lunged again.

This time, he let her go.

"Mommy!"

He followed more slowly, allowing himself another deep breath, pasting on an expression that he hoped didn't look too hesitant, and climbed down from the cab.

Heather had dropped to her knees and wrapped Millie in a swaying embrace that looked so tight it might have cut off Millie's ability to breathe if she hadn't been equally plastered to her mother. He had a feeling the wetness he spied on their faces had little to do with the rain.

He turned away to give them a little privacy, busying himself with Millie's tiny purple suitcase. When at last he looked back, Heather was on her feet with her arm draped around Millie's shoulders as if she didn't dare let go.

Funny. Heather had occupied such a huge place in his mind for so long that he always forgot how tiny she was.

"Hello, Hank. You're looking well."

Her hair was shorter than it had been during the

last visit. He'd thought she might have cut it from the glimpse he got when she Skyped with Mills, but he tried to stay out of the room then, so he hadn't been sure. She wore clothes that made his jeans feel like last week's leftovers, with shoes that he considered a broken ankle in the making, but he had to admit that the happiness pouring off her was something he absolutely recognized.

"Hey. So, are you all settled in?"

They chatted for a couple of minutes, politely and far more easily than he had anticipated. He handed over Millie's thumb-sucking chart and briefed her on what to record and when. Millie pouted. Heather laughed but promised to follow through.

Maybe he was being too optimistic, but he believed her.

Too fast, Millie was wrapping her arms around his neck and giving him a perfunctory kiss on the cheek before ducking into Heather's car. He stood beside the truck with his hands in his pockets, watching them drive away with little more than a token wave in his direction.

"Have fun," he whispered in the direction of the disappearing car.

An HOUR LATER, Hank walked into his empty house, dropped into the kitchen chair and looked around.

"Shit."

He'd thought he was ready for this. He had plenty of practice, both from Heather's previous stays in

Ottawa and from the two or three times each year when he'd taken Millie to Vancouver Island and flown home to emptiness. He'd had a vague hope that it would be easier now, but that wish had been blown to hell the minute he opened the door.

How could a house feel so damned hollow with just one small person missing?

His head knew that this was good for Millie. A kid needed her mother around. A girl, especially. He should be counting his blessings that it looked like Heather might be on hand to handle things like haircuts and shopping and the talks that would be needed in a few short years.

If only the house weren't so damned silent.

He pushed himself to his feet, headed to the sink. A drink of water, maybe blow the dust off the treadmill, then a couple hours' work. That was the ticket. He needed to keep busy, keep his mind from things that he shouldn't be thinking about. *Accept and move on.*

Things like what Brynn might be doing down in the Wolfe cabin.

Standing at the sink with his water, he could see her lights spilling into the wooded areas between them, pushing back the encroaching night. She was down there, probably alone. He was up here, definitely alone. All of a sudden, he couldn't remember why he had ever thought that *alone* was the best way to be.

Dammit to hell. He wanted her, and she had done

a fine job of letting him know that the feeling was mutual. So what was stopping him from walking down that path and kissing her until their knees gave out?

The answer was embarrassingly clear. He was scared. Not of being rejected, but of what might happen if anyone found out. He was standing at his sink, staring at her cabin like the stupidest dork on the planet because he didn't want anyone in his family to smirk and say "I told you so."

Talk about cutting off your nose to spite your dumb-ass face.

"Oh, for the love of…"

This was his *family*. The ones who knew him best, had seen him be a total idiot more times than he could count, and still loved him. They wouldn't think any more or less of him if they learned that he had finally acted on what they all suspected. They would tease him, rub his nose in it for a bit and then they would—

Hell. They would accept it and move on.

Which should have been reassuring, but something about it bugged him. As he tried to push his feet toward the door, it hit him.

He wasn't scared of what would happen if anyone found out.

He was scared of what would happen when Brynn left.

"Oh, *shit*."

All that talk about what would happen to Millie

when Brynn said goodbye? That had been a smoke screen. Yeah, he wanted to protect his kid. But he'd mostly been keeping Brynn at arm's length to protect himself. Because he was scared silly of taking the next step, getting more involved with her and then needing to let her go.

Unbidden, the memory of Millie's reunion with Heather rose again. Millie didn't know yet that her mother might be back for good. He and Heather agreed to keep that quiet until it was definite. As far as Millie knew, her mother was working in the area for a couple of months, after which she would leave again. Yet had she allowed that to dampen her joy?

Dammit to hell. His seven-year-old daughter had more emotional guts than he did.

"You want to be the boss of your own life, North?" He set the glass on the counter with a solid thud. "Get your ass out there and start acting like it."

CHAPTER TEN

BRYNN WAS HALFWAY through her forty-fifth viewing of *Dirty Dancing,* three-quarters of the way through a bag of ketchup potato chips and fully immersed in the kind of pity party she despised. She'd seen Hank's truck pull in a few minutes earlier, heard the sad, solitary slam of one door. She had paused the movie and held her breath and waited, even though she knew she was the world's biggest fool.

But she had pulled off another happy ending. She had helped Taylor and saved Ian from a broken heart and maybe even saved a family. She deserved some kind of celebration, some kind of reward for making herself relive moments of passion to help jump-start her cousin's love life. Was it wrong to wish that the reward involved something other than Patrick Swayze and a bag of grease?

Apparently so, because that solitary slam was followed by…nothing. No footsteps on the path, no knock at the door, no invitations to help while away some child-free hours. Zip, zilch, nada.

Okay. So maybe she had read too much into what

had happened. After all, she was the one who had pounced in the truck, not him. Come to think of it, he hadn't made any overtures since that first kiss. No significant glances. No brush of his hand against hers. She was pretty sure he had continued to watch her, and he sure as hell hadn't offered more than a token protest when she had climbed all over him in the front seat, but still. She had been the only one making a move.

What was it he had said? *Another time, another place.*

Though maybe she was the one who said that.

She snuggled deeper into Old Faithful, grabbed another handful of chips and started the movie once again. Maybe this time Baby wouldn't make the jump and Patrick Swayze would leap off the screen in search of a real woman who—

Something crunched outside.

She sat up straighter.

A squirrel. A chipmunk. Maybe even a raccoon, though, holy crap, that sounded like human footsteps on the—

Someone knocked on the door.

It's probably not him. Or he needs a cup of sugar. It doesn't mean anything.

But her pulse did the kind of leap that usually required at least ten solid minutes of running. And even though her brain knew she was setting herself up for yet another disappointment, as she closed the laptop and hurried to the door, she couldn't keep her body from humming the song from the end of *Dirty Dancing*—the one about having the time of her life.

Of course she looked like hell—no makeup, hair pulled back in a braid still damp from the shower, wearing her favorite old Leafs jersey over yoga pants. Deliberate choices made in an effort to remind herself that nothing would be happening.

Oh, how she hoped she was wrong.

She peeked through the window before opening the door and gave a little yip. Hank stood on her porch in jeans and his leather jacket, hands in pockets, face unreadable. Average, everyday Hank.

Enticing, lickable Hank.

The shaking of her hands slowed her ability to unlock the door. When she finally wrenched it open, she had to slide her hands inside her opposite sleeves, kimono style, to hide the trembling.

"Hey." *Oh, good. Entrance him with your witty repartee, Brynn.*

"Hi." He opened his mouth again, but no further sound came out.

"Did everything go okay?"

He nodded.

"Are you okay?"

He shook his head, nodded, then grimaced and shook it again. She couldn't decide if she should laugh, feel sorry for him or grab him by the jacket, wrench him against her and kiss him silly.

He raised his head to look directly at her, his eyes

dark and decadent. The hell with deliberations. It was action time.

"Hank—"

"Here's the thing," he said, cutting her off at the invitation. "I still have no idea what I'm doing most of the time with this parenting gig. I want what's best for Millie but I don't always know what that is. All I know for sure is that I don't want her to get hurt."

She nodded and looked away so he wouldn't see the disappointment on her face. He was here to talk about his kid. Okay. She should have expected that. He was a good dad, the kind who took his responsibilities seriously. Of course he was confused and adrift.

She could listen. And help. She could brainstorm and distract and try to make this better. It was her job. It was what she did best.

Even as she stepped back, holding the door wide to invite him in, her ego gave perverse thanks that she was dressed like a slob.

But he didn't move.

"Mills was two when Heather left. Barely two. She wandered around the house calling for her, and it killed me because I couldn't make her understand…. Not that I could make any sense of it myself, but I'm trying to convince myself that it's good for Heather to be here again, that this time might not end up with Millie hurting, but I'm scared shitless that it's gonna be the same story all over again."

"I understand." And she did. She would never forget how those first days of longing for her father to come home had transformed into vowing that if the selfish bastard ever returned, she would personally shove his ass to the street—preferably in front of a passing semi.

"And it's kind of the same with you," he said. "Because she really likes you, and if I let her think for one minute that there's something between us, she would start hoping for things that we both know will never happen. But at the same time…"

Wait. *Wait.* Was Hank saying what she thought he might be saying? Hope pounded through her. Or maybe that was just the drumbeat of her libido.

"At the same time," he continued, finally stepping off the porch and into the cabin, "Millie isn't the only one who likes you. And I sure would like to pick up where we left off that night in the truck."

Hot damn and hallelujah. "Me, too."

Would it be too brazen to slam the door behind him and lock it?

He inched forward before stopping again. "I don't want you to think… I mean, I can't—this has to be just sex."

"Just sex is just fine with me. Perfect, actually."

But still he didn't move. Every nerve in her body stood on full alert, waiting for him to step closer, to put his arms around her, to kiss her senseless, but still he hovered in the door like some stranger waiting to be invited in.

Okay. Maybe he was out of practice. He'd been divorced for years, it sounded like he hadn't gone out much since then... He could be uncertain about what to do or say next. She could make this work. All she had to do was get him into the bedroom and—

"Right, then." It sounded like he was talking to himself more than to her. But she didn't have time to wonder because no sooner were the words out of his mouth than he was on the move. He stepped closer and cradled her face in his hands as he had done in the parking lot. She closed her eyes in a moment of total thanksgiving, only to feel a light kiss on her eyelids—one, two, soft and tender, gentle and tentative. She slipped her hands forward and gripped his jacket, planning to urge him forward, but was stopped by his lips on hers, again light and teasing, barely more than a nip. She leaned forward, searching for more, but his hands had slipped to her shoulders and he was keeping way too much space between them. She was all for treasuring the moment but there was a time and a place, and she was pretty sure this wasn't either of them.

"Hank..." she began, but once again her words were swallowed by his kiss. His hands tightened on her shoulders and his heart beat against her touch, and it hit her that he wasn't trying to be tentative or gentle. He was trying to stay in control.

She had never been so ready to kick control to the curb in her life.

She broke off the kiss and looked at him, ready to reassure, to remind him they had as long as he wanted. But no sooner had she parted her lips to tell him not to worry than some shred of…*whatever*… seemed to snap within him. One second he was holding her away from him and the next his arms were pinning her against him and he was there, everywhere, mouth and hands and that long body surrounding her, pulling her against him as if he weren't quite sure she was really there. Her hands went beneath his jacket, running over the muscles she had watched with such longing so many times when he wasn't looking. He was lean and hard all over, pulling her even tighter, clutching her to him like he was afraid she would slip away.

Didn't he know that the only place she planned to go was down the hall to that gorgeous bed?

"Brynn." His whisper was hot against her ear, rough and raw and aching. There were probably words that would be useful but she was damned if she could remember what they were. She settled for tugging at his shirt and arching back to give him full access to her neck. There was a hand in her hair and another at her butt and lips on her neck and then the tip of his tongue tracing the vee of her jersey, sliding in a hot line toward the hollow between her breasts and then, God, pulling her even tighter against his hips while he nudged the jersey aside and nipped at the top of her breast.

The shock made her sway backward. She tried to right herself but there was no need. He clutched her tighter and marched her back against the wall, pressing her against it. She was caught between a rock wall and a rock-hard man and she couldn't think of anyplace she would rather be, except maybe in—

"Bed." She dragged the word from somewhere in the rapidly shrinking rational part of her brain. "Hank. Let's—"

"Good idea," he said, but instead of pulling back he pushed against her again, molding her to him so she could feel every blessed inch of him. Suddenly the bed didn't matter nearly as much as feeling and arching, and oh, God, his hand was inside her leggings, hot against her skin while his fingers hunted and probed and her jersey shifted and his mouth was at her breast, his free hand pulling the bra down while his tongue and his mouth consumed her skin. She needed to catch her breath, to get to the bed and do this the way she had imagined, but then he growled against her throat and her hips tipped forward and she grabbed his shoulders because she was slipping, she was teetering, she was falling, and if they didn't stop she was going to—

"Hank, I'm— We— Let's go to—"

He bit the side of her neck and yanked the lace down and the cold rush of air on her breast was pushed aside by his mouth and his tongue swirled and her hips arched and his fingers slid home and she fell, clutching him as every muscle in her body clenched and grabbed and tightened around him, around Hank, around this man who had...who had...

This man who had pushed her against the wall and reduced her to a jelly-legged mass of deep breathing and the most erotic sounds to ever come out of the back of her throat.

She opened her eyes and looked into his. A smile tugged at the few muscles she had that weren't still reeling.

"You know," she whispered, "six more steps and we could have been in bed. And then I wouldn't be standing here with rock burn on my butt."

"You complaining?"

"You're the one who said I was your test case."

"Sorry." His lips were hot against the side of her neck. "I can't hear you over the glow."

"That doesn't make any sense."

"None of this does." He caught her hand and squeezed. "But I'm not gonna whine about it."

He kissed her again, rocking against her before peeling her away from the wall and backing her toward the bedroom. They stumbled and grabbed and kissed their way until finally, *finally* they tumbled onto the bed. As he landed on top of her and pushed her harder against the mattress, she had two final rational thoughts before slipping into pure sensation.

The first was that she was immeasurably thankful that she had stocked the bedside table with just-in-case condoms before stepping into the shower.

The second was that sometimes, a change of plans could lead to most excellent rewards.

SOMETHING WAS DANCING through his dreams. A dog. A dancing dog? But no, it wasn't a dream, it was... real. Real music. Dog music.

He screwed his eyes tight and groaned.

"Millie, take the toy away from Daddy's head. Now."

Instead of the giggle he expected, the end of the song was accompanied by a soft kiss on his cheek and a very satisfied sigh.

"Sorry, sunshine. It's just me and my alarm this morning."

Holy shit.

Reality hit as his eyes flew open. He saw pink-dotted sheets, dark hair on a pillow and a smile that had him quickly abandoning memories in favor of the moment.

"Hey." It came out morning-rough but she didn't seem to care.

"Sorry about the alarm." She gestured to the Snoopy clock he hadn't noticed last night. Not that he had been capable of noticing anything but her. "It was a gift from Casey. Turns out I like it. And since I have this really horrible job, I figured I need all the smiles I can get in the morning."

"Sucks to be you."

"Doesn't it, though?"

Her smile made a complete mockery of her words. So did the lazy circles she was tracing on his chest.

"So," she said. "Sleep well?"

It was the best sleep he'd had in months, if not longer. "Like some gorgeous enchantress gave me a double-strength sleeping potion."

Strength being the word of the day. Forget running or power tools or any of those other things that made a man feel ready to conquer to world. All he had to do was remember that moment last night when Brynn had come apart in his arms, shuddering so hard that she would have dropped if not for him holding her tight against the wall. That was a kind of heady power that left him ready to leap tall buildings, grapple wild animals and wrestle pesky fears to the ground.

To think how close he'd been to letting this slip through his fingers...

Her smile deepened, revealing a dimple he'd never noticed before. "Not feeling very enchanting this morning. Or gorgeous." She made a face before wriggling close enough to bump up against his knee, sending sparks shooting through him. "However, I can say I'm quite delighted that you knocked on my door last night."

That made two of them.

"But if you want to know the truth…I think if you hadn't come knocking, I might have been the one doing it."

Now, that was intriguing. "Oh, yeah?"

"Yeah. I even… Well, the other day, I picked up some stuff for Millie's thumb. I used to use it, back when I bit my nails. You paint it on like nail polish. It tastes awful but it works."

"Thanks. You didn't need to do that."

She grinned again and ran a finger over his collarbone. "Well, I can pretend I did it out of the goodness of my heart. Or I can admit that when I bought it, I had this image of me taking it up to your place and saying something about wanting to give it to you when Millie wasn't around, because I didn't want to tip her off."

"You had it all planned out, did you?"

Her skin pinked ever so slightly. "Hey, all I was going to do was offer. Whatever might have happened next would have been up to you."

And that, he realized, was one of the reasons why it was so easy to be with her. She had her agenda and her plans but she never shoved them down anyone's throat. Sure, usually by the time she was done he felt like an idiot if he tried to go against her, but she had a way of making it feel like the choice truly rested in his hands.

He was going to have to watch and learn. Not that watching Brynn was any hardship.

"Nice to know you were thinking of us." And by *us,* he most definitely did not mean him and Millie.

"Nice to know I wasn't the only one thinking," she said with a saucy grin. She rolled away, fumbled in the drawer beside her and handed him a small bottle. "Here."

"It might be worth a try." He scanned the instructions. "So far she's playing it safe, saying she'll give up the thumb if I get Angry Birds for her. She knows I think it's too violent."

"It's not violent. It's fun."

"The point is, she deliberately chose something she knew I would refuse."

"Dang. That's a serious attachment."

"Yeah, well, no one ever said that change was easy, right?"

"I think you know the answer to that one already." She kissed him lightly on the jawbone—not to seduce, he knew, but to comfort. Didn't mean he wasn't ready to roll her over and let his own lips do a little exploring, but all in good time.

"I didn't think it would be as rough as it was to drop her off last night."

"It's a pretty big change for all of you. Probably a good one, but even those can be a challenge."

"Yeah, I guess, if we made it through everything so far, we can figure out this one. God knows it won't be anything like when we found out Millie was on the way."

"Or when Heather left?" The words were so quiet

that he knew he could easily pretend he hadn't heard her if he wanted to avoid the topic. Turned out he didn't.

"That one was a kick in the gut, for sure."

"You didn't see it coming?"

He breathed in, willing himself back to those days he tried to avoid remembering. "In hindsight, yeah. It's easy to see how things were falling apart. But at the time— You know, we hardly ever saw each other. We were looking after Millie and working and taking classes, and I guess I missed the signs. No excuse, but that's the way it was. Does that make any sense?"

"I think so."

He caught her hand, let his thumb circle hers. "I should have had more of a clue and she should have spoken up, and we probably should have been about twenty years older than we were. But there's no changing history."

"Did you miss her?"

"That ship sailed a long time ago, Brynn."

"That's not what I asked. I have a pretty good idea that you're not pining away for her these days." A quick pat to his groin emphasized her point. "But back when it happened, when she was first gone… Did you miss her then?"

Had he? He remembered being more furious than he had thought possible, lost and overwhelmed and so scared that he could hardly breathe. He remembered his rage at how she insisted everything was fine, then ran anyway. He remembered long nights of rocking his heartbroken daughter and crying along with her, longing to make things better for her.

But for himself?

"Maybe I was just too angry," he said slowly. "Or too busy. But I don't remember ever wishing that she was still around for me. For Mills, yeah. But not for me."

Funny, but he had never thought of that before. He had liked Heather a lot before things went south. They'd had some good times. And it was kind of nice that he no longer needed a slug or two of whiskey to get through a phone call. Sometimes he was even able to joke with her, to share a laugh over Millie's latest exploits. He liked being able to have that with her.

"My mom did."

Lost in his own past, it took a minute for him to understand what she was saying. "Your mom missed your father? Even after what he did?"

"Yeah. Hard to imagine, huh?" She pulled the pillow close and curled around it, the way Millie did when she had a bad dream.

"Most of the time she hated him, I think. But sometimes one of us would say something, or it would be…I don't know, a birthday, a school thing, whatever. And she would stop and look around the room real fast, like she was looking for him, ready to do that 'can you believe this?' grin that people share when they've been together forever." She swallowed. "You could tell the instant she remembered he was gone. Her face just…I don't know. Crumpled."

He slipped his fingers through her hair, wound a curl around his finger, let his finger slide down her cheek.

"One day—she has no idea I know this—but one day, I heard her on the phone with Taylor's mom. She was crying and ranting and just so… I mean, she held it together through everything. The operations, chemo, the hospital. She was scared and all of that, but she never let it take over."

All of a sudden, he understood how Brynn had become so focused.

"But this one day… You know, I think it was their anniversary. She lost it. Completely. I will never forget hearing her tell Aunt Connie that she hoped to hell he never asked to come back, because she didn't think she would be able to say no. Even after everything he did to her, to us, she still missed him. She still loved him."

He didn't know what to say. It didn't sound like any kind of love he'd ever heard of, but what did he know?

She made an odd little sound, somewhere between a laugh and a cough. "I'm sorry. I don't know why I told you that. She did finally figure out that he'd had no idea how to be a real partner. She's been with a great guy for a couple of years now,

so, you know, ancient history. Please don't tell anyone, okay?"

"Not to worry." He took her hand between his
own. Giving her time. He wasn't sure why she had
decided to share this with him, of all people, but he
had the feeling it wasn't the kind of memory she
could simply bounce back from.

Sure enough, for a few moments she lay silently,
still curled on her side though not as tightly. Her
eyes were open but unfocused, seeing things he
would lay money she would rather not see again.
He rubbed her hand, letting his finger play over her
knuckles and giving her what comfort he could.

After a time she drew in a deep breath, blinked
and gave that quick little head shake and the determined smile he was so familiar with.

"Okay. Enough melancholy for one morning.
Time to move on."

For once he agreed with her.

Her gaze shifted to him. The smile softened. "I
set that alarm so I would have time for a run, but
you know, I've been very faithful to my training
program. I think I've earned a morning of some
alternate exercise."

"Is that so?"

She rose on one elbow and kissed him, a slow
exploration of his mouth that left him ready for
anything she had in mind.

"You're the boss," he said, and this time, he was
more than happy to let her have her way.

By Monday morning, when Brynn was scheduled to have a meeting with Moxie, Hank and Carter to go over some of the festival vendor contracts, she was convinced that she should arrange for a weekend such as she had just had at least once a year. It wasn't as productive as she usually preferred, but whoa and damn, did she feel *good*. One weekend of Hank and she was walking with the kind of deep relaxation that followed a full day of spa pampering and hours of massage. She felt fluid and flexible, ready to attempt the most daunting yoga poses—assuming she didn't immediately melt into a boneless puddle.

Oh, did she know how to pick them.

She glided into Taylor's office, hung up her jacket and pulled out her phone. She'd missed a call from Taylor last night. Okay, she had heard the phone and even checked the screen, but she and Hank had been making the most of his last hour before he had to get Millie and she had known Taylor was safely in Calgary for the conference, so she had muted the phone and let Hank pull her attention back to some seriously nonfamily-centered activities. She could have called Taylor once Hank left but decided it was better to wait until she could be sure she wouldn't break into giggles if Taylor asked what she'd been doing all weekend.

Time to remedy her shocking lapse of family concern.

But before she could make the call, one came in

from the manager of one of the bands slated to perform at the festival. By the time she listened to the other woman's concerns and worked out a solution, she had to scramble to make the meeting on time.

She scooped up her laptop and files with a smile. It took all her restraint to keep from skipping down the hall.

Hank and Moxie were already in the conference room when she arrived. She slipped into her usual chair with a "Good morning" to Moxie and a smile for Hank. He gave her a small, restrained nod, just like always—

And she suddenly, completely lost the ability to speak.

She pressed her hand to her midsection and focused on breathing, relaxing.

Light and easy, Brynn. A good time, remember? Nothing more, nothing less. Friends with most awesome benefits.

After what felt like a lifetime, she turned her attention back to Moxie, praying that she had imagined the spark of curiosity she saw in the older woman's eyes.

"Well, then." Moxie spoke with far more satisfaction than was good for the state of Brynn's mind. "Let's get this party started. Vendors."

Relief was quickly followed by confusion. "Wait. What about Carter?"

"Not here."

Oh, no.

"Is he sick?" Hank sounded only mildly concerned. Brynn clutched her pen and waited for Moxie's answer. A cold. A stomach bug. Something that would have kept him home but he could still be called if they had questions... Surely that was the only reason for his absence.

Please, please, let that be all.

Moxie fixed Hank with an evil eye. "What did I say about checking your emails before meetings, Henry?"

"I thought it was more important to be on time."

"Really." Moxie leaned back in her chair. "Interesting, since this email went out Saturday morning."

Do not blush. Do *not* blush.

Thank heaven, Hank was more in control than she would have been were she in his shoes. "Moxie, you know full well that Millie spent this weekend with her mother. I had a lot more important things to do than read email."

Important. Doing her had been important. Her worry took a backseat for a moment, eclipsed by sheer delight.

"Besides," he continued, "I don't work here anymore, remember? I'll do my part but it comes after my own work."

His shrug was pure "deal with it." Instead of being appeased, Moxie fixed him with a shrewd gaze that seemed to dart in Brynn's direction one too many times for Brynn to breathe easy.

"How was it?" Moxie asked at last.

Brynn's jaw sagged. Moxie hadn't really—

"It went well," Hank said easily. "Millie is a trouper. If you want to talk about it over lunch, I'm free."

Oh. Very nicely done.

Moxie eyed him for another long moment.

"Twelve-thirty. My office. Now let's get down to business." With a quick roll of her shoulders, she moved on.

"But—Carter?" Brynn didn't want to draw attention to the fact that she hadn't read the email, either, *really* didn't want Moxie probing into her reasons for being behind the curve this morning, but the need to know what had happened far surpassed her own potential embarrassment. "Is he sick?"

Moxie sighed and set her papers back on the desk. "Listen, you two. I am old and running the whole damned place, and I still found time to be up on everything pertinent before I came to this meeting. I suggest you both remember your priorities next time instead of doing…whatever it was that kept both of you from being prepared for the same meeting."

Brynn ducked her head in hopes of hiding the pink she knew was taking her face hostage. Moxie was fishing. That was all. That had to be all.

"Friday night we got a call from Dana, who was at the conference with Taylor. Death in the family. We'd paid for two registrations and it seemed a pity to waste it."

No. No.

"I called Carter and told him what happened, and he stepped up. He flew out Saturday night. He's there now with Taylor."

CHAPTER ELEVEN

OF COURSE TAYLOR wasn't answering her phone.

Brynn scowled at her cell for about the three hundredth time since Moxie had dropped her bomb. She'd spent the day calling and texting, doing her best to distract herself with work.

No luck.

Nor did it matter how many times she reminded herself that Taylor was in meetings and workshops and wouldn't be checking her phone anyway. All she could think about was Taylor and Carter, alone together in an anonymous conference hotel. All she could do was pray that she had done a good enough job of rekindling Taylor's feelings for Ian that this would be nothing more than…than a test. That was right. This was a test, and Taylor would make it through, and when she came home she would know deep in her bones that she was truly, passionately, forever in love with Ian. They would be married by Christmas and start popping out babies and live happily ever after.

At least that was the plan.

She had decided against going back to the cabin

to work, opting to camp out in Taylor's office. She figured she had more chance of accomplishing anything festival-related if she stayed here as opposed to where she had spent the weekend having hot humping-bunny sex while Taylor tried to call her....

Oh, God. Please let it have been nothing more than an update call.

Brynn pulled out her dance notebook and began making notes. She'd scribbled a few thoughts during rehearsals, ideas about how to ramp up the moves and highlight all her dancers' strengths, but now she needed to integrate them. Perhaps if she shifted things so Carter was up front...

She was so absorbed in her plans that she gave a little start when she heard a sharp knock at the door.

"Oh!" She looked up to see Moxie eyeing her with that canny expression that always made her feel like she was doing something wrong. She jumped to her feet. "Mrs. North, sorry, you—"

"Brynn, I am tired of telling you to call me Moxie. If I have to say it again, you're fired. Got it?"

"Got it. Yes. Sorry. So, Moxie." Brynn leaned back against her desk to steady herself. "What can I do for you?"

"Well, you can show me what had you so lost to the world that you nigh-on had a heart attack just now."

"Sure. I was going over the dance. The original lineup was a good start, but I thought if we played around with where some folks are standing…" She showed Moxie the various options, debating the pros and cons of Millie's cuteness versus Carter's flair. Moxie, as always, had some thoughts that managed to give Brynn a new perspective.

"You know, I think that's exactly what I was looking for. This is great. I should have known you would have the perfect solution."

Moxie sniffed. "That CEO thing isn't just honorary, you know."

"I'm seeing that more and more."

"I bet you are." Moxie straightened, placing a hand to her back but waving away Brynn's offer of a chair. "So tell me. Do you think Hank is going to pull off this cabin thing in time?"

"Me?"

"Yes, you. You're living there, too. You can see what's going on. Is he on target?"

What was this about? Brynn had spent enough time at Northstar to know that Moxie felt perfectly comfortable hopping back and forth from work to family and combining them at will.

She tipped her head to the side and measured up the older woman. "Are you asking this for official dairy reasons, or as his grandmother?"

Moxie's grin was all the proof Brynn needed that something was afoot. "Both."

"Well, then, I can assure you—the head of

Northstar—that he is giving one hundred percent to all his endeavors." Especially those endeavors that left her limp and barely capable of stringing two words together. "But I would tell his grandmother that I'm not part of the family and suggest that if you're worried, you talk to him yourself."

"You always this political?"

"Not usually, no."

"I didn't think so." Moxie chuckled. "You have a good head on your shoulders, Brynn. You see things other folks don't, and you put them together in ways other folks can't. Probably because the rest of us are too close. But you—you have a fresh eye. Good instincts, too, I'd wager."

"I really hope you're not planning to ask me to spy for you, Moxie. I'd hate to have to say no to someone who has such a high opinion of me."

Moxie sighed. "Damn. I knew you'd see through me."

"Seriously?" Oh, dear heaven. "You weren't really—"

"Oh, God no, girl. Get over yourself. I wouldn't do that to my own family. Besides, I do all my own snooping. More accurate and a hell of a lot more fun."

And that was supposed to be reassuring?

"Let's just say that you have insight into Hank that the rest of us don't."

If Moxie suspected anything, Brynn could bid farewell to secrecy, privacy or subtlety.

"Be that as it may…"

"Relax. I don't want you to do anything devious. But I worry that he's burning the candle at both ends and all that crap. That boy always did push himself, first from trying to keep up with his brothers, then from doing the single-parent thing. No help allowed. Bit of a damned fool, if you ask me, 'cause who doesn't need a hand every once in a while?" She shook her head. "It almost killed him to move back in with me and his folks after Heather left. I prit near fell off my chair when I found out he was letting you help with Millie. That's not his usual style."

"I had that impression." Now she was doubly glad she'd made him see reason.

"I don't want him to work himself sick. If I say anything, he'll tell me everything's fine, but he listens to you. Talk him into taking a few days off. Maybe the next time Millie goes to her mother's. He thinks he can't, that he has too much to do, but I believe I saw a difference in him today."

How the hell was she supposed to respond to that one?

"Interesting. Well. How about… Look, family stuff is off-limits for me, but I can promise to talk to him. One adult to another. But that's as far as I can go." Except, of course, for doing her level best to make sure that his next solo weekend was even more rejuvenating than this one had been.

"Fair enough. I suppose I can't ask for anything else." Moxie smacked her hands together and headed toward the door. When she reached the entryway, she turned back and gave Brynn a pointed look. "By the way, you might want to adjust that scarf a bit if you want to keep pretending you're wearing it just for show."

She winked and moved into the hall far faster than anyone her age should ever be capable of doing. Brynn clapped a hand to her neck and lunged for her purse. She pawed through the contents until she found a pocket mirror. She held it out, yanked the scarf out of the way and angled it so she could see the length of her neck.

Nothing.

She closed her eyes and offered a prayer of thanks. Moxie definitely didn't play fair.

But Brynn couldn't keep herself from admiring the hell out of her anyway.

Seven o'clock in the freakin' evening, and Taylor still hadn't called back.

Alone in the communal laundry room that served the cabins, Brynn glared at her phone even as she ordered herself to calm down. There had been a quick text—Breathe—but that hadn't been much consolation. Even as she reminded herself that conference days were jammed, that Taylor was probably in break-out sessions followed by appointments followed by dinner meetings with no chance to return to her room for the privacy this kind of call would require, her panic meter was going off the charts.

Because Carter was there. And Brynn wasn't. And she was pretty sure Moxie had chosen Carter deliberately.

She grabbed a blouse from the dryer. Yes, in some ways it had made sense to send Carter. He was single, he was family, he was peripherally involved in much of what Taylor did at Northstar. But only peripherally. There were other people who would have gained much more from these sessions.

Instead, Moxie had sent her main legal eagle to the conference. Which was almost as scary as remembering that Carter could easily have said no. The fact that he had willingly gone along with this made her fear that he had an agenda of his own, and that between him and Moxie there was going to be a whole hell of a lot of heartache running through the North family very soon.

"You are such a control freak, Catalano." She yanked a bra from the dryer and tossed it into her hamper. They said that admitting you had a problem was the first step to defeating it. Too bad this was the exception to the rule. Because if you had to acknowledge your problem to gain control of it, but the problem was that you couldn't let go of the need to be in control in the first place…

"Argh!" She tossed a pink argyle sock on top of the dryer to await its mate. As she reached back into the still-warm clothes, her phone rang.

"Finally!"

But when she glanced at the display, she saw that the call was from her sister-in-law.

"Hey, Libby. What's up?"

"Not much. Have you got a minute? Casey wants to say hi."

"Absolutely."

Brynn boosted herself up on the dryer and waited for the wet breathing that always accompanied her nephew's phone conversations. He didn't bother with a greeting but immediately launched into a story about the dog, his nursery school teacher and SpongeBob SquarePants. She had learned long ago that trying to understand Casey's calls would only increase the frustration level, so she leaned back, drumming her feet softly against the dryer while listening to the rise and fall of his adorably breathy voice, repeating a few of his words whenever she could understand them. All in all, probably the most satisfying conversation she'd had all day.

After a minute or two she heard him shout, followed by a crash in her ear as the phone fell, and then the sound of Libby's laughter.

"Sorry about that. Finnegan took off after something, so of course Casey had to follow."

"Not a prob. But next time could you catch the phone on the way down? I'd like to keep my hearing as long as possible."

"Sorry. I'll make it up to you. Dinner tomorrow night?"

"Sure. What should I bring?"

"I don't know. It's Sam's night to cook, and I have no idea what he has planned. But why don't you stop at that new bakery and get some of their stretchy bread? I've been craving that for days now."

"Sure." But something Libby had said had tweaked her curiosity. "You really don't know what he's cooking?"

"Probably chicken of one kind or another. I saw some defrosting in the fridge. Why, have you decided to go radical vegan or something?"

"No, not that. It's just… I never would have expected a fellow control freak to not have the menu planned for the next month or so."

"Who says I don't?" Libby's laugh was light and playful—and, Brynn suspected, probably aimed at Sam. "But just because I plan it doesn't mean your brother will follow it."

"And you're okay with that?"

"Do I have a choice?"

Car lights flashed through the window. Brynn sat up straighter and glanced at the clock mounted above the vending machine that would soon be filled with one-load boxes of detergent. Hank and Millie were home.

God, she hoped she could get through the evening's hellos and goodbyes without doing a lovesick-teenager imitation.

With a start, she realized Libby was still speaking. "…comes a point when you have to ask yourself if something is worth the energy. So if we eat chicken four nights in a row, does it really matter? No."

Brynn remembered Taylor crying out her confession that she thought she was in love with the wrong brother. "But what about when it *does* matter?"

"Oh. Well, then I ask myself, do I really have any control over this? Because sometimes I do, but most of the time, it's just me being a worrywart. Or, you know, obsessing about something that doesn't matter because it's easier than thinking about things that scare the crap out of me."

"Fixating on fixing someone else and ignoring your own issues? You, Libby?"

"Oh, never." This time there was a decidedly rueful tone to her laughter. "Of course, sometimes I'm just a tad convinced of my own superhuman abilities."

Do I really have any control over this?

Brynn leaned forward and stopped drumming her feet, stilled by the impact of Libby's words.

Do I really have any control over this?

She didn't. Not anymore. She had done what she could and helped where she was able, but she wasn't in Calgary and she wasn't Taylor. And when push came to shove, this was Taylor's life. Not hers.

"But doesn't that feel like a cop-out? Like you do what you can and then say, okay, out of my hands now? What about seeing things through, or pushing to make sure something happens, or—"

"Or convincing yourself that the fate of everyone you ever loved rests in your hands?"

It was almost like there were thought balloons floating around Brynn's head, and Libby had a telescope trained dead on them. This was the last time she would look for advice from someone who was on such a similar wavelength. "Well, when you put it that way…"

"Brynn. You're not God. Sometimes, you have to do what you can do and then trust other people to do what they can do." She added, more gently, "You want to tell me what has you so worried?"

An unexpected lump came to Brynn's throat. "I… Not right now. But thanks. I might take you up on that someday."

"Anytime, hon. The door is always— Oh, crap. Casey! *Finnegan!* Not that, it's dead! Gotta go, Brynn. See you tomorrow."

She hung up before Brynn could stop laughing.

After a moment Brynn shoved the phone back in her pocket and forced herself to resist the urge to check for missed calls or messages. She scooted to the edge of the dryer and dropped to the floor.

Libby was right.

Yes, this situation mattered far more than Libby realized, and the potential problems were greater than she knew. But for at least this moment in time, there was absolutely nothing that Brynn could do about it.

She had done her best to help Taylor. It was time to let go of this, to accept that whatever happened next was out of her hands.

She didn't like it. Hated the very thought. But as she hefted her hamper on her hip and headed into the early evening cool, she couldn't help but look up at the house where she would soon be welcomed by Hank and Millie. Hank, who had forced himself to ask for and accept help even when it was the last thing he wanted. Who was willing to risk making an idiot of himself onstage to show his kid how to rise above bullies. Who was giving his ex a second chance to make things right with their daughter, no matter how much it terrified him.

Hank had proved to be an expert in helping her lose control. Maybe she could learn a few things from him about letting go of it, as well.

ON WEDNESDAY NIGHT, Hank bounced down the driveway after dropping Millie off with Heather, pulled into his spot and checked for Brynn's car almost by reflex. No sooner did he realize what he had done than he gave himself a mental kick.

Get over yourself, North.

They hadn't made plans. At least, no official ones. God knows he'd spent plenty of time since the weekend thinking of the many ways he and Brynn might pass the hours until Millie came home.

But she hadn't said anything, though he knew she was well aware he would be free. She had kept her distance. Which was fine—Millie was around all the time, and he was the one who had said that Millie couldn't suspect anything. But he had kind of been hoping she would issue an invitation. Not because he had been the one to make the big move over the weekend, though that was in the back of his mind—hey, he was only human—but because Brynn wasn't the type to leave things to chance. If she had wanted to spend the evening with him, she would have let him know.

But she hadn't.

The way his body reacted to the sight of her little hatchback pulled up snug against the side of her cabin told him just how much he wished she had.

Okay. So maybe she had something already planned. The festival was just three weeks away, Taylor had been gone for days, Brynn was probably swamped with details and phone calls. He sure as hell had enough on his plate to keep him busy for the next few hours.

Of course, everyone could use a little special relaxation now and then....

He hopped out of the truck, shook off the temptation to wander down and say hello, and headed into his place. A load of throw rugs had been delivered that day. He would distribute them among the cabins before returning to the main project of the moment, hauling rocks from the river shore to build up the crumbling sections of the stone fence that surrounded the house.

He spotted the rugs beside the new medicine chest he had to install in the Grindstone cabin. Okay. He wouldn't do that now, but he could carry the rugs and the chest down to Grindstone and leave them there on his way to the shore. It would make sense, save him a trip later.

The fact that it would take him right past Brynn's cabin was purely a coincidence.

Arms fully loaded, he set out. But just as he passed Brynn's place the night was rent by a blast of music, something loud and booming and so unexpected that he jerked and sent his careful stack crashing to the ground.

"Shit!"

He cursed again, silently this time, because he knew what was going to happen next.

Sure enough, no sooner had he bent to scoop up the muddied items than Brynn burst out of her cabin.

"Hank? Is everything—oh."

She stopped in front of him. He made the mistake of looking at her.

Oh, hell. She had been doing yoga. She was wearing some skintight thing that was red and bared her shoulders and had lines in places guaranteed to draw a man's eyes right to the forbidden zone. The pants didn't do much to conceal her other assets, not with the way they molded the curves that had given him so many happy memories.

Worse than her clothing, though, was her face, all pink and slightly sweaty and filled with barely suppressed laughter. She looked rumpled and lush and ready to be made sweatier and messier and pinker.

And she wasn't even trying.

"I have a horrible suspicion I contributed to this," she said without a hint of actual repentance in her voice.

"Let's just say you picked a lousy time to let loose with the John Williams fanfare."

"I'm sorry. I was channeling my inner Princess Leia, and I wanted the right music."

"Do me a favor and go for Yoda next time, will ya?"

Her laughter was his undoing. She let loose with that full, throaty laugh that made him remember other moments he had coaxed it from her, and the next thing he knew the medicine chest had slipped from his grasp again to slam his toe. And he didn't give a rat's ass because he had danced away from it and was holding her again, pulling her close and kissing her and filling himself with Brynn.

She wriggled closer, sliding her arms around his neck and tilting her head so he had full access to that mouth that kidnapped his brain, telling him without words that she had missed this as much as he had. Maybe even missed him as much as he had missed her.

Because he *had* missed her. More than he wanted to admit. A smart man would back away now while he still could.

Yet his arms insisted on tightening when they should have been letting go.

She was the first one to back away. No surprise there.

"Hey." At least she left her arms looped around his neck, her forehead resting against his so he was still surrounded by her scent. "Much as I would love to stick around and play, I have to leave in about ten minutes."

Leaving. It kind of scared him to realize that he'd expected her to say that. It scared him even more to admit that he wished *leaving* was dropped from his personal Brynn vocabulary. *Leave, walk away, go. Move on.*

But he wasn't supposed to think about her that way. Wasn't supposed to get worried that *leaving, walking away, moving on* were words that he'd heard her utter way too often. After all, it wasn't like he was looking for anything more than some good times. It wasn't like she had ever pretended that leaving wasn't in the cards.

Get with the program, North.

"Big plans?"

"I have to go to Ottawa. Taylor's flying back tonight." Some of the happiness leached from her smile, giving him a moment's pause.

"Everything okay?"

"Fine. No worries."

Right. And he had been totally free of ulterior motives when he set out for Grindstone.

But it was hard to worry about what she wasn't saying when her hands were resting on his chest, one finger sliding back and forth along the top of his T-shirt.

"Is it wrong to admit that I wish I hadn't told Taylor I would pick her up?"

Ah. So she wasn't leaving by choice this time. She had a family thing. That, he could well understand.

Amazing how one little question could make him see everything in a new light.

"Only if it's wrong to admit that I know a back way to the airport that would save you, oh, fifteen minutes."

She leaned back and looked him up and down as if she were trying to determine his truthfulness, when in fact he was pretty sure she had already made up her mind. Maybe because her fingers had slipped inside his shirt and that her backward tilt was accompanied by a forward slant to her hips.

Or maybe because he knew her. Not as well as he would like. Probably more than was good for the sake of his continued happiness, given the fact that she would be leaving town in less than a month.

"Fifteen minutes isn't exactly confidence-inspiring."

"Planes are usually late."

"This is true." She swayed from side to side,

brushing up against him, interfering with his ability to breathe. Not that he was complaining.

"Of course," she continued, "I still need to grab a shower."

"Not a problem."

Her eyes widened, all fake innocence. "You mean you understand that I need to have a long, steamy shower instead of having a long, steamy you?"

"Nope." He slipped his hands beneath her yoga pants, pulling her flush against him while biting that sweet curve where neck met shoulder. "I mean, with all that yoga you do, I think you're flexible enough that we can make that shower do double duty."

"I knew there was something in it for me besides inner peace."

This time when she laughed he joined in. A little rusty, maybe, but still a laugh. Something he'd been doing a hell of a lot more since Brynn came to town.

He was going to miss the laughter almost as much as the sex. Maybe more.

"Come on, Princess. We'd better get moving if we want to pretzel you up before the *Millennium Falcon* has to take off."

"Ooh, Captain, I do believe there's a lightsaber in your pocket!"

Yep. Sex, laughs… Definitely a toss-up.

It wasn't until they had christened the shower

and he had done his best to keep her from getting dressed and she had hit the road with wet hair and a very satisfied smile that he thought to wonder why anyone would need to channel warrior Princess Leia to do yoga.

A LITTLE OVER an hour after kissing Hank goodbye—for about the fourteenth time—Brynn took one look at Taylor walking out of the secure area at the airport and knew she had failed.

So much for Libby's advice to trust and let go.

Not that this came as a surprise. Taylor had avoided all calls and texts, allowing no contact other than a brief voice mail left at a time when she knew damned well Brynn would be in a meeting. And somehow, a cryptic, "Everything is as it should be" wasn't the most reassuring of messages.

But the lecture she had planned to deliver during the drive to Comeback Cove was pushed out of her head by the sight of Taylor, looking somehow smaller and more fragile than Brynn had ever seen, walking toward her with her arms tight around her middle. It looked like she was trying desperately to hold herself together.

Brynn hadn't felt this sick since the horrible day when Sam called her to tell her Casey's mother had died. And looking at Taylor, she was pretty sure she was seeing another death happening right in front of her.

If Cupid were to flutter past her right now, she

would grab him by the wings, haul the little bastard to the security checkpoint and tell the agents that he was packing arrows. That would throw him out of commission for a while.

"Hey." She stepped forward, ready to take a carry-on, offer an ear, but Taylor stopped her with an upraised hand.

"Don't hug me or I will completely and totally lose it."

Shit.

"'Kay. You have a checked bag, right?"

"Yes."

"You want to wait for that while I get the car?"

Taylor's nod was small. "Good plan. Thanks."

Too many possibilities raced through her head as she hurried through the dusky night. Whatever had happened, it obviously wasn't pretty.

Taylor was at the curb by the time she pulled around, but looked like she was about to keel over at any second. Brynn threw the car in Park, took the suitcase and all but pushed Taylor into the seat.

"Buckle up." It felt odd to say it to an adult, but honestly, Taylor seemed to be drifting further away by the minute.

Oh, God. Love sucked.

"You ready to talk?" she asked as she pulled out of the airport lot.

"There's not much to say."

"Yeah, well, the fact that you look like someone just hooked you up to a vacuum and sucked out your soul makes it hard for me to believe that, you know?"

"I'm sorry."

It wasn't the words that made Brynn's heart twist. It was the broken whisper, the hitch in the breath, the way Taylor hunched further into herself as if waiting for life to deal her another blow.

Just the way Mom used to be.

Brynn spotted a golf course and turned into the deserted parking lot, where she steered to the farthest, darkest corner and killed the engine. Shadows and silence wrapped around them.

"You want to stay in the car or sit outside? I have a blanket in the back."

"This is fine."

"Okay." Brynn cracked the windows and filled her lungs with the cool night air before touching the back of Taylor's hand, lightly, quickly. "What happened?"

Taylor stared out the window. Brynn could barely make out the moment her face began to crumble.

"Carter and I…"

"Tay, no. You didn't."

Every worst-case scenario reared up and grabbed Brynn by the throat, easing only slightly as Taylor shook her head.

"We didn't. We…we agreed we couldn't hurt Ian that way."

"What happened?"

"I tried my best to stay away from him. He asked

me to dinner, I said I had plans. He sat beside me at lunch, I faked seeing someone I knew at another table and moved. He knocked on the door of my room and I pretended I wasn't there. I tried so hard, Brynn." She wiped a tear from her cheek. "But he followed me off the elevator and to my room. I told him I wasn't feeling well but he…he said he knew I was avoiding him and he needed to know why. I pretended I didn't know what he was talking about, but he looked at me, and Brynn, oh, my God, it was all there in his face, everything I'd been feeling, too…and he said he could only think of one reason why I would be doing my best to stay away from him. Because it was the same reason he'd been doing his best to stay away from me the past year."

Oh, no. "So why did he speak up now?"

"Because of the conference. He said he promised himself he would never say anything, but when we both ended up there, he felt like maybe it was some kind of sign. Permission from the universe. Then when I wouldn't let myself be near him, he knew he had to speak up." Her voice cracked. "He loves me, Brynn. Just like I love him."

Everything in Brynn wanted to insist that this wasn't love but some twisted quirk of a malevolent fate. But even as her brain spit out explanations, her heart told her that the time for pretending was over.

Taylor had been right all along. She didn't love Ian the way she should. That damned sicko Cupid had won again. It was time to accept what had happened and move on.

But hell and damnation, she was so sick of that little so-called god messing up the lives of people she loved.

"Tay, baby. I'm so sorry."

"Don't be. I'm glad."

"You're *what*?"

"I mean, I'm not happy about any of this. Every time I think of Ian, of Carter, of all of it, it's like someone reached inside me and shoved glass into my heart, you know?" She clutched herself again, bringing a tightness to Brynn's throat. "But even with all that hurt, there's this stupid happiness. Because he loves me. It's the most horrible mess I could ever imagine and it hurts so much I want to…I don't know… But there in the middle of it is the fact that he loves me. And that makes the hurt worth it. Because knowing that if things were different… You don't know what kind of joy that gives me."

Love that could go nowhere, but still gave joy? Oh, yeah. That made perfect sense.

Yet even as she tried to scoff, she remembered the moment in the shower with Hank when the hot and heavy was behind them and the water had beat down on them and she had stood for a minute. Not moving. Not doing. Just being. It had passed almost as fast as it had come, replaced by a joke about aching muscles and a quick kiss and the reluctant need to get going. But for that one moment, she had been so…well…happy. Completely, undeniably happy. Not because her world had been rocked to the rafters, but because she was with Hank, and he was holding her, and that had been everything she needed.

Not that she was in love. Good Lord, not that. Hers was a simple case of lust mixed with friendship and a healthy dose of laughter. The perfect combination for some springtime fun, and thank God for that.

So why was it that seeing Taylor glowing through her tears left Brynn almost jealous?

"What happens now?"

Taylor stared through the windshield. "We do exactly what we have to do. When Ian comes back, we get through the festival, I tell him I'm not in love with him, I leave."

"And Carter?"

The words were barely audible. "Will stay."

Brynn's eyes filled with the tears Taylor seemed determined to hold back. Of course. This was the only path they could pursue.

"What do you need me to do?"

"Remember when we first started this and I said you might need to take over my job for a while after I leave?"

"I—" The agreement died on her lips as the implications hit her. Yes, she had promised to do that. But that was when she truly believed that Taylor loved Ian, before she knew the Norths, before she knew Hank. Before she understood that her promise meant that—if Moxie and the others agreed to let her fill in as needed—she would be spending the weeks until cousin Paige went on maternity leave at Northstar while everyone around her knew that she had been party to this.

She would be a walking reminder of all the hurt that had come to the family, and that was even without Carter's role being made public. They would dread the very sight of her.

And Hank—Hank would probably think she had been lying all along.

"Brynn? You promised."

Fake it 'til you make it, Brynn.

"Of course, hon. If they want me to fill in, of course I will. As long as I can."

"Thanks." Taylor pressed her fingers to her eyes, but when she spoke, her voice was almost frightening in its steadiness. "Most of all, I need you to promise you'll help him."

"Who, Ian?"

"No. I mean, yes, of course, but his whole family will be in his corner. They'll get him through this. But Carter—" her voice caught on a sob "—he won't have anyone he can talk to. Except you. He knows that you know. Everyone will be so focused on Ian, and that's fine, but no one will have any idea that Carter…"

With that, Taylor finally broke.

Brynn reached across the console to pull Taylor close and rubbed her back, promising that she would help Taylor, help Carter, help all of them.

Even if she had absolutely no reason to believe there was any way anyone was going to get through this without a broken heart.

CHAPTER TWELVE

HANK WASN'T SURE when he had started to look forward to the dance rehearsals. Maybe right after he realized that it meant watching Brynn shake assorted parts of that body in different and enticing rhythms. Maybe it had happened last week, when Millie snatched the ever-present blue notebook away from Brynn and led her on a giggling, shrieking chase through the halls that led to a giant family game of tag.

Or maybe it had been a couple of weeks ago when he realized he had stopped worrying about the steps and the audience and the past, and was simply enjoying the moment. Yeah, that had been a breathtaker, all right.

Whatever the reason, the truth was, he kind of liked it now. The dancing. The laughter. The feeling that he was part of his family again. Not that he had ever stopped, of course. But when they were moving through the sequence, each in their own spot but still together, it was easier to think that maybe he had found his place. Maybe he could figure out how to be part of them without always feeling like he was a step behind.

He would never have believed it, and there was no way in hell he would ever admit it, but he was glad Brynn had guilted him into dancing.

The weekly planning meetings, however, were still a pain in the ass. Especially this morning, when ten-fifteen rolled around with no sign of Carter.

"Must be getting reacquainted with Jenny in Accounting," said Cash, leading to assorted snickers around the table.

Ma rolled her eyes. "He's probably still on Calgary time."

Moxie snorted. "Not that one. He bounces back faster than spandex on a porn star. Nope. It's gotta be something else."

Huh. The last time Moxie had made excuses for Carter she'd been covering for him while he negotiated the last-minute purchase of the Brockville plant.

"Well," Brynn said, "he's not the only one who has to adjust." She glanced at Taylor, who looked like she was ready to slide into a puddle at any moment. No spandex there, that was for sure.

As if to prove how out of sorts she was, instead of being pleased by Brynn's comment, Taylor pressed her lips together and frowned. Like she was…angry? With Brynn?

Oh, geez. If this was because he'd kept Brynn

from being on time at the airport, he was going to have some fast talking ahead of him, for sure.

Thinking back to how he'd made her late, though—yeah. Any groveling would be well worth it.

"I'll call him," Cash said, but just as he reached for his phone, Carter stomped into the room, dropped his laptop on the table with a thud that made Moxie wince and yanked his chair out.

"Son of a—" Cash clamped his mouth closed and glared.

"What?" If Carter made the word any sharper, it could have pierced ears.

"Take it easy. You slammed your chair into my knee."

Carter shrugged. "You've been crowding my space since before we were born. Not my fault you're a slow learner."

"That's enough." Ma pointed at the twins. "Carter, you are late and obnoxious. Get a grip."

"Give it up, Ma. There's no laundry room here."

"Carter Wilfred North—" Dad began, but Brynn placed a light hand on his shoulder.

"Carter, you've had a busy few days. Do you need to skip the meeting this morning?"

He scowled. "No."

"Well, then, we're glad you could make it. Please don't do anything to make us change that opinion."

Hank tried but couldn't completely repress his snort. Carter sat up straighter and glowered. Hank met his gaze, only to be distracted by something smacking into his ankle. Since he was sitting beside his mother, he had a pretty good idea of both the source of the smack and the message behind it.

Fine. He could take the high road.

Besides, if he stepped back, that gave Brynn more freedom to take Carter down herself—something which she could do ten times better than he had ever managed.

"Let's get started." Brynn put on her glasses. "Reports?"

As each North brought the rest of the family up to date, Hank alternated between taking notes and sneaking peeks at Carter. He certainly wasn't channeling his usual smooth legal-eagle self and Hank could almost see the waves of anger rolling off of him. He didn't know what had Carter so pissed at the world, but he sure as hell wouldn't want to be on the receiving end of it.

"I've finalized the schedule for folks to move into place at the cabins," Brynn said, flashing it on the screen. "I'll send it out after the meeting. Hank, yours has more details than this but I'm sure there will still be questions. Let me know what I might have forgotten and I'll make sure you get the answers."

He nodded and pushed down the panic that reared up when he thought of how much still lay ahead of him. He had committed to this. He would make it happen.

"That's everything for this week." Brynn set her pen back on the table. Did she even know she always grabbed a pen when she had to talk? "Things are falling into place nicely, folks. This is going to be—"

"Hang on there, Brynn. We're not done yet." Moxie leaned forward. "I have an idea."

Hank shot a quick glance at the clock, noted the time and stifled a sigh. Moxie was going to eat a major chunk of his day; he could guarantee it.

"We have lots of good things planned but I want to add something. Stop shaking your head, Cash, it won't cost a lot of money." Moxie sighed. "You people have no faith."

"What were you thinking, Mrs.— Moxie?"

"Well. We're talking a lot about the history and the community and all that, but I was thinking we need more of a human touch. So I thought back to when I was a girl. Our ice-cream bar in town has always been a place for folks to get together. I think we need to have folks send in pictures of themselves from times they've been there. Soccer teams and birthday parties and such. Maybe have them give us stories of how the dairy has been part of their life." She shook her head and chuckled. "When I think of all the first dates that have happened there over the years…"

"Oh." Brynn sat back. "Well. That's, um, yes. We could put together panels of photos and stories. I like it."

So did Hank. But he couldn't help noticing that Brynn's scrunched-up expression lacked excitement.

"We could do it by decades," Ma suggested, but Moxie waved the suggestion away.

"Nah. That'll be like everything else we're doing. Let's do this one by theme. You know. The teams, the parties, the sweethearts. Haven't we had a couple of proposals there, too? I think we need to—"

She was interrupted by the crash of Carter's chair hitting the ground. All eyes turned to Carter, who gripped the edge of the table as if it were the only thing keeping him upright.

"Carter?" Janice rose halfway from her chair, but he shook his head and stepped back.

"Sorry. I'd better—" He clapped his hand over his mouth and sprinted out of the room.

"Oh, dear." Janice sank back into her chair before focusing on Taylor. "Was there a bug going around at the conference?"

"I don't—" Taylor bit her lip, shook her head then stopped. "Maybe."

"Well, hell. He breathed on all of us, too. Everyone go home and eat chicken soup." Moxie sounded mighty damned excited for someone offering up a gloom-and-doom prediction.

"Cash, go check on your brother," Janice said.

"Right. We're finished here." Brynn seemed distracted. "Moxie, could you email me the details of your idea? I think we could do something with it."

She scribbled something on her notepad. Chairs scraped and there were a couple of laughs as everyone gathered their things. They were all so busy that he was probably the only one watching Brynn as she looked at Moxie with narrowed eyes. Almost as if she were trying to read her mind.

T MINUS 17 DAYS.

The permanent countdown in Brynn's head had started inching up in volume as they drew closer to the festival. Every sign of spring—the first shy crocus peeking through the last snow, the day she saw the faint green shimmer on the trees that meant the leaves were budding, the morning she stepped outside and then tossed her jacket back in the cabin because she was too warm—all of these usually welcome moments had been a mixed blessing this year. At first, each one reminded her that the festival was drawing closer and the time for getting through her ever-growing list of tasks was shrinking before her eyes.

Then each sign was a jab to her bubble of happiness, a whisper that soon she would be leaving—something that usually didn't bother her, but this time around was proving more difficult than she'd expected. Maybe because she loved the work. Maybe because she had family here.

Maybe because laughing with Hank made her feel like she wanted to grab the moment and freeze it.

And now, ah, now. Here it was, almost May, and all she could think was that they were mere days away from a season colder than the cruelest winter. In seventeen days they would begin the festival, in nineteen days it would be over, and in three weeks Taylor would be gone and Ian and Carter would be nursing broken hearts and Hank—

Hank probably wouldn't be laughing with her anymore.

Scowling at the robins hopping around the trees that circled the Northstar parking lot, Brynn shoved sunglasses on her face and headed for her car. She'd spent the morning alternating between festival calls and Taylor pep talks, and all she wanted was to drive to the river, sit on the shore and eat her sandwich. Alone.

And maybe come up with a way to postpone the festival a few weeks so she wouldn't have to be permanently alone quite so soon.

Of course, she'd no sooner hit the pavement than Moxie pulled into the lot and waved at her. Damnation! She'd been so close to escaping. Instead, here she stood, waiting while Moxie unfolded herself from her vintage MG.

"Oh, mother of spawn, that sucker gets closer to the ground every time I have to get out of it." Moxie put a hand to her back and straightened. "Don't get old, Brynn. Death is a hell of a lot easier on the vertebrae. Now, tell me, where are you headed?"

At least the minutes spent waiting for Moxie to

get herself upright had given Brynn time to create a good cover story. She had a feeling that if she told the truth, Moxie would want to come along. "I'm going to Town Hall to make sure all the permits are in order." Not a total lie. She had already planned to do that on her way back.

"Good thought. Are you counting the days until it's over? Or are you down to hours yet?"

"Um…minutes, maybe. At least, I know I would like a lot more of them."

Moxie let loose with her trademark barking laugh. "Get used to it, sweetie. That's a feeling you'll have more and more as you age. But listen." In a flash she had flipped back to being Maxine North, CEO. "I know your contract is only through the festival, but I've said it before—you have a good head on your shoulders. We need your kind of smarts around here. Is there any way we can convince you to stay on when this job is done?"

It felt like the pavement jumped up to smash Brynn's stomach. "I… Sorry…what?"

"Carter said something to me a while back, and I've been thinking it over. There's always projects popping up, good things, great opportunities, but we have to foist them off on someone who might not be the right person, because they have the job that's the best fit. Or they're new and have the most time on their hands. Whatever." She swatted at a kamikaze fly. "It's not the best way to handle it. I'm thinking we need someone to take them over, be the grand poo-bah of special projects, and I think you're just the gal for it. You interested?"

Interested wasn't the word. It was the kind of job Brynn lusted after, the kind that would keep her always hopping, always learning.

And she couldn't take it.

"Oh, Mrs. Nor— Moxie," she amended quickly as she caught the beginnings of a glare. "You don't know how much I wish I could say yes. But I… It's not possible. I have…I have other commitments."

"Humph." Moxie eyed her with far too much insight. Brynn had to force herself to stand still. "You're not playing hard-to-get, are you?"

"I'm not that good an actress. Seriously, if I could do it, I would probably embarrass myself by kissing your feet or something. But I…I just can't."

"You have something else lined up?"

Thank God for Paige.

"More like family obligations."

"Ah." Moxie stared for a moment or two, just long enough that Brynn felt like she was going through an airport scanner. She shook her head and sighed.

"You know that family obligations are the one thing I can't interfere with, don't you?"

Brynn nodded.

"From what I've been told, you've had a lot of those over your lifetime."

What? Who told her that?

"No more than anyone else, I would imagine."

Brynn squared her shoulders. "And I have always been…grateful…for the ability to help."

"Really."

"Really."

Moxie's gaze sharpened, then abruptly softened. "Well then. Guess it's our loss."

"Actually, it's mine. But that's, you know…life." Before she could think about the many ways she would like to change life at the moment, she faked a smile.

Accept what's happened and move on.

Fake it 'til you make it.

Funny how her trusty mantras weren't giving her nearly as much comfort as usual.

"Thank you for the offer. It means more than you know. But right now, I'm still part of Northstar, so I'd better get back to work."

Moxie nodded. "Go on, then. But if things change, speak up. The job is yours if you want it."

"Thank you."

Brynn hurried to her car, slammed the door and stared up at the roof.

"You know," she said to whoever might be listening, "we need to have a little chat about overkill."

HANK KNEW THERE was trouble the minute he walked into Millie's after-school program and spotted her drawing multicolored frowny faces on a dry-erase board.

"Hey." He tapped the board with one finger. "Heck of a rainbow you've got going there, kid."

"It's not a rainbow."

"Yeah, I figured. That was supposed to be a joke."

She kept her focus firmly on the fat blue marker in her hand. "Not funny, Daddy."

"Well, how about we go home and you tell me all about it while we have dinner?"

She drew another circle, squeezing it in the space between two eye dots on a larger one. "What's for dinner?"

"Uh…" Call him a pessimist, but he had a feeling that Kraft Dinner, salmon cakes and peas probably wasn't the answer needed to turn this saga around. "Chicken and ribs from the drive-thru."

She glanced up. Her eyes sparked for a moment, and he held his breath, hoping he'd won.

She set the blue marker down, selected a red one and added a blood-dripping frown to the face in progress.

He sighed. "Come on, Mills. Let's go home."

If he hadn't been worried before, her silent acquiescence sealed it.

She stayed quiet all through the ride, barely answering his questions as to whether she wanted fries or baked, white milk or chocolate. When they pulled up to the house she hoisted her backpack on her shoulders and trudged inside, head down, shoulders and hair and even her jacket drooping.

He had a bad feeling about this.

As soon as her hands were washed and they were seated at the table with the food transferred onto plates—his nod toward sophisticated living—he decided the buildup had gone on long enough.

"So. Are you going to tell me, or do I need to guess?"

She picked up her fork. Two fat tears plopped onto her junior ribs.

Ah, hell.

"Mills. Talk to me, kiddo." Taking a wild stab in the dark, he said, "Was it Noelle again?"

"Oh, Daddy!" The sobs came in earnest. Shoulders heaving, she described a picture he could see all too easily—a game in gym, a ball not caught, a chase at recess that ended with accusations of stupidity, babyhood and the taunt that the ball would have been caught and the team would have been victors if not for a misplaced thumb.

By the time the story was out Millie was on his lap, his shirt was soaked and his dinner was cold. Surprising, since he was pretty sure his anger was hot enough to heat anything within reach.

This had gone on long enough. Millie still refused to wear her lab coat to school or anywhere but home. He had half hoped that Heather's return had meant Millie hadn't needed the stand-in as much. Then came the morning he found the shirt wadded up beneath the covers at the end of Millie's bed and he realized she was sleeping with it.

She still needed it. But thanks to Noelle, she was afraid to wear it in public.

Now the thumb. Yes, Millie needed to give it up. He knew it. She knew it. But he would be damned if he would let some little brat-mouth shame Millie for it.

When her sobs finally subsided, he lifted her chin and looked her in the eye.

"Mills. I need to tell you something."

A wet sniffle was her only response.

"When I was in high school, I went to a dance and tried out some moves I'd seen in a movie. It was pretty ugly. People teased me about it for a long time. You know what I did?"

"What?" It was barely more than a whisper, but it was a start.

"I did the wrong thing. I should have told them to take a hike, but I listened to them. I believed them. I stopped going to dances and I didn't let myself dance except at home with you. And that was really stupid, 'cause you know what? I like dancing."

"But you're doing the dance with Brynn."

Thank God she'd made him see the light. "You know why I said yes?"

She shook her head.

"Because I figured if you were brave enough to keep going to school every day, even though Noelle was being mean to you, well, I should be brave enough to go out there and dance again."

"Really?"

"Really." He pulled her close and kissed the top of her head. "Those kids were mean, but I was just as wrong. I let them be in charge of what I was doing. And you're making that same mistake."

"But I don't like when she calls me names."

"I don't blame you, and I'm going to call the teacher again tomorrow. In the meantime, if you think you're ready, there's something we can do about the thumb." He would let the lab coat wait. One battle at a time. "Noelle is wrong to tease you about it, but the fact is, you do have to stop. So how about you take charge of this? Not because of Noelle, but because you're ready to do it for you."

"What?"

"Brynn gave me stuff we can put on your thumbnail. Like nail polish. It'll taste yucky, but she says that it's the best thing to get you to stop."

"She did?"

"Yeah, babe. And you know Brynn would never lie to you." He took her hand and kissed the poor offending digit. "You and your thumb have had a good run, but it's time to move on, kiddo."

She drew a long, shuddering breath and burrowed her face deeper in his chest. But he distinctly felt the slow nod of her head as she gave her permission.

A LITTLE AFTER MIDNIGHT, Brynn realized that half the reason she was unable to focus on the book she'd been staring at for the past hour was because the lights were still on at Hank's place.

She'd had a meeting with the puppeteers who would be doing shows at the festival, so she hadn't been able to take Millie after dinner. But she'd seen Hank and Millie down by the river when she drove home. They had been standing on the dock, pointing at something on the water, and she had been so damned close to hightailing it to the shore to join them. She'd longed to walk out on the swaying boards and kiss Millie's head and slip her arm around Hank's waist and rest her head on his chest while Millie caught her up on her day.

The temptation had been so strong, the image so vivid, that she had stood at the side of the car for endless moments, afraid to move because she couldn't be sure her feet wouldn't carry her down the slope. When she finally forced herself to pick up her bags she had to keep her gaze glued to her shoes shuffling down the gravel path to her cabin.

She was in over her head. She, who prided herself on keeping her work relationships light and her sexual ones even lighter, was getting sucked into a work–family blend that was all the more forbidden because of the complications coming down the pike. She needed to keep her distance. Not just for herself but for Hank and Millie and all the others who were going to have enough other upsets to cope with.

But after an evening of losing herself in notes

and yoga followed by an hour of tossing and another hour of attempting to read, she conceded defeat. The lights from Hank's house called to her. Mocked her.

And, after another hour, worried the hell out of her.

Because more lights were coming on. Someone was moving from Millie's room to the kitchen to the bathroom. Then the living room light went on, and Hank's room…then the kitchen again…

It was 1:37 a.m. and every light in Hank's house was on.

Something was definitely wrong.

She grabbed her phone. Her finger hovered over Hank's number.

Texting would be the smart thing to do. Shoot him a message, ask if everything was okay, feel like a dork when it turned out all was well, go to bed reassured. Sleep, wake, move on.

But she couldn't. Because what if something was wrong with Hank? What if he had fallen or was sick and Millie was alone up there, crying and afraid and—

Brynn knew she was being an overdramatic idiot even as she reached for her jacket and pulled it over her cow jammies. Millie was smart enough to get her if there was a true problem. Hank certainly knew that he could call anytime. There was no need for her to grab her flashlight and slide her feet into clogs and make her way toward the lights that had her so troubled.

Yet here she was, knocking softly at Hank's door. Because she was a totally overdramatic worrywart who—

"Brynn?"

Brynn had never been much for zombie movies but she was pretty sure that Hank's white face, red eyes and feet that could barely shuffle were as close to the walking dead as she ever wanted to come.

"I saw the lights," she said. "Is Millie—"

A heartrending sob pierced the night. "Daddy, Daddy, Daddy…"

"The fingernail stuff. We put it on." He scrubbed his face with one slow hand. "She can't sleep. Because, you know, she's never fallen asleep without it. Her thumb, I mean."

Brynn closed her eyes while the guilt washed through her. Was there no end to the ways she could screw things up for this family?

A most pitiful moan greeted her as she entered the room where Millie lay curled in a ball, her blankets a thrashed-up mess, her face puffy and streaked with tears.

"Brynn." Millie sat up, arms outstretched. "I want my thumb!"

Hank sank to the edge of the bed, the picture of exhaustion. Brynn took the other side and pulled Millie close.

"It's so yucky. It makes my mouth all dry and squishy." Millie shuddered against Brynn's chest. "And I can't get to sleep."

"No sleep at all?"

"Not really," Hank said. "She dozed on and off for a couple hours, then she woke up when I was getting ready to call it a night." His eyes closed before opening slowly, as if he were dragging them back into place. "We've been awake ever since."

Dear God, no wonder they both looked like death warmed over. "Have you tried hot milk?"

"Yep."

"Drugs?"

"Nighttime cough medicine," he said in a tone that verged on snappish. Not that she could blame him. "We rocked. Rubbed her back. Let her cuddle up in Daddy's bed. I even read to her from an old economics textbook, okay?"

The unfamiliar edge to his voice told her she needed to tread carefully. None of them were operating at peak performance at the moment.

A few swipes of nail polish remover would do the trick, but she had to offer it in such a way that Millie didn't understand. "I, uh, have some acetone-based liquid at my place that could eliminate the offending substance. If you get my drift."

Bleary eyes blinked in her direction. "Ace— Oh. That." His hand settled protectively on Millie's trembling back. "No. We're not backing off now. We've come this far, we're not surrendering or moving on or any of that."

She blinked. Why had that felt like it was aimed more at her than at Millie?

As if reading her thoughts, he shook his head. "Sorry. I just… If we give up now, we'll never get a second chance."

Of course. He was absolutely right. It was just exhaustion making him irritable.

"How about the plug-in drug?" she asked softly.

"You mean the electronic babysitter?"

"Right."

"Didn't try that. I thought it might be too much of a distraction."

She nodded toward Millie, who was whimpering softly in her embrace. "I don't think it could get much worse."

He heaved a sigh. "What the hell. I'll try anything." He staggered to his feet. "But for the love of all that's holy, I'm picking the movie."

Millie's head popped up. "What movie?"

Brynn shook her head. "Uh-uh. *I'm* picking. *You* are going to bed."

Hank stared at her as if he weren't able to process the words. She untangled one hand from Millie and made a shooing motion.

"Go. I had a catnap already, and this was my idea. I can handle this one."

"And I can handle my own kid."

Get out of here, Brynn. You're not needed.

Silence hung in the room, thick and choking. Then he heaved a sigh and ran his hand over his face.

"Damn. I didn't mean… That came out wrong. I'm more whupped than I realized. I'm sorry."

She couldn't manage anything other than a reflexive nod. Hurt and confusion clogged her throat. Words flitted through her head—*this was partly my fault, I just want to help*—but she couldn't squeeze them past the wall of guilt and pain that had sprung up between them.

"I wanna watch a movie with Brynn."

Thank God for Millie's shaky whisper. If ever Brynn had needed a distraction, this was the time.

"Go," she said to Hank, a little more forcefully than intended. "Sleep. We'll be fine."

Without so much as a glance in his direction, she tugged Millie from the bed, grabbed a blanket and headed for the door.

"Come on, Mills. *Tangled* is waiting for us."

"Again? You always choose that one."

"Trust me, honey. It's got great music and the hottest hero Disney ever created. There's no such thing as too much *Tangled.*"

She piled onto the sofa, pulled Millie close and started the movie. Within half an hour the familiar story and exhaustion took their toll. Millie's eyes closed and her breathing grew more regular. Her fist settled at the side of her mouth and her knuckle slipped between her lips, but the thumb itself stayed clear.

Mission accomplished.

But it took a lot longer for Brynn's eyes to finally close.

Hank had snapped, but she really couldn't blame him. She knew he didn't like to accept help, yet she'd barged in and started throwing around suggestions anyway. That wouldn't go down well at the best of times. Toss in hours of frustration and fatigue, and he'd had every right to be testy. He wasn't the only one who should be apologizing.

She could understand his reaction. It was her own that would have had her tossing and turning if not for Millie tucked in beside her.

She'd offered help before, he'd declined, she'd shrugged and moved on. Not this time. She'd been on the verge of tears, and much as she tried, she couldn't convince herself that it was simply because his words dredged up her father's brush-offs. No, it was because she *needed* to fix this problem.

Because she had contributed to it? Partly. Because every bit of her ached at the thought of Hank and Millie hurting. Because she needed to help them more than she needed to sleep. Because she knew there was no way she could be completely happy if their worlds were out of whack?

Oh, hell.

CHAPTER THIRTEEN

THE ALARM MUST DIE.

Hank fumbled for the source of the offending noise and smashed it with his hand, groaning. Images from the past few hours swam into his consciousness: Millie weeping giant tears over being unable to fall asleep, the hours of fruitless attempts, Brynn knocking on the door and saving his ass.

And speaking of asses, he'd certainly done his best imitation of one last night. He had some serious apologizing to do. Maybe even a little groveling.

I'm not very polite when I'm half-asleep....

I know you were trying to help, but sometimes I'm an idiot about that....

I know you meant well, but when you offered the nail polish remover it made me worry that you can't stick with anything, just like when you told Mills to walk away, just like when you say you have to move on, and I don't want that to be true, don't want it to be you...

He grabbed his glasses, shoved them on his face and reached for his phone to check the headlines.

The world hadn't exploded in the night. Which meant he needed to get moving and face the music.

Having avoided the inevitable as long as he could, he grabbed the blankets, jerked them back and sat upright. He staggered toward the kitchen with no thought more coherent than his immediate and all-encompassing need for caffeine, but was stopped en route by a most unexpected sight. Brynn was still sacked out on his sofa, Millie snuggled against her. Millie's thumb rested against her cheek, but for the first time he could remember, it wasn't in her sleeping mouth.

Holy shit.

He wasn't sure which sight made him happier. Millie without her thumb—wow. It was what he had hoped for, but that didn't mean he had believed it would work. Or that it would last. But, damn, it was a hell of a great start.

And Brynn… She was here. Still here. In his mix of pissed-off exhaustion when he hit the hay, his last thoughts had been that she would probably get Millie settled, watch over her for a while and head back to her own cabin. He hadn't expected her to sleep on the sofa, *really* hadn't expected to find her still here this morning.

That's 'cause you were too busy being an idiot to think things through, dumb-ass.

He let himself watch the sleeping beauties for a moment. Millie's hair spilled over Brynn's cow jammies. Brynn's arms wound under and over

Millie, as if even in sleep, she wanted to be sure Mills didn't slip off the sofa. They breathed in tandem, one chest rising as the other fell. Like they were connected.

Like they were family.

Whoa.

Head spinning—and not simply due to lack of sleep—he continued on to the kitchen and hit the button that would bring the elixir of life to him. Muffled rustling pulled his attention back to the sofa. Brynn was waking up.

Time to start groveling.

He filled a travel mug with coffee, added the double cream but no sugar that she preferred, then started a fresh serving for himself before tiptoeing in her direction. He bent over the back of the sofa and offered her the mug.

"Thanks," she whispered, pushing herself upright and accepting his offer. "You're a saint."

Not.

"How ya doing?"

She winced. "My back isn't very happy with me, but it looks like she made it."

"Yeah. Give me a second and I'll carry her to her bed."

"You're sure she won't wake up?"

"She might, but you're going to need to move soon anyway, right?"

"Yeah, probably." She shifted. Her hand rose as if to settle on his cheek, but she turned it into a not-very-convincing stretch at the last moment. She glanced away but not before he caught the way her face had pinked up. He would have thought she was embarrassed—but there was more to the way she was avoiding his gaze. It was like she was hiding from him.

Or slightly ticked over his behavior.

He bent lower, all the better to speak softly. "I was a horse's ass last night. I was rude and stupid. I'm sorry."

"Not to worry. None of us were at our best."

She was saying the right words, but she wasn't meeting his gaze. Not good. He ran one tentative finger along her hairline. She stilled beneath his touch, but not in a good way.

"What's wrong, Brynn?"

"What? Nothing. Everything is fine."

"Are you mad at me? Not that I don't deserve it, but—"

He stopped. He hadn't known it was possible for someone who was lying down—with someone else wrapped around her, no less—to curl into herself. Yet she managed to do it.

"Hank." She still wasn't meeting his gaze. "Please don't. It's too la— I mean, too early in the morning for anything that requires thought, okay?"

Right. It was damned early and he knew it, but he would bet the farm that she had been about to say it was too *late*.

Which made no sense whatsoever, especially at this ungodly hour. But there it was.

But too late for what?

THERE WASN'T ENOUGH yoga in the world to unkink Brynn after her night on the sofa, not nearly enough caffeine to wake her and not a hope in hell of clarity despite hours spent wondering and worrying. But one step into Taylor's office, one look at Taylor's too-wide eyes in her very white face, and Brynn snapped to attention.

"What is it?"

"Close the door." Taylor's voice shook. Brynn closed it, locking it for good measure, and hurried to the chair in front of Taylor's, pulling it so close that their knees touched.

"I just got an email from Ian. He was able to move his flight up a day." She closed her eyes. "He doesn't want me to tell his family. He has…plans… for those twenty-four hours."

The breath left Brynn's lungs in a giant whoosh of comprehension. "Shit."

"My thoughts exactly. But I can't put that in my reply, can I?"

"Give me a second." Brynn bit her lip and looked around the room for inspiration, but whiteboards and wall-size calendars only emphasized the fact that the day of reckoning was rapidly approaching.

"Okay. Brainstorming time." If only her sleepless night hadn't stolen her capacity to think. "Let's toss out some options. Remember, no protests or objections. So. You could meet him at the airport and hide away for a day as requested."

"I am not—"

Brynn raised a finger. Taylor clamped her lips together.

"You could break up with him as soon as he lands."

"Too close to the festival."

"No commentary, Taylor."

"Bite me, Brynn."

God, couldn't this have waited a day? "I'm trying to come up with an idea to save your ass."

Taylor crossed her arms.

"Think carefully about not sleeping with him. It could—" Out of habit, she had been about to say that it could reignite Taylor's passion for Ian, but no. That ship had long since sailed. If Brynn wanted any chance of rescuing this situation, she had to remind herself that it was now Taylor and Carter. Except it wasn't, and never would be.

"It might be an easier way to say goodbye," she pointed out gently. "I know you think I'm living in fantasyland, but—"

"It's not an option, Brynn."

"Then you're going to have to either break up with him now or come up with a hell of a convincing lie."

"I thought you were supposed to be helping."

"Well, what do you expect? Did you think I could just wave my magic wand and make it all better?"

Taylor's eyebrows pinched together as she stared at Brynn. Then she whirled around in her chair.

"Forget it. I'm sorry I bothered you."

Oh, hell. Now Brynn had some more guilt to add to her collection.

"Tay, I'm sorry. I had a lousy night and didn't get much sleep and I'm not at my best right now."

"Yeah, no shit."

The urge to dump it all on Taylor was almost physical—to say, "Hey, I know I'm a bitch, but this morning I woke up on Hank's sofa and he bent over and gave me coffee and for a minute it was all so damned perfect that I can't think of anything else. Because it can't happen again. And it won't. And all I can think is that I'm losing out at a chance on something so amazing that it scares the crap out of me."

But that wasn't why she was here.

She set her briefcase on the table and laid a hand on Taylor's shoulder. It took a second but Tay's hand grabbed hers and squeezed.

"For the record," Taylor said in a thick voice, "I don't think you have a magic wand. Just a kind heart and a really good head on your shoulders. If I've been taking advantage of those, I'm sorry."

Her words pulled the plug on Brynn's confusion. "Oh, sweetie. I'm an exhausted shrew today. Slap me or something."

"No way. I still need you to help me figure out what to do about Ian." Taylor swiveled round with a faint but determined smile. "But first you're going to tell me why you had such a lousy night."

"It's nothing," Brynn began, the familiar words coming automatically. Then she reconsidered.

What was it she had laughed about with Libby? Something about focusing on fixing everyone else and ignoring her own issues?

"I got up in the night and all the lights were on at Hank's place so I thought something was wrong, and I went up there and Millie was an exhausted wreck because he painted her nails with the no-thumb-sucking stuff I gave him. So I sent him off to sleep and I stayed up with Mills and we all made it through but I'm kind of bitchy this morning and I shouldn't have taken it out on you. And I'm sorry."

Taylor blinked. "Whoa. Okay. Bitchiness is definitely allowed after that."

"Yeah." And that was as far as the revelations were going to go. But it felt good to get that little bit off her chest.

"So anyway, enough of me. Back to Ian. Let me grab my magic wand." She grabbed a pencil, twirled it between her fingers. "You're going to need a foolproof reason for not sleeping with him, and simple cramps won't cut it in this case."

"We could drug him so he passes out."

"Good thought, but what happens when he wakes

up? No. It has to be something inarguable. And you have to be so miserable that he can't even suggest some alternatives. Unless you think you might be able to…"

"No. It would feel like I was cheating on Carter."

"Oh."

"Yeah, oh." Taylor shook her head and sighed. "So I need to be in the hospital or horribly injured or puking my guts out."

"I think those are your choices, yeah."

"I'd rather be choosing between London or Paris. Chocolate or vanilla. Hugs or kisses."

Brynn flashed back to that moment on the sofa, still half-asleep, the first hints of coffee teasing her nostrils and Millie warm against her and Hank bending over her with that sleepy apology that had twisted her inside out. She had been so close to pulling him down for a kiss. Millie was asleep, it would have been safe and secret and perfect.

And that, of course, was why she had changed direction at the last moment. Because it had been so automatic to reach for him, so natural, that she had known she was on the brink of falling into something she had no right to claim.

Just sex, he had said that first night, and she had agreed. Happily. But she had been lying through her teeth, even if she didn't know it. There was no such thing as *just sex* with Hank, and this morning had been the proof. There had been nothing sexy or seductive about those few moments. That had been all about comfort and gratitude and sharing a lousy experience but coming through it better—battered, but better—because they had pulled each other through.

There was a word for those kinds of moments, those kinds of feelings. A word that had her closing her eyes tight and whispering, "No, no, please, no" inside.

"You have to tell him the truth."

"Brynn, we—"

She shook her head, cutting Taylor off midobjection. The words had slipped out without forethought, but something about them seemed so right....

"It's only a couple of weeks now." Brynn leaned forward, warming up to her topic. "In fact, this might be perfect timing, you know? Long enough that he has time to process the news before he comes home, but not so long that he has to deal with it forever. He would get through the worst of it, then he'd come home, be with family, have the festival... You could be gone already so he doesn't have to deal with seeing you and you don't have to lie to him anymore...."

The more she talked, the more she realized that this might just be the solution they all needed. The truth would come out. The lies would end. The complications would cease and she could get everyone through the festival and under control, and then leave. They could all move on that much faster. Taylor, Ian, Carter…her.

Hank.

No more lying to Hank. No more guilt. No more slipping out of control and struggling to hold up the wall that was keeping her from falling for him.

"I don't know…."

"Take a day to think it over." She placed her hand over Taylor's. "It could be the best way out."

Taylor's head bowed. "I think you might be right. It's just that…it will be so final, you know? Not that I want this to drag out—it's killing me, it's killing Carter—but at least while I'm here, I'm still with him."

"Oh, honey. You know that the longer you stay, the harder it will be, right?" Taylor nodded. Brynn turned the chair so Taylor was facing her, knelt and clasped shaking hands between her own.

"Sweetie, Carter is going to need time, too. If you wait until Ian comes home, people will expect him to be sympathetic, and if it's all fresh for him, too, that might be too much to expect."

"I know." Taylor silently mouthed the words.

"They're going to be brothers for the rest of their lives." She squeezed. "Maybe the best thing you can do is give them the time to deal with this privately, so they don't end up losing each other, too."

HANK CHECKED THE CLOCK for the third time in ten minutes, then pulled his phone from his pocket yet again to be sure the clock was correct. Yep. Still working. Which meant that Brynn, the queen of promptness and efficiency, was fifteen minutes late for Millie time. Fifteen minutes late and she hadn't responded to the text he sent at the ten-minute mark.

All of a sudden he had a glimmer of what she must have felt the previous night, seeing his lights blaring through the darkness.

Her lights were on and her car was in its usual place, so he knew she hadn't left. She must be caught up in something. Or maybe—crap—still pissed at him for his behavior last night. Not that he didn't deserve it, but he didn't think that was her style.

He would give her five minutes and then he would—

The door burst open. She blew in, cheeks red, hair swirling around her face. Tension left him in a rush, leaving him glad he was leaning against the back of the couch.

It was a good thing he knew he was wiped out from the hours awake with Millie. Otherwise he would have to talk to himself about overreacting.

"Sorry! Sorry, I turned my phone off earlier because I was planning some things with Taylor, and I forgot to turn it back on and I…well. Here I am." She breathed in, gave him a slightly lopsided grin. "Unfortunately late, but better than never."

Whatever had been bothering her in the morning seemed to have been forgiven. Damn, it felt good to let go of that worry. "Not a problem. I'm actually not working in the cabins tonight."

"Oh?"

"Yeah. Mills, off the laptop—Daddy needs it now. I'm too tired to be trusted with a hammer tonight, so I figure I'll work on the website."

"Makes sense. Millie, how are you surviving?"

Millie didn't even bother looking up from the screen. "Thumbs are for babies. Ha! You are gonna die, pigs!"

Brynn snorted. "You're kidding me. Angry Birds?"

He hoped his shrug came off more casual than it felt. "It was a reward, okay?"

"Of course."

"And it's not as violent as I thought."

"Mmm."

"And it, uh, is kind of fun."

"Seems to me I've heard that before."

"All right, okay. I was wrong, you were right, I'm sorry."

She gave a little bark of laughter that veered off into a weird kind of hiccup. Or was it—was she *crying*?

"Hey, are you okay?"

She bit down on her lip, seemed to gaze into the distance for a second before shaking her head. "I, um, no. I mean, yes. Fine. Guess I'm still kind of tired, too."

Of course she was. He wasn't the only one who had been up half the night.

"Look, maybe we should take a pass. Early bedtimes all around."

"Daddy, no! Brynn promised she would make my nails pretty after I stopped my thumb!"

There was an edge to Millie's voice that served as a sharp reminder that she, too, was running close to empty. Lucky for him, before he had to negotiate, Brynn was tweaking Millie's nose.

"That's right, kiddo! I bought some super awesome nail polish just for this occasion. Also some glitter paints and sequins to decorate your jeans for the dance. Your lab coat, too, if you want to wear it."

Millie's smile dimmed a little as she placed a protective hand over the shirt, but she sat up straighter and eyed the bag in Brynn's hand.

"Are there sparkles?"

"Would I forget the sparkles?" Brynn's hand settled over her heart. "I am hurt, hurt, hurt."

Millie's giggle told him she would be okay for a while. Brynn, however, still worried him. *Fragile* wasn't a word he would have ever used to describe her, yet that was how she struck him now. Not just because of the circles under her eyes and the lack of wattage in her smile, but because of something he couldn't quite identify. She seemed almost hesitant. In other people, that wouldn't be an issue, especially after the previous evening, but with Brynn?

"Mills, finish up that level. Brynn, can you give me a hand in the kitchen?"

The sudden wariness in her eyes did nothing to reassure him. "Sure."

He waited for the door to close behind her before crossing his arms and studying her. "Okay. Out with it. Is this because of last night?"

"What? No, I told you, there's no need to worry about that. I understand and I'm fine. Just a little tired. You take care of business and I'll hang with Millie and everything will be right as rain."

"Yeah, and that would explain why you sound like you're going to fall apart any minute now." Too late he realized that he had all but dared her to cry. Shit. Millie tears, he could handle. Brynn tears were totally different.

He'd guessed wrong, though.

"Fine. Fine! I was trying to spare your male sensibilities, but since you're so determined to know the truth, it's hormones, okay? I'm PMS-ing and everything makes me cry. So hush up and leave me alone and go do your thing."

He almost believed her. Almost. If she hadn't thrown in the line about wanting to spare him, he might have bought it. As it was, he had a strong suspicion that the woman who grew up with three brothers was trying to play him.

"Okay. Sorry I asked." He raised his hands in mock surrender. "There's some leftover Easter chocolate in the freezer if you need it."

She hadn't expected that one. He could tell by the sudden widening of her eyes. His alert level was veering from pink to red—*crap, she's gonna cry*—when she lunged forward, caught his lips between hers and kissed him with a kind of desperation that had him pulling her tight and molding her to him and wishing, God, wishing—

"Daddy, I killed the piggies!"

He jerked back, automatically swiveling toward the door, but Millie was shouting from the other room. Thank God. Because Brynn was flushed and he was breathing hard and the last thing he could have handled at this moment was an explanation.

"Sorry," she whispered.

He shoved his fingers through his hair, mostly to keep them busy so they wouldn't latch on to her again. "Yeah, well, if you hadn't done that I probably would have, so don't beat yourself up."

She closed her eyes. When she opened them again, a faint smile played over her lips.

"Thanks."

"My pleasure. Believe me."

She ran a hand down his chest, lightly, but it was enough to make him step closer. When he realized what he had done he pulled back, but her touch left a trail that was leading him to places he knew he shouldn't go but wanted to follow anyway.

"Brynn…"

"What?"

He hesitated. These were words that couldn't be unsaid. But he wanted to say them anyway.

"You never said what you're going to do after you're done here."

She averted her gaze, a gesture he was learning to hate. "I have plans. Family stuff."

"In the area?"

She kept her focus firmly on the floor, but the hunch of her shoulders told him everything he needed to know.

Okay. It had been a good thought, but obviously there was no future in this. Not that he was looking for a future.

Except he might be. Not a full-fledged future, nothing definite or permanent, but if things were different…if she were going to be around…

Knowing that she wasn't going to be there much longer made it more important to say what was in his heart. "If you were staying…"

He stopped. He had to touch her while he said this. He didn't dare go for skin, so he reached for her hair, feeling the little kinks and curls wind around his fingers just like the way she curled herself around him after they made love.

"If you were staying, I would want to keep seeing you," he said softly. "To see where this might lead."

Her eyes closed, but not before he saw the sorrow building in them. "I would have liked that, too."

It was the truth. He could tell. She wasn't leaving

because she wanted to but because she was promised elsewhere. Because her family needed her.

He could have accepted that a lot easier if he hadn't seen her sleeping with Millie and for one brief moment they had felt like a family themselves.

THE NEXT DAY, as soon as the clock hit noon, Brynn saved the file she'd been working on, checked to make sure there were no urgent emails or festival-related messages and, certain that the coast was clear, turned to Taylor.

"Ready if you are."

Taylor paled a bit but nodded. "Let's go."

They exited the building together and walked to their cars. A few minutes and one drive-thru later they were at Taylor's apartment, huddled over her tiny excuse for a kitchen table.

Brynn peeled the foil from her container of curry chicken. "Okay, kiddo. Let's go over this. Have you decided what to say to Ian?"

"I think so." Taylor stared into her bowl of lamb tikka masala and wrinkled her nose. "This will be a good day for it, I think. He's coming to the end of his biggest project and doesn't have anything major on the horizon. The end is nigh, and all that crap." Her soft sigh echoed through Brynn. "Okay. So I was thinking I would let him spill about his day like always, just in case something horrific has happened, but—"

"No." Brynn slugged some water and shook her

head. "Unless somebody has died, which I highly doubt, there's no way his day could be bad enough to keep you from doing this."

"Oh."

"Yeah. Your plans are set. You're as ready as you can be. And remember, hon. Every day you put it off is another day you're lying to him." Her throat tightened. *Hank*. "Lying to someone you care about… That sucks. For both of you."

Taylor nodded. "You're right. So, I say hi, I make sure he's alone, and then I say, Ian, I'm so sorry, but even though I care about you very much, I don't love you the way I should for us to have the kind of marriage we both want. So I'm ending our engagement and—" here, for the first time, her voice faltered "—and leaving Comeback Cove."

"He'll have questions. And he'll try to change your mind."

"I know. I'm ready."

"He's going to ask if there's someone else."

Taylor nodded. "I still don't have a good answer to that one."

"I know. If you stick to the party line about not loving him the right way, he's going to see right through you. If you flat-out deny, he probably won't believe you."

"And I don't think I could say it without breaking down."

Oh, hell, this was going to be tricky. "You'll probably be crying already."

"Yeah, I will. But I still think he's going to see through it."

"Maybe..." Brynn scooped up some curry, chewed, made a face. "Maybe you could pull a half-truth. Tell him that you have been faithful, but that you have found yourself being, I don't know, drawn to someone else. And that's what made you realize that this wasn't meant to be."

"Because if I was truly in love with him I wouldn't be having those feelings about another guy. I could get through that one, I think. And it's true."

"He's going to ask who."

"I'll tell him it's irrelevant. Nothing happened, nothing will ever... Oh, crap, if I say that I'll really fall apart."

"Then don't. Just tell him there's no point in naming names because all that matters is what's between the two of you."

Taylor nodded. "I can do that."

"What are you going to do about the ring?"

"I'll give it to Moxie when I hand in my resignation."

"And when will you do that?"

"Right after I hang up with Ian." She smiled weakly. "And maybe have a quick belt of vodka, because Moxie scares me."

"Okay. You got your most important things out of the office, right?"

"Right. And here's the list of what I'd like you

to grab. Moxie will probably let me pack up, but I won't be thinking too clearly."

"True." Brynn tapped the back of Taylor's hand. "Carter?"

Taylor swallowed. "He's in Brockville today."

So no goodbyes. "That's probably the best way to handle it, hon."

Taylor nodded silently. For a moment the only sound was her breathing, short and choppy. Then she shoved her take-out box aside.

"God, I hate lamb tikka."

"I like it." Brynn eyed the box longingly. "But I'm not going to finish it. I don't want to associate it with today."

"Which is why I said Indian instead of burgers." Taylor's mouth crumpled and she bent over, cushioning her face in her arms. "Oh, Brynn. I don't know how I'm going to get through this."

Brynn dropped her fork and moved to kneel beside Taylor, pulling her close. "I know, sweetie. I know. Just keep reminding yourself that once you get through this, you're going to get on that plane and the worst will be behind you."

"It feels like I'm running away. Like I'm throwing everyone into a horrible situation and flying off to Bermuda."

"For one thing, Charlottetown is very nice, but it's hardly Bermuda. For another, once you've said your piece, would it help anyone to have you here?"

"No." She sat up and wiped her eyes. "I know that. But…everyone I love is here."

"I know. And someday… Someday, maybe, you can come back. But you have a good friend waiting there for you. It won't be home but you'll have her, and she will get you through the worst."

Taylor nodded silently and mopped more tears. "I will be so glad to hit the point when I stop crying every other minute."

If you were staying, I would want to keep seeing you. To see where this might lead.

"Yeah," she whispered. "I know."

They sat silently. At last, Taylor breathed in.

"I, um, guess I'd better get to it."

"You're sure you want me to leave?"

Taylor nodded.

"Text me when you're done."

Another nod.

"If you need me to do anything else…"

"Right."

How could one little word carry so much pain?

Brynn reached, but Taylor shook her head, her hand pressed tight to her mouth.

At that, Brynn's gut twisted. All the words she longed to say crowded together in her throat, but for Taylor's sake, she swallowed them down.

"Love you," she whispered, and closed the door.

CHAPTER FOURTEEN

BACK IN THE OFFICE, Brynn was too restless to focus. She filled a box with the items from Taylor's list— a plant, a couple of books, some funny cartoons— and hid it beside the desk.

She opened a file. Typed two sentences. Closed it.

Checked her voice mail. Nothing.

Checked her email. Two things, neither of which she trusted herself to deal with at the moment.

Opened her drawers. Pulled out a pencil decorated with Angry Birds.

Hank.

She dropped the pencil, buried her face in her hands. God, this sucked so bad.

She longed to tell him the truth, to make this easier for him. But she couldn't. She had promised Taylor and she had to keep that promise. And she couldn't, absolutely *couldn't* let him know the whole story, the parts that would only lead to more pain.

But oh, God. To think that last night was to be their last time together? With her a weeping fool and Millie killing pigs on the other side of the door?

No.

She couldn't do anything more for Taylor, or for Carter or Ian or anyone else who was impacted by this whole damned mess. But she could do something for Hank. Something for her.

She could give them one more memory before reality pushed in on them. One moment to stop faking and be real. One stolen hour to let herself show what she wished to hell wasn't true.

One brief moment to let herself be in love with Hank.

HANK WAS IN THE Grenadier cabin with the windows open, the music cranked and his shirt off—all the better to enjoy the first truly warm day of the year. There was nothing like sawing and sunshine to work up a sweat. After months of snow, cold and damp, he was more than ready.

"'Here comes the sun,'" he sang, wondering if George Harrison had ever suspected how many folks would think the song was written with them in mind. Because as he measured and cut, hammered and sweated, all he could think was—yeah. He'd had his winter, and it had been a bitch. But maybe now the sun was coming back.

Or maybe it had been there all along, but he'd needed some help cracking the door to let it in.

This floor was the last major repair on his list.

He still had about twelve thousand little things, but they would be easy to knock off, and none of them were essential. The festival folks could set up next week and he could breathe easy knowing that the inaugural guests would have safe, solid accommodations for the Victoria Day weekend.

Barring some kind of disaster, and despite the curveball of hosting the festival, he might actually pull this off.

He was setting the final floorboard in place when a shadow blocked the sunbeams pouring through the door. He looked up, startled, and settled back with a smile when he saw the cause. Brynn stood in the middle of the light, her hands in the pockets of the full skirt that was rippling in the light breeze.

"Hey. What are you doing here in the middle of the day? Playing hooky?"

She glanced around the cabin, her gaze lingering on the sawhorse, the wood scraps, the pile of sawdust. She walked to where he sat on his haunches, looked at the floor and dropped down, her skirt spreading around her like a puddle of pink roses.

Whoa.

"I had something that was best done away from the office," she said.

"Oh, yeah? What's that?"

Instead of answering with words, she leaned forward and caught his lips in a kiss.

Taken by surprise, blindsided by the movement and the rush of heat, he lost his balance. Instinct had him clutching her as he swayed. She sighed against his mouth and grabbed his arms and tipped with him to the ground. He landed awkwardly, half on his side, half on his back, but still she stayed with him, clinging, kissing, driving the breath from his lungs.

He pulled his mouth away.

"Whatever you were working on before you got here, I really, really approve."

She made an odd sound—almost like she was holding back a sob—but then she kissed him again. Not the teasing kind of kiss he would have expected given the fact they were in the middle of an unfinished cabin in the middle of a workday, but frantic ones laced with some underlying tension that had his arms closing tighter around her even as his brain whispered, *Hang on, something's off here.*

"Brynn?"

She shook her head and silenced him with another kiss. Her breath came in harsh gasps that echoed off the bare walls. Something was definitely wrong, but before he could ask she pushed him flat on his back and straddled him and, sweet Jesus, she wasn't wearing anything under the skirt.

His head started spinning. Something wasn't right, she was too intense, but she was tugging her shirt over her head and—oh, God—there was nothing under there, either, except skin and heat and invitation. She curled forward so her hair spilled across his chest and moved against him, and if he'd had any doubt of her plans, it was knocked aside by her hand at the snap of his jeans.

"Brynn?"

"No words," she whispered against his heart. "No questions."

A mighty fine offer, but there was one thing he would never let himself forget.

"Brynn. Babe. I don't carry condoms in my tool-box."

She sat up, thighs gripping his hips as if she feared he might try to leave, and pulled a most welcome foil packet from her skirt pocket. She pressed it into his hand and curled his fingers around the edges. The corners dug into his palm but he didn't care because she was bracing herself against his shoulders and curling against him and he knew that as soon as he could make himself let go of her, his jeans would be history.

His palms ran along the smoothness of her thighs, cupped her cheeks and pulled her tighter, urged her forward until her breasts settled in his hands and his thumbs were sliding across her nipples and she was making that sound again, the one that had haunted him all through the long days since the time he pushed her up against the wall, the little half gasp that made him feel strong and hot and so damned complete each time he remembered it.

She drew back. Kissed and nipped her way down his chest. Made short work of his jeans and the condom and then, ah, then she was sliding over him, taking him into herself, her skirt still flowing around them like some kind of weird curtain, but it didn't matter because it was Brynn and she was all round him and she needed him and—

Something trickled onto his chest. Soft. Powdery. He opened his eyes and tried to make sense of it but it didn't make sense because he could swear it was—

"Sawdust?"

She tipped her hand so more of the fine powder dribbled over his skin and back to the floor. She rubbed it into him, mixing it with his sweat, pouring it over her own chest and bending to kiss him again.

"Every time you're working, every time you smell sawdust, you're going to remember this. You're going to remember us." She rubbed her cheek against his jaw and kissed him right below his ear. "You're going to remember me."

His breath was still coming in ragged gasps and Brynn was collapsed on his chest when Hank gripped her shoulders and pushed her upright, trying to see into her eyes. The fact that she kept her face averted sent a new and most unwelcome kind of shudder running through him.

"Hey. Not that I didn't appreciate what just happened, but this wasn't… You aren't— What's wrong?"

She rounded her shoulders, shrinking away from him and reaching for her shirt. She pulled her top over her head without once meeting his eyes. Gone were the teasing, the laughter, the saucy smiles that he associated with Brynn afterglow. He was getting colder and more fidgety by the minute, and lying on the ground half-naked sure as hell wasn't helping the situation.

"Brynn." He pushed to his knees, tugged his jeans into place. "What's going on?"

She started to stand but crumpled back to the floor. He reached for her but she shook her head and shrank away from hm.

"Don't. Please. If you do, I'll never get through this."

"Get through—"

"Taylor is breaking up with Ian."

"What?"

She drew in a deep breath and twisted her hands together in front of her. "She was calling him as soon as I left. She's leaving the dairy and flying to Charlottetown tonight."

"She— Wait. What? Why is she— Why are you— I mean, I know she's your cousin, but why are you—"

"Because I told her to do it."

Brynn told Taylor to leave. Cold dread crept through him even as he shook his head. "But that doesn't make any sense. And why did you— Start over, okay? From the beginning. Because I'm not following this."

She stared out the window and spoke in a voice so flat that he would never have believed it was hers. "Back in January she came to me and told me she wasn't in love with Ian anymore. I told her she was wrong, that she just missed him. I told her I could fix it. Because, see, I can fix everything, and I was sure that it was just a matter of reminding her of things, getting her head on straight...." Her voice thickened. She looked up, swallowed, tried a couple of times before speaking again. "I was so certain...I talked her into it. She convinced you guys to hire me so I could be close to her. The whole time I've been here, I've been trying to force her to fall back in love with him, because I thought, hey, all I had to do was find the right switch and everything would be better." She slumped back against the wall, covered her face with her hands. "I was such an idiot. I had no idea...no idea at all what I was playing with. No idea what love really means."

He pushed to his feet, knees still weak and untrustworthy. "So the last four months have been a lie?"

"For Taylor. Yes." Her eyes filled. "But not for—"

"Don't." If she tried to bring them into it, her and him and Millie, he would never get back to what mattered. To Ian.

He grabbed his shirt, pressed it to his face for

a second, let it fall to his side. "You told Taylor to leave. To run away." It was like a neon sign in his brain, red and glowing and blocking out everything else. *Run away. Walk away. Move on.*

No. Ian. He had to think about Ian.

"Why now? If she's known this for months, what changed?" His gut twisted. He knew what had changed, and it had nothing to do with Ian and Taylor. But that made no sense. He had to be wrong, there had to be something—

"There's more to this, isn't there?" About Taylor. Taylor and Ian. Because Brynn couldn't really be doing this over the two of them. Could she?

She didn't move.

"God dammit, Brynn, what else? Did she steal from the dairy, or cheat on Ian, or—"

"No! No, God, no, Hank. I swear to you, she hasn't—hasn't taken anything or done anything wrong. She doesn't love Ian but she cares about him, she never… Her biggest mistake was in listening to me."

The way he had listened?

"Then why the rush? Why now? Why not wait until he's home?" He rose to his feet. "What are you hiding, Brynn?"

She crossed her arms over her stomach and pressed, so hard that he could see the push of her biceps. There was something else and she knew it and she wasn't going to tell him.

"I'm moving out of the cabin. Going to Taylor's."

It shouldn't have hurt. He should have expected it. But hearing the words made it worse. Harder. *Real*.

"Of course you're leaving."

She scrambled to her feet and looked at him, really looked at him for the first time since walking into the cabin. He saw the tears, saw about a hundred shades of regret and sorrow and hurt and, damn him, he wanted to hold her and tell her it would be okay, *they* would be okay.

But he couldn't. She was running away, just like he had known she would.

"Leaving is what you do best, isn't it?"

"What?"

"Come on, Brynn. You're not leaving because of Taylor."

She took a small step back. Shook her head.

But didn't say a word.

"I told myself you weren't leaving by choice. I thought, oh, if things were different… But I was wrong. Leaving is your thing."

Her mouth moved in a silent *no*.

"Oh, yeah, Brynn. Maybe you can keep lying to yourself, but I can't. Not anymore. The temp jobs, the 'walk away, Millie,' the 'accept and move on,' the 'oh, yes, I would want to keep seeing you'— you see a pattern here?" He balled up his forgotten shirt, threw it into the corner. "You know what? Leave. Now. Go ahead. It's better this way. At least

I won't be walking around for the next two weeks wondering how much time, wondering what if…"

"You knew. You knew we were never going to be more than this."

"Yeah, I knew. But I wasn't spending the whole time we were together planning how to get away." He stalked to the corner, grabbed his shirt, shook off the sawdust that clung to the fabric. "Tell the truth. If things had been different and you could have stayed, how long would it have taken? How long until you got bored with me and Millie and invented some reason to take off?"

"I wasn't…"

"Last night, when you stood in my kitchen and said that if you were staying, you would have wanted to see where this might lead—were your bags already packed, Brynn? When you were crying and kissing me, were you busy thanking Taylor for giving you a ready-made excuse to get out before things got too serious?"

She walked to the door, leaving him reeling in the middle of the empty space with her words pounding through him and the scent of sawdust all but choking him. When she reached the threshold, she stopped and turned back.

"I know you won't believe me. I don't blame you. But you and me… None of that was a lie. Not one minute."

With that, she walked away, her footsteps sounding softly on the porch and then fading as she stepped to the ground. He watched through the door and then the window as she walked up the path and disappeared into the stand of maples.

She was leaving. She was going to pack up her car if she hadn't already, and he was going to be left here, without answers, trying to console his child, who wouldn't understand.

And even though his head kept telling him that his brother had been handed a far worse blow, his heart was having a hell of a time believing it.

BRYNN WOULDN'T HAVE thought it possible to be even less focused when she returned to work than before she ducked out. Turns out it was.

The building was quiet. People were leaving for the day. She would normally have been preparing to hit the road herself, but today she dreaded the thought. Taylor's apartment was so filled with memories and sorrows that she could scarcely breathe when she was there.

But she couldn't stay in the cabin. Couldn't look out the window and see the lights of Hank's house and know they were forever closed to her. Choking on memories was infinitely better than drowning in regrets and hearing the echo of Hank's accusations and wondering—

"Well, Miss Catalano. It's been quite an afternoon around here."

Brynn whirled toward the door, where Moxie stood as stiff as a guard at Buckingham Palace.

Though Brynn doubted that even the most devoted sentinel could defend the queen as ardently as she was sure Moxie was about to protect her family.

Brynn started to rise but Moxie pointed to the chair.

"Sit."

Brynn sat.

Moxie advanced slowly. "I'm not going to bore you with the details, because as I understand it, you have known about them far longer than I would have believed. What matters now is the future."

Brynn nodded.

"I understand that you are willing to continue on here through the festival, ensuring it goes off as planned."

"That's correct."

"And that Taylor has briefed you on the most pressing of her duties, leaving you prepared to carry them out until such time as we can hire someone new for the position."

Again, Brynn nodded. There seemed to be no point in using actual words. Moxie was well aware of everything and anything Brynn would have tried to say.

"It seems you two gave this a great deal of thought."

"We wanted to keep the disruption and…and the hurt to a minimum."

"So I understand." Moxie ran a finger over her wedding band. "I'm guessing this is the family commitment you referred to when you turned down the job."

"Yes, ma'am."

"Well, at least that part makes more sense now."

It was the first thing Moxie had said that wasn't true, for none of this made sense. Not one bit.

"For the love of God, I hope this is the last commitment on your plate." Moxie peered at her. "Or should we be bracing for another explosion?"

Carter. "This should be the end of it."

Moxie frowned. "Interesting answer."

"It's the most truthful one I can give, I'm afraid. Reading the future has never been one of my talents."

Moxie gave her that look again—the one that left Brynn feeling like she was being put through a combination X-ray/MRI scan.

"You are a careful one, aren't you?"

Oh, shit, oh, shit, oh, shit. Moxie knew there was more. Or at the very least, she was highly suspicious.

"Not careful," she said softly. "Just…trying to make the best of a lousy situation."

"Humph. Going for the understatement-of-the-year award, are you?" Moxie shook her head. "Tell me the truth, girl. People are going to be pissed as hell with you, especially being as how Taylor isn't here to face the music. Do you think you can shrug that off and keep running the festival?"

"I've worked through worse."

"Fine. I understand you have about a month to help us while we get someone new here. Until then, I expect you to give three hundred and ninety-eight percent to this company with every breath you take. Is that clear?"

"Very." And probably more than she deserved.

"Then that's what we'll do. But let me give you fair warning, miss." Moxie leaned forward, her gaze boring into Brynn's. "If anything goes wrong, I'm holding you responsible. And believe you me, that's not a position I would want to be in at all."

A COUPLE OF DAYS after his world went to hell, Hank ended his call, shoved the phone back in his pocket and let loose with all the curses that had filled his brain during his conversation but had remained locked up because, geez, who says those kind of things to his grandmother?

Feelings temporarily vented, he yelled down the hall.

"Mills! We have dance rehearsal tonight after all."

She flew out of her room, lab coat flapping, and pushed her glasses up on her nose. "But you said—"

"I know." He had been sure the dance would be nixed now that Taylor was gone. Who could expect Ian to get up there and high-step it when everyone watching would know that he had just had his heart handed to him on a silver platter?

Apparently, Moxie had no trouble with it.

"Your great-grandmother says we need to do this no matter what. So let's get going."

Millie skipped down the hall. "But this is good, Daddy! Brynn will be there and we haven't seen her since she left. I miss her!"

You aren't the only one, kiddo.

He grabbed his shoes and shoved his feet inside, directing all his swearing abilities at himself now. He'd been an idiot. A complete and total numskull. He'd known something was up and he'd talked himself into believing Brynn wasn't the kind to walk away.

Yeah. That had worked out really well.

His logical brain insisted on pointing out that really, all Brynn had done was speed up the inevitable, that she would have left no matter what. It didn't help. He'd been doing a damned fine imitation of a zombie ever since Brynn packed up her hatchback and drove off to Taylor's place. And to be honest, half the reason he'd been hoping they would shit-can the dance was because he didn't know how he was supposed to be in the same room with her, knowing what she had done but wanting her just the same.

Damned Moxie. Damned festival. Stupid damned idiot self.

Half an hour later he was in his familiar place in the Northstar lobby, doing his best to avoid looking at Brynn. She stood alone by the floor-to-ceiling windows, sketching things in that blue notebook, scratching them out and drawing again.

Millie, of course, had burst in and overflowed with hugs and stories. He had settled for a nod. The only consolation was that no one else seemed to know how to deal with Brynn, either. If it were possible to measure sidelong glances and lowered voices, he was pretty sure the Norths would set a new record tonight.

"There's Uncle Car!" Millie stopped twirling in circles and ran to throw her arms around Carter, who had scooted in from the interior stairs. He must not have seen her coming for instead of catching her in his usual bear hug, he stumbled backward and almost landed flat on his ass. In fact, if Hank didn't miss his guess, Millie was the one who kept them both upright.

It seemed Carter was losing some of that pornstar snap in his old age.

"Sorry I'm late." He steadied Millie, who wrinkled her nose and backed away.

Brynn studied him for a long moment before shaking her head and heading to the table.

"Okay." Her voice was pure steel. She glanced at her notebook, bit her lip, but tilted her chin up. "Here's the new lineup."

He'd heard more enthusiasm from Millie on the way to her last dentist checkup. They made it through the warm-up and then the first verse with barely a stumble. A miracle, considering he was pretty sure none of them were focused on the moves tonight. Midway through the chorus, Carter missed a step and slammed into his side.

"Ow!"

Carter glanced at him. "Jesus, Hank. Watch where you're going."

"I didn't—" he began, but Brynn shook her head.

"Keep going. It's good practice in case there's a problem when we're live."

He scowled but counted the beats and stepped back into the song, feeling a tiny burst of pride at being able to find his place again. One thing was sure: Brynn's line about being ready for anything that might happen during the actual performance was pretty accurate. If they could make it through this rehearsal they could get through any—

"Shit!"

He saw Carter heading for him just in time to step out of the way. Too late for Carter, though, who grabbed for him, missed and promptly kissed the tiles.

"Jesus H.—" Carter's words were lost in a rush of questions from the rest of the clan.

"Carter, are you okay?"

"Uncle Car, you fell!"

"For the love of God, boy, go home before you hurt someone."

Brynn's voice, low in his ear, was the only one that registered. "Help him up. He's drunk."

What the hell?

Shoving aside the reflexive jolt of pleasure at her nearness—*over, dammit*—he reached for Carter, bent extra low and sniffed. Sure enough, Carter's breath was laced with rye and Coke.

He glanced at Brynn, hating himself for turning to her, but not too proud to admit that she was the one with the clearest head. She bit her lip and leaned in close.

"Get him out of here, please." Standing, she said loud enough for all to hear, "Oops. Guess that stomach bug decided it wasn't finished with Carter. Let's call a halt. If anyone wants to stay and practice one-on-one, I'll stick around a while. Everyone else, sorry for dragging you out. I should have realized this was too much to ask tonight."

"Bossy bitch, isn't she?" Carter said from his oh-so-dignified perch on the floor.

"Carter North!" Ma tried to get in close, probably to dispense a whap across Carter's thick skull, but Hank leaned in to play barrier.

"Let's go, Carter."

"Why? Just because she said so?" Carter leered up at Hank. "Do you let her boss you around like that when you're—"

Hank didn't pause. Didn't think. Just grabbed his stupid brother by his crisp white shirt and hauled him upright.

"We're leaving because you're a dumb-ass, Car. Now move it."

He gave Carter a none-too-gentle shove toward

the door. Carter took a couple of slow steps before stopping and turning back to the family clustered together.

"Sorry, folks." Some of his bravado slipped away. "Seems I made a royal mess of things again."

Again?

Hank glanced at Brynn. While everyone else seemed puzzled or surprised—or, in Moxie's case, slightly sad—Brynn looked mostly resigned. Like she'd been expecting something along these lines.

She met his gaze, shook her head the tiniest bit and put her hand on Millie's head. *Home,* she mouthed. He got the message.

He followed Carter out the door and headed for the parking lot, curious, worried and hoping against hope that Carter's next royal mess wouldn't land all over the front seat of the truck.

BEING BACK IN Hank's home hurt.

Brynn had known it would be awkward to step back into the house where she and Hank and Millie had spent so much time laughing and learning about each other. She had expected the wave of sadness that hit her the minute she walked into the kitchen and saw Hank's plaid jacket hanging from the hook by the door.

But she hadn't realized how much it would hurt. How each step through the familiar rooms and the sight of Millie's Angry Birds drawing on the refrigerator, and the lingering scent of Hank's beloved dark roast coffee, would drive home the message of loss.

Standing in his living room, holding a picture of him and Millie from last Halloween—Millie in a SpongeBob costume, Hank wearing a goofy smile and a Han Solo vest and blaster—the ache gripped her throat.

Dear God, but she missed him.

It made no sense. She'd known him barely three months. How could he have become such a part of her in such a short amount of time?

But running her finger over his long frame in the picture, remembering moments when she had held him close, she knew.

This was why Taylor had wanted to be near Carter, even when she couldn't be with him. This was why her mother had said she didn't know if she could send her father away again, even after he made a mockery of their marriage.

But it was more. It was why Sam and Libby smiled each time the other walked into the room. Why Hank's parents looked first to each other during meetings. Why, even though it had made no sense at all for her to ask Hank to take care of Carter tonight, he had been the first one she turned to.

Because he was part of her. Knit into her by love.

And she had the horrible feeling that he might have been right about the real reason she had urged Taylor to end things when she did.

IT WAS JUST a minute or two after she kissed Millie good-night that the door opened. She risked a peek from her spot at the kitchen table. He seemed tired and worried and frustrated, his hair was a picture in wildness, and the moment he spotted her she could see his emotional shields snap into place—yet she had to force herself to stay seated instead of sliding her arms around his waist and resting her cheek against his shoulder the way she longed to do.

"Millie asleep?"

"Probably not. The lights went off just a couple of minutes ago."

He nodded and peeled off his sweatshirt, giving her a moment to drink in the sight of his chest, the strip of skin where his T-shirt rode up. It would be warm, she knew. And she was so very cold…

"How's Carter?"

"You tell me."

"Sorry?"

His shrug was far too casual. "Come on, Brynn. You're the one who knows all my family secrets, and you sure as hell didn't look surprised when he showed up plastered. Seems to me you probably have a better idea than I do."

How was she supposed to fake it through this one? She couldn't think of anything to say other than the truth—the one thing that would do more damage than good.

She chose to go with a much older fact.

"My father used to come home drunk sometimes. I got good at spotting the signs very fast."

He studied her for a second before nodding. "I'll give you that one. 'Course, that doesn't explain *why* my tight-assed brother decided to hide out in his office after work and get shit-faced."

"He didn't say anything on the way home?"

Hank snorted and shoved his hands in his pockets. "The only thing he said was, 'Pull over, now.' Not much of a conversation."

Thank God.

"Will he be okay alone?"

Hank stared at her, his face unreadable. He probably thought she didn't really care, that she was simply trying to deflect the conversation. Could she blame him?

"Cash was on his way over," he said at last. "He said he could babysit."

"Good." She didn't want Carter to be alone. She had called him once after Taylor left, but he had made it clear that she was more of an unwanted reminder than a help. All her calls and texts since then had gone unanswered. She had planned to follow him home after tonight's rehearsal, just to be sure he really was okay—Taylor kept asking—but that plan had blown up in her face, too.

It was all slipping through her fingers. No matter what she did, she was only making things worse. Twisting knives. Breaking more hearts.

"I should leave," she said, but Hank's hand shot out and gripped her arm.

"The hell, Brynn? Is that your answer to everything?"

No. She wanted to say it, but she couldn't because she wasn't sure. Not anymore.

"Maybe I was too blown away to let that happen after Ian and Taylor, but not again. Something is wrong with my brother and you know what it is, and even though walking away is the only thing you know how to do I'll be damned if I let you—"

She saw the moment he put it together. It was all there in his face, so heartbreakingly easy to read. The sudden halt as he made the connection between what she had said after Taylor's departure and Carter's actions tonight. The moment of wide-eyed disbelief. His small, instinctive step back, as if he were trying to distance himself from the truth. And then...oh, then, the hopelessness in his eyes as he shook his head and looked at her, begging her to tell him he was wrong without saying a word.

Brynn's last, slender hope snapped.

"No." His voice was rough, hoarse, as if he'd dragged the words free. "That can't be."

She closed her eyes, hoping he wouldn't read the answer she knew he didn't want to admit.

His hand tightened on her arm. "Tell me, Brynn. Tell me I'm wrong, that Carter... That Taylor..."

Her eyes were still closed. It didn't matter. She knew his face too well. The image was raw and clear in her mind, magnified by his fingers tightening on her arm.

He knew. He knew, and now the one hope that had given Taylor some measure of comfort—that the family would be fine—had been shredded. As long as it had been simply Carter's secret there had been hope, but Hank—Hank wouldn't be able to keep this to himself. He would try but it would leak out, maybe not in his words but perhaps in his actions. His mother would pick up on it. Or Moxie, who already suspected, she was sure of it. They were all going to find out. They would all know.

"Brynn, for the love of God…"

There was nothing she could do now—for Taylor, for Carter, for Ian, for any of them.

Except—

She could tell Hank everything. All of it. There was no point in pretending anymore. She could tell him, and maybe make him see that even though she had stayed silent it was for good reasons. Make him see that she had truly been trying to help. Then maybe, just maybe, he could understand why she did it. Maybe, someday, he could forgive her. Maybe they could find a way past this, could get back to that point when he held her in this very room and said that if she were staying, he would want to keep—

No.

She had failed Taylor in every way possible. She would not—*could* not—fail her now. Even though it wouldn't make a difference. Even though it wouldn't change anything.

Even though it would cost her that last fragile possibility with Hank.

"I'm sorry," she whispered.

This time, when she tried to pull her arm free and run away, he made no move to stop her.

CHAPTER FIFTEEN

HANK FELT LIKE the walking dead when he pulled into the Northstar parking lot the next morning. He hoped his head would be clearer after he did what he'd come to do, but given the way things had been spinning lately, he didn't hold out much hope.

He double-timed it toward the building, not even faltering when he passed Brynn's car. He'd seen it at the cabins a dozen times the past few days while she supervised the setup for the festival. He was immune.

At least that was what he told himself.

Moxie's door was open, as usual, so Hank sailed past her assistant with the bare minimum greeting required by politeness. There were times when being family came in damned handy.

Moxie raised a hand as he approached, her gaze never leaving the computer screen. She pulled headphones from her ears. "Hold on. I'm almost done."

"But—"

"Henry. Patience. I need two more minutes."

It was so much like the way she used to talk to

him when he was a kid that he couldn't protest. Instead, he sent a pleading glance at the portrait of Grandpa Gordon hanging behind the desk and closed the door. He edged behind Moxie's chair in the hope of seeing what was so vital, fully expecting her to give him hell for spying on a top secret document. Instead, he saw that she was watching an episode of *The Big Bang Theory*.

"Seriously?" he asked once the final credits appeared and she pulled off the headphones. "You made me wait for the 'Soft Kitty' guy?"

Moxie, of course, was totally unmoved. "When you're my age, you know that things can change in the snap of a finger. I like that show. If I died without knowing how that episode ended, I'd have to haunt you for all eternity."

Not that he believed in ghosts, but the thought of having Moxie hang around him for the rest of his life was enough to make him think that maybe she had been doing him a favor.

"Listen." He grabbed a chair, flipped it around and straddled it, his arms resting on the top of the backrest. "I found out something last night, and I don't know what to do with it."

"This have anything to do with Carter's bonehead move?"

"Yeah. I think—"

"Did he say anything to you when you took him home?"

"No. But I—"

"Dammit to hell, I thought he might finally "

"Moxie, would you let me finish?"

She gave him an evil eye that quickly morphed into something a whole lot warmer.

"Well, well, well," she said with far too much satisfaction.

"Look." He gripped the rail of the chair. "If you want to play Zen master, you go ahead, but I have a to-do list twelve pages long. So maybe you could save the questions for a minute."

She waved her hand in a spot-on imitation of the queen. "Continue."

"Brynn said something last night." He frowned as he replayed the conversation for about the five millionth time. "Well, actually, she didn't. But I said something, and remembered something else she said, and I think…" He took a deep breath, checked to make sure the door was still closed. "I think the reason Taylor broke up with Ian is because—"

"Because of Carter."

Thank God—she hadn't phrased it as a question. It meant he wasn't the only one who had put things together in this seriously twisted way.

On the other hand…

On the other hand, if Moxie thought it was true, then dammit to hell, it probably was. And God, but he had hoped he was wrong.

Didn't it figure—the first time in his life he was

the one who had the inside scoop, and he would give anything to not know it.

Moxie let out a long sigh and swiveled to stare at the photo of her and Gramps that sat at the corner of her desk. "Well, one good thing. You coming in here today saves me from going down the hall to choke the truth out of Brynn."

"You wouldn't have got very far."

"Oh?" Moxie could say more with one word and a quirked eyebrow than most people could with a novel.

"Last night, even after I put it together, she still wouldn't admit it."

"'Course not. She likely promised Taylor she wouldn't breathe a word."

"But I already knew."

"You already suspected." Moxie pointed at him. "Big difference. And your Brynn might be a lot of things, but she's not one to let down her family."

"She's not my—"

He stopped, sidetracked by Moxie's words. *Family.* That word kept whispering in the back of his brain whenever he thought about her. If he could only think about that for a moment…

But there was no time because Moxie was off and running.

"No, siree. If she said she wouldn't tell anyone, then that's the way it's going to be. The only way to get the truth out of her is to make her see that it's for the better."

"How could anything be better about this?"

"You leave that to me." She turned in her chair once more. "I have to say, of all the things I thought might be coming down the pike, this wasn't one of them."

"Seriously, Moxie? I know you think you're the great and powerful Oz, but you can't convince me that you saw this coming."

"What, Carter and Taylor? Of course I did. Why do you think I sent him to the conference?"

Thank God he was already sitting. "You're kidding. You knew about this and you sent him anyway?"

"I didn't know. I suspected, same as you. And yes siree bob, that was exactly why I sent him. Anyone with eyes and seventy-odd years of experience could tell that something was fishy with those two. They just needed the chance to admit it."

"Forget the dairy, Moxie. You should be working with the Mounties."

She shrugged. "I never looked good in red. Now, leave Carter and Taylor to me. It's time to talk about you."

Brynn. "Remember that to-do list I mentioned? I think it's time I got back to it."

"No," she continued as if he hadn't spoken. "I can't say I'm surprised that you figured out what was up with those two. What really threw me for a curve was you walking in here all worried."

Well, that was unexpected. "You think I wouldn't worry about my own family?"

"It wasn't the worry that took me by surprise. It was the walk." She pushed up from her chair and leaned across the desk, giving him the stare that had launched a thousand nightmares. "It wasn't that long ago, Henry William North, that you were so hell-bent on doing things yourself that it was like you'd built a wall between you and the rest of the family. One with lots of windows, mind you, but a wall all the same. Yet today you waltzed in here because you knew something was wrong. Three, four months ago, you would have sat back and waited to see how it played out. Today, you're trying to make it better."

He wanted to say she was wrong but given her track record, he figured he should save his breath.

"I guess, now that Millie and I are in the cabins, maybe it's easier—"

He was interrupted by a very loud, very rude snort.

"You're not stupid, Hank. Don't try to fake it now."

BRYNN ENDED HER CALL with the electrician, rubbed her forehead—wiring would be the death of her yet—grabbed her bottle of water from the desk and almost choked when she tipped her head back to take a drink and spotted Moxie lounging in the doorway.

"You know," she wheezed as soon as she caught her breath, "the stealth ninja thing is really getting old."

"Not as old as I am, kid."

"Yet you move faster and more silently than my mother's cat."

"Is that so?" Moxie's smile was decidedly unsettling. "In that case, Brynn, I'm giving you fair warning. You just turned into a mouse."

"What do you—"

Moxie stepped into the room, pulled the door closed. "No more secrets, girl. Tell me the real reason Taylor left."

Oh, *shit*. This wasn't going to be pretty.

"Don't bother acting like you don't know what I'm talking about." Moxie dropped into Taylor's chair with a groan. "Something's wrong, and it's time to deal with it once and for all."

"Why do you—" Brynn began, but Moxie leaned forward and pointed her finger.

"Listen to me, girlie. There's two things on the line here—my company and my family. I can and will get the dairy through this. People leave all the time. But my family is a different story altogether. I can't make this work unless I know what I'm dealing with, and as far as I can tell, you're the only one who can help."

Brynn shook her head. "It will only make things worse."

"Let me be the judge of that."

The temptation was strong. She had a pretty good idea that Moxie had figured things out already. But if she hadn't confirmed things with Hank last night, she certainly wasn't going to do so now with Moxie.

Moxie sighed. "You ever have a splinter, Brynn?"

The question was so unexpected that Brynn nodded in agreement before she even realized it.

"Good. So you know that while the splinter is stuck, it hurts like a mother. If you pull it out, things might be tender for a while, but eventually it will heal. But if you don't pull it out, what happens?"

"It gets infected." The sick feeling in her stomach strengthened her suspicions. Moxie's cat-and-mouse comparison had been spot on.

"That's right. It festers. And what are you left with? A messy, slimy wound that's worse than it had to be. Takes a hell of a lot longer to heal, too. So what of it, Brynn? Are you going to help my family get rid of this splinter now, or are you going to push it underground until it explodes?"

What did explosions have to do with splinters?

"I'm guessing you promised Taylor you'd keep silent. I respect that. Just nod. Is she in love with Carter?"

Brynn was certain she gave nothing away—she didn't so much as blink—but Moxie crumpled a little anyway.

"Ah, hell." The chair creaked as she leaned back. "I wouldn't have minded being wrong just this once."

"But I didn't—"

"That's right. You didn't do anything because you knew what I was going to ask. If I was wrong, you'd-a been jumping out of your chair asking what the hell I was smoking."

Despite everything, Brynn couldn't help but smile. "I can truthfully say that I never would have asked that."

"And that's all you're going to say?"

"If you suspected something like this—" Brynn chose her words carefully, seeking to avoid flat-out confirming Moxie's theory "—why did you send Carter to the conference?"

"The truth had to come to light. If it hadn't, and Taylor went ahead and married Ian… Well, there's your slimy mess, for sure."

"But you didn't say anything."

Moxie snorted. "Good God, child. You think anyone would have listened to me? One wrong word and they would have been so deep in pretending there was no problem that there would be no getting to the truth. It had to come from them. All I could do was put the pieces in place and let them make the moves."

Why did those words have a familiar ring to them?

"But it doesn't matter anymore. Taylor is in Charlottetown and—"

"I know that. The question is what's going to happen next."

"What?" The ache in Brynn's stomach turned into an uneasy roll. "But there is no next. She's gone."

"Oh, and here I thought you were smarter than that." Moxie leaned forward. "Taylor isn't the splinter. Carter is. Well, his feelings for her. Those aren't going to go away just because she's taken her cute little behind to the east coast."

Oh, hell and damnation.

"But surely with her gone…"

"Leaving isn't always the answer, Brynn."

Walking away is the only thing you know how to do.

Moxie leaned forward, cutting through the memory of Hank's angry words. "Listen to me, girl. I know nobody meant for this to get so messy, and that you two cooked up this solution to keep from hurting Ian any more than necessary. That's understandable. But what do you think will happen when Ian comes home and everyone is looking after him because he lost the woman he loved, and there's Carter, who lost her, too, but can't say a thing?"

Mentioning that Taylor had asked her to help Carter would only add fuel to Moxie's fire. Luckily—or not—Moxie wasn't waiting for feedback.

"That's gonna hurt, Brynn, and it's not the kind of hurt that goes away easy. It's going to eat at him. It's going to make him resent his brother, and Ian won't know why, and if we try to hide this, even though you'd think it should help, I'm telling you, it will only make things worse."

She was right. Brynn bowed her head as the truth sank into her. Moxie knew love and she knew her family. If she thought it would be worse to stay silent, then the odds were that someone needed to speak up.

"What do you suggest?"

Moxie sighed. "There's going to be hurt no matter what. The question is how many people are going to end up hurting."

"You don't— Are you saying I should tell Taylor to come home?" Home to *Carter?*

"Hell no, girl." Moxie reached forward and knocked Brynn on the forehead. "I'm going to tell Carter to haul ass and go after her."

LATER THAT AFTERNOON, Hank was adding bits of river rock to the stone fence surrounding the house when he heard the slam of a car door. No surprise, given that the cabins had become Comeback Cove's version of Grand Central as the festival approached. Stages were being assembled. Vendor booths were going up. The cooking tent was in place and the Grenadier cabin had been turned into a living history display, overflowing with photos and memorabilia and period clothing. Hank had gone in there when he returned from his little chat with Moxie, checked out the exhibit she'd suggested on Northstar Sweethearts and shook his head at how she had used it for her own nefarious means.

With all the comings and goings, a slamming door was par for the course. But Brynn had texted to say she was on her way and he wanted to be sure he was out of range when she arrived.

Cowardly? Hell, yeah. But even though he had thought he couldn't get any more confused when it came to her, it turned out he'd been wrong. Ever since he walked out of Moxie's office he'd had the weirdest feeling in his gut—like he was missing something big. Something about Brynn. Something about family.

It was probably nothing. It wasn't like he'd been getting enough sleep lately to be working with a clear head. But until he had a better handle on it, he thought it might be smarter to avoid her.

Though when he spied the Saab sitting in his parking lot, he almost would have preferred Brynn.

Carter had his hands in his pockets and his head down as he picked his way through the tangle of sticks and wires.

"Careful," Hank called. "You don't want to fall someplace you have no right landing."

Judging from the way Carter flushed, Hank's meaning hadn't gone unnoticed.

"I know you think I'm an ass—"

"Oh, I'd say it goes a lot further than just thinking." Hank picked up a slab of limestone, eyed it critically. "Come to think of it, *ass* is a pretty mild description, too."

"Believe it or not, Hank, there's nothing you can say that's worse than what I've said to myself every minute of the day for the past year."

"A year?" He hadn't expected that one. "But that was before Ian left."

Carter placed a hand on the smooth hunk of stone that was currently on top of the portion in progress. "Probably longer, if you want to know the truth. There was always something special about Taylor, but the timing was never right—she was in school, then I was in law school, and there were other people in there. By the time I was done with law school and came back, she was with Ian." He pressed down on the rock. "My God, Hank, you have to believe I never meant for this to happen. I tried to make it stop. I saw other women, I stayed away from her, I spent extra time with Ian when he was here to help me remember that he's my brother.... I did everything I could except move, and I was even going to do that once Ian came back."

"So what changed?" Hank didn't want to feel sorry for Carter, but damn, if what he was saying was true, it was hard to keep him firmly in the villain camp.

"What changed was that I could see she wasn't happy. Then Moxie sent me to that conference, and

Taylor was doing her damnedest to avoid me and I decided I had to know."

"You took a hell of a chance." Hank wasn't sure if he should be impressed or distressed by that gamble, so he opted to stick with confusion. "Did you think she would ditch Ian and run off with you, all from one little conversation?" At least, he hoped it was just a conversation.

"She had already decided to leave Ian. She said she was on the verge months ago, but Brynn talked her into giving it another shot."

The worst thing she ever did was listen to me.

No. He couldn't let Brynn into his head now.

"She went along with it because she thought maybe it would work and everyone could end up happy. Except she didn't know that I…" He picked up a small bit of limestone and threw it hard, sending it sailing through the air.

"It sucks all around, Hank. I know that. I hated myself, called God some pretty sick names, let poor Jenny in Accounting think we were going somewhere when all I was doing was using her… If there was a good way to handle this, I didn't find it. I've been such an ass that I don't understand how anyone could even put up with me, but she does. She loves me, Hank. And believe it or not, knowing that is enough to make all the other shit worth it."

Believe that one? Yeah. He did. After all, how many times had he himself found himself thinking that meetings and rehearsals were easier to get through because they gave him a chance to hang with Brynn? And that hadn't even been love, just sex and laughs. The real thing would probably take over a life. Transform it. Make a man look at everything in a whole new way.

Kind of like what Moxie had said this morning about him.

Hank whirled around and blindly chose a piece of stone, glad for the ache in his arm when he lifted it too fast. It beat the hell out of thinking about what Moxie had been implying.

"So why are you here?"

"First, to apologize for last night. For being an ass in general and for what I said about you and Brynn. I know you were trying to keep that under wraps and—"

"Save your breath. There's nothing to wrap or unwrap."

"Really?"

"Really. And I have a lot of work to do, so if you have anything else to say, could you spit it out and move on?"

"I'm flying to Charlottetown tonight."

Hank set the stone down too fast and narrowly missed pinching his fingers. "Son of a— What the hell, Car?"

"Moxie marched into my office and read me the riot act. She said… Well, to be honest, most of it didn't make sense. She kept going on about splinters and infections and—anyway, she made me see that keeping quiet, pretending, could be worse in the long run than being honest."

"Sure. I bet Ian would say so, too."

"No, he didn't."

That one left Hank gaping. "You told him?"

"Yeah."

"Why?"

"Because he's my brother. And I don't want to spend the rest of my life resenting him for something that wasn't his fault."

"But why would you—" Hank began, then shook his head. "Let me guess. Moxie?"

"It made more sense when she said it."

That, Hank could believe.

"How is he?"

Carter gave the limestone a shove, setting it wobbling. "About how you'd expect."

"But you're going to Charlottetown anyway?"

"Yeah. I am. And if I'm luckier than I deserve to be, I'll be staying there with Taylor."

Hank was getting tired of feeling like he'd just taken a fist to the gut.

"It's the only way," Carter continued. "We can't be here, not with Ian. Nothing good could come of that. Maybe in a few years, once we've all had time to get past this…" Carter made a strangled sort of noise that Hank assumed was supposed to be a laugh. "Listen to me. Making plans when Taylor doesn't even know I'm coming out there."

"So help me, Carter, if you don't stop dropping bombs on me, I'm gonna shove one of these rocks onto your foot. And I don't think fancy lawyer shoes have steel toes."

Carter's grin was a mere shadow of its usual warmth, but it was familiar enough to set something a bit more securely inside Hank.

"Let me get this straight. You and Taylor have a thing—"

"It's called love, little brother. We're out of elementary school. You can say it."

"Whatever. So you've had a thing for her, and you waited too long to man up and talk to her, but you finally did. She decided to do the honorable thing so she broke up with Ian and moved away. But now Moxie has a splinter and that means you had to spill it all on Ian, and you're flying to Charlottetown to talk to a woman who doesn't even know you're on your way?"

Carter's eyes flitted back and forth as if reading some internal script before he nodded. "In a nutshell."

"Nutshell. Huh. That sounds pretty accurate."

"Yeah, it does."

They both fell silent. Hank squinted at the limestone in front of him, pretending to be noting its shape and size when all he wanted to do was grab it and hold on, because it sure as hell was the only solid thing about this day.

At last Carter spoke. "I know it's a lot to take in. My head is still spinning, and I've gone over it more times than I care to count today, what with Moxie and Ian and Cash and Mom and Dad. But I just keep coming back to something Moxie said—something about, sometimes the only way out of something is to go straight through it."

"Say what?"

"When Taylor and I decided that nothing could ever come of this—well, we were trying to go around the problem. We thought that if she left, if we kept quiet, then we—the North family—could move on. Except I still love her. That could turn into the elephant in the room someday, and God, Hank, I don't want to lose Taylor but I don't want to lose my brother, either. The only way we can get past this is to drag it out in the open, admit it's there and then find the way through."

Accept and move on.

Oh, God. Had she been right?

He inhaled, short and sharp. There was a difference between moving on from a bad situation and plain running away. Wasn't there?

"I gotta be honest, Car. I don't like any of this." Especially the fact that he wasn't sure if he were talking about Carter or himself. "But I think you have a point."

"Thanks."

"And I hope— Well, I hope I don't see you soon. Know what I mean?"

A sad sort of grin split Carter's face. "I think that's one of the nicest things anyone has said to me all day."

"Yeah, well, don't let it go to your head." Hank glanced up at the sun. "I'd better get back to work now. It'll be time to get Millie pretty soon."

"Yeah. Say goodbye to her for me?"

Oh, that was going to be a picnic. Millie was still trying to understand why Brynn had moved out and Taylor wasn't going to be Auntie Taylor anymore, and now he was going to have to explain that the aunt thing might happen after all.

"I will. But the way things have been changing around here, I might start by telling her you're on vacation."

"Can't blame you for that one." Carter shifted. "I'll get out of here, then. Bye, Hank. I'll keep you posted."

Hank nodded. "Have a safe flight."

Carter stepped forward, hesitated and turned around. Hands in his pockets, he trudged back toward his car.

Hank looked from his brother to the wall taking shape beside him.

"Shit."

He pulled off his work gloves and sprinted down the path. "Car! Wait up!"

When Carter turned around, the hope on his face was almost more than Hank could stand to see. He solved the problem by throwing his arms around Carter.

"Good luck." He thumped Carter on the back, hard.

Carter nodded against his shoulder. Hank was pretty sure he knew why his well-spoken brother was staying silent.

After a moment, he stepped back, his hands still gripping Carter's shoulders. "One piece of advice."

Carter cleared his throat. "Yeah?"

"If you want to make this work, for the love of God, keep your hands off her Pop-Tarts."

CHAPTER SIXTEEN

It was the damned tulips that did her in.

Brynn was holding it together fairly well, all things considered, until she arrived at Sam and Libby's on Sunday night for a quick visit. She had way too many tasks on her list to be paying a visit to anyone other than contractors, electricians or vendors, but apparently Casey had started believing she was gone again. She would be leaving soon enough. She didn't need to cause her one and only nephew extra distress right now.

She rearranged her schedule, woke an extra hour early to deal with some of the never-ending emails, did a quick site check—taking care to time it for when she knew Hank and Millie would be at church—and then drove to Sam's place. She pulled into her usual spot and hopped out of the car with a determined smile on her face. She would be cheerful, dammit. Cheerful and laughing and totally focused on Casey, who needed her.

Nice to know someone still did. Though if she were being honest, she would have to admit that Casey wasn't the neediest one in this equation.

But as she walked down the rock-lined path to the house, her eye was caught by a burst of color beneath the leafy maple. The first tulips had opened. Fiery red, sunshine yellow, deep orange—they tugged at her, practically demanded that she wander over and drink them in.

Until she saw the purple ones. Double tulips, streaked with hints of pink, so fat and full they could easily be mistaken for peonies. And her brain decided to throw a memory in her path, just in time for her to stumble over it: her and Mom, the first spring after that terrifying fall and winter, when they were just starting to believe that Mom might beat the cancer after all. Mom had sat on a blanket in the mild May sunshine and instructed Brynn as she weeded around the purple tulips that had popped up that year.

Somehow they had drifted from discussions of weeds to talking about Brynn's father.

"He was never a strong man," Mom had said. "He was never good at coping with reality. That was why he had those drinking spells, and why he was forever taking a nap. And in the end, it was why he left. Because things got too intense and he got scared and he ran away."

Things got too intense and he ran away.

Leaving is what you do best.

The flowers blurred before Brynn's eyes as the tears she'd been pushing down came crashing back. All she could remember was waking up on Hank's

sofa to see him smiling down at her. For one mo
ment her world had been so brimful of love that
there had scarcely been room left to breathe.

Is that your answer to everything?

Then reality had caught up with her. And she realized she was heart-deep in something she couldn't
control, something too intense. And she had run.

Just like her father.

HANK STILL WASN'T SURE why Ian had asked for him
to be the one to meet him at the airport, but he
wasn't about to debate protocol with a man who had
been through four flights, God knew how many
time zones and a double whammy to the heart. He
rearranged his schedule, asked his mother to take
Millie for the night and steered the truck toward
the airport.

Even with months of frequent Skype calls,
Hank wasn't prepared for the changes in his oldest brother. Ian's beard looked fuller and bushier
than when they were talking via computer. He was
thinner, too, his face more drawn and weary. Hank
suspected that the flights could be blamed for only
a part of that.

The biggest surprise came when Ian folded him
into a bear hug that went on and on. Hank had a
feeling that the hands clutching his shoulders were
those of a man who was just now letting go of the
rope that had been keeping him upright. He patted

Ian's back as he would to Millie and glared at the people casting them curious looks.

"You're looking good, Hankie." Ian peered behind him. "No shadow?"

"Not tonight. She wanted to come but I figured it was even odds you'd be delayed, and it's a school night, so she's with Ma."

Ian's grin was almost like the one Hank remembered, but a little slower, a little less enthusiastic. "You're such a Mr. Responsible now."

"Yeah, well, that's the good part about being the youngest. All the sense and brains trickled down to me."

Ian needed to stop at the first coffee stand they passed, and his moaning over the half-and-half made Hank feel like a voyeur. Steaming large drink in hand, they staked out a place at the baggage carousel, making small talk about the flights, the people they saw, the overwhelming brightness of the fluorescent lights after months in a country where brownouts were the way of life. Hank figured they could get into the serious stuff once they were in the car. Not even then if Ian wasn't up to it. But he'd forgotten that his brother had never been one for laying low.

"So Heather is back, huh? How's that going?"

Well, hell. Hank hadn't anticipated that he might be the one under the microscope. "It's easier than I expected, at least so far. I think… Yeah. I think if we had tried this when she first left, it would have been a miserable flop. Too close, too soon, all that. But now, you know, the worst is behind us. We can do the water-under-the-bridge thing and focus on what's best for Millie."

"Guess that's how it should be." The hollow sound of Ian's voice told Hank which direction his brother's thoughts had veered. He held his breath, staring very intently at the gray rubber flap where the baggage would appear, as if wishing fervently for a wild African animal to come through the opening.

Thank God the first bags started popping through at that point. The crowd moved forward and conversation became limited to such important questions as, "That blue one yours?" There were times when routine and small talk were a hell of a savior.

It wasn't until they were in the car, with a drive-thru behind them—apparently, Tanzania had neither McDonald's nor Tim Hortons, judging from the way Ian was slobbering over his food—and an hour of quiet road ahead, that Hank dared to really talk again.

"So you're staying with Moxie and the folks?"

"Yeah. That seemed like the best option, all things considered."

Hank could understand Ian not wanting to go back to his own place yet. Too many memories, too many plans. Yet another experience he wished they didn't have to share.

Ian crumpled the take-out paper and tossed it in the bag. "I'm going to regret that meal in about a half hour, but damn, it was good."

That sounded like the brother he remembered. Maybe Ian would come out of this okay after all.

"I figure I'll stick around for the festival, let Moxie feed me a bit, spend some time with all of you. But then, I think… I haven't told anyone yet, so keep this quiet, okay?"

Hank's hands tightened on the wheel.

"I sent Carter an email. Told him that since folks at the dairy were already used to me being gone, and I don't feel like being everyone's pity project, I'm gonna move on. Carter and…and her… They can come back here."

For as many times as he'd been smacked by reality the past couple of weeks, Hank still wasn't used to it.

Nor was he ready to have this conversation while he was driving.

"I knew there was a reason I took the back road instead of the highway," he said as he cranked the wheel and steered into the parking lot of a farm supply store. He slammed into Park, killed the engine and twisted to face Ian.

"You're going to leave again." Didn't anybody ever stay put anymore?

"That's right."

"So they can come back here and get off scot-free?"

"I'm not doing it for them, Hank. Trust me. There's no martyr complex here."

"Then why—"

"I told you. I don't want to spend the next two years walking around, knowing everyone is whispering about how sad it was that my brother ran off with my fiancée. And you know God damned well that's what'll happen." He glanced out the window. "Let *them* hear the whispers. That's fine with me."

"But…shit, Ian. It's not right."

"You want to tell me any part of this that is?"

There was no good answer for that.

Ian slumped in the seat and closed his eyes, reminding Hank just how tired his brother must be in so many different ways. He reached for the key, intending to get home as fast as possible, but Ian's voice stopped him.

"I was already thinking about leaving the dairy."

"You?"

"Yeah, me. The stuff I was doing in Tanzania— it worked for me. The dairy did, too. I was glad to be there, but when I was in Africa, I knew I was making a difference."

"You're not thinking about going back there, are you?"

One eye cracked open. "Did you miss the part where I said I wasn't a martyr?"

"Must have forgot it in all the excitement."

"I have some ideas. Nothing definite yet. I'm gonna take my time and do this right. As long as I end up doing good, and not doing it here, I'll call it a win."

"So are you looking at this as a permanent move?"

"I'm looking at this as… I don't know. Coping. Making the best of a lousy situation." He waved in the general direction of the steering wheel. "Moving on."

Accept what's happened and move on.

Dammit!

Hank fumbled for the key and cranked the engine, wondering if he could rev it loud enough to block out the memory of Brynn's voice, the hollow hurt that grabbed him every time he thought of her leaving. No luck.

"Hey, Hank?"

"Yeah?"

"How long does it take?"

Hank chanced a sideways glance. "How long does what take?"

"For it to stop hurting."

"You're asking me?" He shook his head. Like he was any expert. All it took was a mention of a yoga class, the sight of a woman pushing her hair from her face and he was back to aching for Brynn in a way he could never have imagined. He felt like he was one of those idiots in the circus who stands up against a target while someone throws knives at them. Every word, every thought was another blade headed his way, and most of the time he forgot to duck.

Though maybe that was because he would rather feel the hurt than lose the memories.

"Yeah, I'm asking you. I don't— I mean, I didn't think you were still holding a torch for Heather...."

Heather? When had she come into this conversation?

Hank stared through the windshield. Replayed the conversation. Then hit the brakes and turned into yet another parking lot as the truth slapped him in the face.

Ian had asked him how to get past the hurt and his first—*only*—thought had been for Brynn. Not for the ex-wife who had borne his child and walked out, but for the woman who had danced into his life mere months ago, rearranged it and turned it into something he barely recognized but knew deep down was the one he was supposed to be living.

Hank couldn't tell Ian how to get over the loss of the woman he loved because he had never done that. He'd gone on without his child's mother, yes.

But he had no idea how he was supposed to get over losing Brynn.

Two days before the festival, Brynn looked up from a stolen moment of peace by the river to see Moxie striding toward her.

"What fresh hell is this?" she muttered as she scurried to meet Moxie at the intersection of Insane and Exhausted. Which actually was a place she welcomed, as it made it easier to push away her appointment at the corner of Heartbroken and Lonely.

"Hey, Mox— Mrs. North. Everything's proceeding as expected. A couple of last-minute snags, nothing I can't deal with, but we're on schedule and should be in great shape for the kick-off Friday night."

"'Course we will." Moxie glanced around the site, her gaze lingering over the stage, the trees, the cabins.

"And we got lucky with the weather. Have you seen the latest forecast? Clear skies, warm with a light breeze on Saturday, slightly cool at nights. We won't have to worry about postponing the fireworks or moving any of the events."

"No surprise there—not after all the time I spent reminding my Gordon that half the reason he's up there in Heaven without me is so's he can do the things I can't do down here." She shrugged. "'Course, I guess the bacon had something to do with it, too. Now, who did you find to do the wagon rides?"

For a few minutes they went over the final details, Brynn bringing Moxie up to speed on some of the more recent developments, Moxie putting things in historical and priority perspective. There were tweaks to be made, of course, but, again, nothing Brynn couldn't handle.

"Sounds like everything is under control." Moxie

nodded as she looked around. "You never can tell what's coming down the pike, but so far, so good."

As far as Brynn was concerned, that pike had already handled more than enough.

Moxie pointed downriver. "You know what you'll find if you go that way a mile or so?"

"What?"

"The cove. The one this town is named for. Comeback Cove."

"Was it a fishing village in its early days?"

"Nah. Well, maybe. But it really took off because of the rumrunners."

Well, *that* was a welcome distraction. "Seriously?"

Moxie nodded. "My uncle Bart made a pretty penny running hooch to the States during Prohibition. He said they used to carry blocks of salt with them when they were making their runs. If they thought the law was after them, they would tie the bottles to the blocks, toss 'em overboard in the cove and let the Feds catch them."

Laughter bubbled inside Brynn, light and welcome. "Let me guess. Then they would come back when the salt had dissolved and harvest the bottles where they floated?"

"You got it."

"A town built on illegal booze. I love it."

"Well, there was a lot more that went into it over the years. But it just goes to show—sometimes, good things can grow out of something you would never believe could bring any—"

Her words were interrupted by the beeping of Brynn's phone, signaling an incoming text.

"Sorry," she said as she reached for it. "I hate to be rude, but with everything approaching, I'm amazed it hasn't gone off five times already."

"Not to worry. Take it."

One look at the name on her screen—*Taylor*— and Brynn was ready to put the phone aside until Moxie was gone. Then she noticed that it was a photo message. On impulse, she opened it.

"Holy crap!"

The words were out of her mouth before she remembered that she was standing beside her employer. Moxie being Moxie, however, she didn't seem the least fazed by Brynn's outburst. Instead, she shuffled sideways to peer at the screen.

"Well, I'll be." Moxie's voice was the gentlest Brynn had ever heard. Not that she could blame Moxie. She herself was blinking rapidly at the picture in her hands: Carter in shorts and a very loud Hawaiian shirt, Taylor in a T-shirt that spelled out *Vegas* in sequins, both of them sporting smiles brighter than all the lights of the Strip.

"Would you look at those grins," Moxie said.

Brynn palmed a tear that refused to stay put.

"They look so happy." She touched the screen, her finger settling on Taylor's smile, and she realized she had got what she wanted: Taylor, happily together with the man she loved.

"Ten to one they get married while they're there." Moxie sighed. "Those grandsons of mine. I don't think any of them are ever going to give me the chance to dance at their weddings."

"Hank didn't—"

No. Don't ask about him, don't think about him, don't—just don't.

"Him? Ha. He ran off to Vegas, too. Didn't even let us know anything was up until they came back and told us. Surprise!" She punctuated her words with a sharp clap of her hands. "Though this time, it would be the right call. It wouldn't be proper to have a big wedding with this one."

"You know," Brynn said slowly, "Taylor spent her whole life planning her wedding. She wasn't obsessed, but she knew that someday she wanted to get married, and when the time came, she wanted to do it right. When she first got engaged to Ian she pulled out the files and was happy as a clam. But then she stopped talking about it."

"Guess that was a sign."

"Yeah. I guess you're right."

"When it's the right man, all the rest fades away." Moxie's voice was soft, but the words went straight to Brynn's heart. Some of the worry she'd been carrying for the past few days lifted, leaving her lighter and happier in a way she hadn't expected.

"Thanks, Moxie. Hearing that—it makes me feel a lot better."

"You've been toting a load of guilt over this, haven't you?"

"I—"

"Don't bother pretending, girl. You're too much like me. I can see right through you." Moxie poked Brynn's arm. "Can't let your family down, can you?"

Thoughts of her father flashed through Brynn's head. She pulled herself a little straighter. "Not if I can help it."

"No need to get your back up. There's nothing wrong with doing what you can. Long as that's what you're supposed to be doing, of course, and not just a reason to keep from doing something else."

That sounded like what Libby had said, about obsessing over things that didn't matter because it was easier than thinking about things that scared the crap out of her. Except this was Brynn's family. What could matter more than that?

Moxie had far too sharp a gleam in her eye. "You told Taylor you would help her fall back in love with Ian, and that never happened, so you feel like if you had done a better job, things would have turned out different. Right?"

"It sounds kind of silly when you say it like that. Egocentric, too."

Moxie shrugged. "Nothing silly about taking

your job seriously or telling yourself you can do something. Hell, how do you think I got through the first couple of years in charge at the dairy? But take it from me, Brynn. Some things are out of even your control. You can plot and plan and work all you want, but those other people are out there doing the same thing, and sometimes they're going to win." She patted Brynn's arm. "Especially when there's love involved."

IT WAS WELL PAST midnight by the time Brynn had a chance to check email that night. She had spent the entire day on her feet, running from one fire to another, and as much as possible, she had enjoyed it. This was the part of a project she loved best— the days before the launch, when everything came together and all the little issues bubbled to the surface and she had to fly from one crisis to another. She was working on the edge, pushing her brain and resourcefulness and creativity to the limits. She felt strong and capable and more alive than she had in ages. She wouldn't want to live at this pitch all the time, but every once in a while, it was a rush like none other.

At least, it usually was a rush. This time she wasn't able to revel in the excitement. This time, each item crossed off the list was another reminder that her time here was coming to a close. On Sunday morning she would wake up and the festival would be over. In another week or so, Taylor would be back—a development that still knocked her sideways, but one she could well understand. Her opinion of Ian had climbed even higher once Taylor told her about his decision. She hoped he would find someone—soon—who could love him the way he deserved.

But Taylor's return meant there was no need for Brynn to stick around. There would be a few loose ends to tie up after the festival, but as of the middle of next week, she would have no reason to remain in Comeback Cove.

Snuggled deep in Old Faithful's embrace, she opened her laptop with thoughts of finding…she didn't know what. Distraction, definitely. Hope? That was probably too much to ask for.

She scanned the messages, deleting the ones asking for her assistance in acquiring money from Nigeria and opening the most pressing of those related to the festival. Nothing that couldn't wait until the morning. When the Northstar ones had been set aside she was left with a reminder from her mother that Trent's birthday was coming up, a good-luck message from Libby and one from Paige. Her maternity leave plan had been approved. Brynn could start anytime after June fifteenth.

Brynn sipped her tea slowly, trying to soothe the tightness in her stomach. She had liked Paige's work. Liked the company and the other people working there. And they were located not far from Kingston, which was always a bonus, as was the salary. Plus, it would be a chance to reconnect with and lend a hand to Paige and her growing family.

But the tug was missing.

"I don't want to go," she whispered to the screen, to Old Faithful, to any deities that might be listening. "I want to stay."

The words were out of her mouth before she really grasped what she had said. But they were still sounding in her ear when the impact hit her so strongly that she bolted upright, almost knocking her tea to the floor.

She wanted to stay.

Always before, by this point, she was ready for new faces, new adventures. Not this time. This time, the thought of packing up her hatchback and hitting the road, even to family members who needed her, made her want to rip up her résumé and slash all her tires and glue her shoes to a patch of ground right here in Comeback Cove.

For the first time ever, leaving—even for family— felt wrong. Because no matter how much she cared about Paige and all her cousins and brothers and everyone else, the family she wanted was here.

But Hank didn't think she was capable of staying. He thought she had hurt his family. He wanted nothing more to do with her.

She closed the laptop and rubbed Old Faithful's worn leather arm. "What am I going to do?"

Her tea was cold and she was stiff from sitting. She set the laptop aside, pulled herself from the depths of the chair and took her teacup to the sink. Maybe if she kept her hands busy, her mind could wander freely and come up with a miracle.

Hey, it was worth a try.

She put her laptop back in her briefcase. Checked to make sure the folder with her notes was still there. Ran through the day's agenda in her head, tossed in a couple of nut bars that would stand in for lunch and grabbed her dance notebook.

"One more night for you."

On a whim, she flipped through the pages. Everything was here—the list of song possibilities, the steps she'd had to write down because she didn't know how else to remember them, the lineups that she had rearranged more times than she cared to remember. The history of her time here in Comeback Cove could be found in those lineups—the ones that included Ian, the ones without Taylor but with all the Norths, the new one with Ian but without Taylor and Carter...

She stopped. Flipped back through the pages. Remembered Moxie's words about good things coming from bad, about no one being able to predict love. Remembered Hank in his kitchen offering her Easter candy and saying he would want to keep seeing her if she stayed.

Hank had said that leaving was what she did best. And yes, she had panicked when she realized she was falling in love with him. Things got intense and she got scared and she had pushed Taylor to end things with Ian, knowing full well that to do so would mean an end to her and Hank. But that had turned out to be untrue. She still loved him. She still wanted to be with him.

She wanted to stay with him.

And that, she realized with a lightness in her heart, was what made her different from her father. He had seen trouble, walked away and never come back. But even though she had set things in motion, she hadn't wanted it to end. In fact, the only things pushing her to leave now were her plans with Paige and the thought that she couldn't be in Comeback Cove with Hank.

Her father would say that staying now would be too hard, too intense. But she wasn't him. And even though seeing what he had done to her mother and their family had left her wary of Cupid's arrow, she didn't have to let that fear push her away from the place that she knew was right for her.

She had told Millie to walk away from a bully. She'd preached the gospel of accepting and moving on. But what had she done? She had used that as an excuse to walk away from places, from people, before she could grow too attached. She had let the lingering effects of her father's cowardice come between her and the best thing that had ever happened to her. It was like she'd handed over all control of her life to a man who had turned his back on her when she needed him most.

"The hell with that."

She wasn't her father. She was good at a lot more than leaving. Like facing down a challenge. Helping people find new solutions to problems like hosting a festival or staffing a maternity leave. Planning.

She might not be able to make Hank want her again, or believe that she was capable of staying. But she could help him see that she had been acting from good intentions. That she had been trying to help his family, not hurt them.

It was a start. The first step in standing her ground.

No more faking it. It was time to get real.

She put the kettle on for another cup of tea, grabbed her notebook again and began planning.

CHAPTER SEVENTEEN

HANK WAS IN THE Grenadier cabin, helping people from the Comeback Cove Historical Society unpack the displays of period costumes, when he noticed Brynn hovering in the doorway. To tell the truth, he sensed her presence before he saw the historian lady smile and wave. He knew it was Brynn before he turned around. Knew, and tried to suppress the jolt of pleasure that came with the realization that she was near.

It was like trying to change the course of the river with a stick and some leaves. It might work eventually, but it would be a hell of a long time coming.

He braced himself and turned to face her. Not to look at her, though he couldn't keep himself from noting the dark circles beneath her eyes or the way she managed to appear bubbling and efficient despite the fatigue that was as obvious as the deep turquoise of her shiny T-shirt. She looked exhausted and excited and eager, all at once, and when he remembered other times he'd seen that mix of emotions in her, he had to glance away so no one could read the pain he knew was showing in his eyes.

"Hi, guys!" She ventured into the room, fussing over the outfits, asking questions about lace and material and other things that left him wondering how she knew so much about so many different things. She was more of a sponge than anything that ever came out of the ocean. She had certainly soaked up as much of him as he could give her. When he remembered being on the receiving end of that focus—

Stop. He couldn't keep doing this to himself. He had cabins to run, a daughter to raise, a family to help. He couldn't afford to waste any energy or emotion or—or anything on memories and dreams. Even if he did wish with every breath that he could push Historian Lady out of the cabin and lock the door and pull Brynn down to the floor the way she had done to him, right here, mere days earlier.

"Hank?"

For a second he thought he was imagining her voice. He'd certainly done that enough over the past few days. But no—when he tilted his head in her direction, she was watching him, stepping toward him.

"Could I see you outside for a minute, please?"

Oh, no. Alone with Brynn was a dangerous place.

"What do you need?"

"I have to go over some things with you."

He grabbed a box, deliberately turning in her direction so she would need to step back. "Fire away."

She glanced at Historian Lady and back at him. "Outside would be better."

"I'm busy." And dying inside, but there was no way in hell he was going to let her see that. He might have blown everything else but he still had the cold comfort of his pride.

Historian Lady, who had been watching the interaction with a bright smile and eyes that were a little too curious, looked at Brynn and seemed to make up her mind. "Oh, my. I do believe I left some notes in the car. I'd better go get them before I forget again. I'll be back in about ten minutes, Hank. Could you stay with the clothes, please, to make sure nothing happens to them?"

"I don't—"

"Of course he will," Brynn said. "We'll take good care of things, Mrs. Collins. You go right ahead."

As soon as the older woman had departed—carefully closing the door behind her—Hank snorted and turned away. "How much did you pay her to conveniently forget her notes?"

"No payment needed. She's Casey's child-care provider. She adores me, and I think she's amazing."

Trust Brynn to already know more people in town after four months than he did after a lifetime.

"Tonight is the final rehearsal to get Ian worked into the dance." She set a worn blue notebook on the nearest box. "I can't be there. You'll need to lead things."

"Me?"

"Yes, you."

He turned back to the boxes. "Forget it."

"You know the steps. You know the music. There are detailed instructions."

"Doesn't matter. It's enough that I'm doing the damned dance. I'm not going to try to lead everyone tonight. Give it to... I don't know. Cash, maybe."

"Cash isn't here right now. Neither is Moxie or Ian or your parents. You are the only one, and, believe it or not, I don't have time to hunt people down." She picked up the notebook and shoved it in his direction. "Take it. Pretend you're someone else, if that's what you have to do to get through it. Maybe you can talk Millie into leading it. But I need to know I can count on you."

There was an underlying edge to her voice that made him decide it was wiser to agree than to risk pushing her over whatever cliff she was on.

"Fine."

Some of the tense lines around her eyes disappeared. "Thank you."

He shoved the book into his toolbox, putting aside the warmth that had sprung up inside him at making her world a bit easier, and squatted in front of it. Brynn stayed in the center of the room. He didn't need to see her to know that her eyes were tracking his every move.

"Something else?"

Her deep breath seemed to pull all the oxygen out of the cabin. "Yes. Could you give Millie a message from me?"

He grabbed a screwdriver he didn't need and stared at it. "Depends what it is."

"Fair enough."

Footsteps told him she was coming closer. He braced himself for her voice, her touch. Instead, she knelt beside him. From the corner of his eye he caught the deep blue of her jeans, the brighter top that clung and curved, the way her fingers twisted together on her lap.

"Please tell her that when I said she should walk away from Noelle, I was wrong. Leaving… There are times when it's right. This wasn't one of them."

Deep in the muddle of longing and sorrow and hurt and want and crazy love swirling inside him, one piece stilled. Hope reared its stupid, persistent head.

Get real, North.

"Easy to say."

"Harder to do. I know. And I know I've been kind of boneheaded about that. But you can tell her that I'm not as smart as…as other people." Her voice dropped. "And that sometimes, people don't even know they're afraid until it slaps them in the face."

She was afraid? *Brynn?*

He didn't dare say anything, certain that if he tried, all reason would be hijacked by the voice urging him to *let it go, believe her, tell her you love her.* Maybe if his family hadn't been involved... maybe if he hadn't already carried Millie through one desertion...maybe if it were only him and his heart on the line...

A small sigh escaped her. "Okay." She pushed to her feet. "Thanks again for taking over tonight. The sound guys and the vendors and I all owe you."

That was rich. She owed him?

He set the screwdriver back in his toolbox and pawed sightlessly through a collection of nails to keep his hands busy. The vibration of her departing steps echoed through him.

"Hank?"

He risked a glance over his shoulder. She stood in the doorway, fingers twisted together. For the first time ever she seemed uncertain. Vulnerable. Scared.

"I don't think I ever told you, but before everything happened, Moxie offered me a permanent job at the dairy. Given everything that I knew was coming down the pike, I said no."

Hope peeked out from behind a wall of fear. He tried to push it back into place.

"I thought I was turning her down because of Taylor and everything, but since then, I've figured out that Millie wasn't the only one being bullied.

Except she was smart enough to know it was happening. I was kind of a clueless participant."

What the hell?

"So I decided that I wasn't going to let my life be run by some irresponsible idiot anymore."

"You're not—" He blurted the words out, twisted to look at her more directly, then realized what he was doing and shut both his eyes and his mouth.

A soft, short laugh surrounded him. "Actually, I was talking about my father. But thanks."

Her *father?*

A man who'd had one curveball after another tossed at him over the past few weeks should have learned how to anticipate and duck by this point. Seems he was a slow learner.

"Anyway, my point is…this morning, I told Moxie that if the offer was still good—you know, considering all that has happened—I would like to take the job. Because it turns out…" Her voice cracked.

So did a piece of his heart.

"It turns out I really want to stay here in Comeback Cove."

She wanted to stay?

Thank God he was squatting. It made the dizziness that much less dangerous.

"I thought you had plans. Maternity leave for your cousin, Moxie said."

"Yeah, well, when I called to tell her I might not

be able to do it, she said she had just decided she wasn't going back after this baby."

His hand tightened around a fistful of nails. "What did Moxie say?"

"She is, understandably, not quite as enthusiastic about the idea as she was when she made the offer. And she's kind of distracted today. Also understandable." She wrapped her arms around herself. "She's going to get back to me."

Oh, God. He knew what that meant.

Moxie was leaving this up to him.

AN HOUR LATER, alone at his kitchen table, Hank thumbed through Brynn's notebook. His ham sandwich sat untouched on the table and the beer he'd allowed himself as a reward for making it through Brynn's revelations intact sat untouched.

She wanted to stay.

It made no sense. Why had she waited until everything fell apart? Why did she want to stay here, where her name would be associated with one of the biggest gossip-worthy events to hit town since Heather walked out?

Why now, when he knew exactly what he felt for her and how much was on the line by even thinking that they might have a chance after all?

It had taken every bit of strength to stop himself from saying anything more after her bombshell, to keep himself parked by his toolbox when she made a funny little noise and whispered goodbye and walked out the door. He'd waited for a slow count of five before jumping to his feet and watching out the window as she walked slowly up the path. Away from him.

Yet she said she wanted to stay.

He flipped a page, ran his thumb over the notes she'd scribbled beside her stick-figure lineups. Maybe her decision had nothing to do with him. After all, she had a brother here, a nephew, Taylor. Family.

Family.

At that first meeting when Taylor had proposed they hire Brynn, she had said that Brynn was all about family. He'd seen that himself. Family determined all her actions, guided her every move. She could well be choosing to stay here because of her family.

His gut told him there was more.

And what had she meant when she said that she'd been letting her father control her life?

He grabbed the beer, let about half of it slide down his throat. The woman had turned him inside out since she'd arrived. In the past weeks he'd learned that no one was who he'd thought they were—that even his own brothers were hiding things. The ground beneath his feet seemed so shaky these days that he might as well be in California.

But for a while there, before it all fell apart, he had been happy.

He shoved the beer aside, grabbed the sandwich, turned to the notebook. Sitting here thinking was only making things worse. He had people running all over his grounds and lights he had to install and now, on top of everything, a new dance lineup to learn so he could freakin' teach it tonight. All so he could show his kid that you couldn't let some idiots keep you from doing what you wanted.

Except it was more than that now.

He shook his head and focused on the notebook. In the first pages, the Norths had been merely *X*s on the page, gradually progressing to stick figures with names and notes. *Move Millie up front—cute. Moxie hips? Hank=great butt. Make him shake it.*

He paged through the various lineups, the changes she'd made as she got to know them, as the Ian-Taylor-Carter story had played out. Lineups were *X*'d out with slash marks. Names were crossed out and erased. People were rearranged and notes were blurred in a pattern that he was pretty sure came from tears.

The final version—the one he was supposed to put in place tonight with his family—was neatly outlined on the last page. No more *X*s or names now. She had printed out pictures of all the Norths and glued their faces into place. One glance and he could easily see the new lineup: Millie and Moxie in front. Him, Mom and Dad behind them. Cash and Ian staggered in the back. Not so different from what they'd been doing. All he had to do was get Ian worked in and they'd be all set.

But the more he looked at the faces smiling up at him, the more he realized it was wrong. Something was missing. Some*one*. Not Carter or Taylor.

But someone who was definitely supposed to be part of the family.

He grabbed his phone, punched a number and waited.

"Hi, Moxie." Deep breath. "I need some help."

THE DAY OF THE festival was everything Brynn could have asked—sunny, dry, warm enough to wear clothes that fluttered but not hot enough that the fluttery bits would stick to sweaty skin. There was enough of a breeze off the river to cool her as she raced from one cabin to the next, answering questions, tracking down supplies and assuring Moxie that everything would be ready on time.

Please, God, let everything be ready on time.

She was glad of the pace, grateful for the questions and crises. They formed a buffer between her and the hurt, made it possible for her to look past the fact that there had been no word from Hank. In fact, while she had seen every other North and had even been introduced to Heather, who was being dragged all over the grounds by an ecstatic Millie, she had yet to lay eyes on him. It was as if he had disappeared. Or was avoiding her...

No. She couldn't let herself think that way. She

had done her best. Now it was time to take Moxie's advice and let the pieces fall where they may.

Especially because there was love involved.

The day seemed to alternate between dragging and flying, speeding up and slowing down depending on which crisis needed her at that moment. By the time the grounds opened to the public she was pretty sure that regular minutes and hours had ceased to exist. Instead, she had entered a parallel universe where time was driven by how loudly the person in front of her was yelling.

Moxie had declared that she would spend much of her time at the gate, thanking and welcoming people as they arrived. Brynn worried it might be too much for her, but when she ran to the entry she saw that Moxie was getting a bigger charge from the duty than a cell phone got from an outlet. She was telling stories and kissing more babies than a politician, and the only downside was that she was slowing down the line to get in.

After wading her way through the crowd of listeners and reminding Moxie that she would need to be onstage fifteen minutes before the dance—a whisper that was met by an uncharacteristic snicker from Moxie—Brynn power-walked back to the main grounds. If she hurried she could manage one final tour before the opening celebration.

She should have known.

Every person, it seemed, had a question, almost all of them unnecessary. The first-aid people needed the Wi-Fi password, which she was sure was on the note given to all vendors and providers. The teens running the hayride weren't sure what time they were supposed to start, though it was clearly marked on the schedule. The woman in charge of the face painting grabbed Brynn, physically tossed her into the chair and had a butterfly outlined on her cheek before Brynn could think to say no. At that point she had to stay, because running around with a butterfly outline would be almost as attractive as running around with half of her makeup washed off.

By the time she was allowed to leave the face painter, she was wishing she had the wings of her new multicolored best friend. She would be lucky to make it to the stage in time to give the Norths a pep talk and see them in their costumes.

On the other hand, maybe it was better this way. It had ripped her up enough to be around Hank before she told him she wanted to stay. Now that she had laid herself bare before him...

Her musings were cut short by a text from the sound guy, wanting to know where she was and how soon she would be at the stage because the crowd was building.

Ack! She tucked her phone back into her pocket and flew up the path, waving and smiling as she dodged clumps of folks who were eating, laughing and blocking her way. The fact that the biggest crowd was the line of folks waiting to have hockey paraphernalia signed by Sam was little consolation.

Out of wind, hot and flustered, she paused for a deep, centering breath before pulling up a smile and striding to the backstage area. She had almost made it when the sound guy cut her off.

"Come on, Brynn. To your seat." He took her arm and tugged her toward the front row of benches. "Everyone is ready."

She stopped, stumbled a bit when he kept moving, then planted her feet and braced herself.

"Hold on," she said. "I need two minutes."

"And I need the paycheck that Moxie said I wouldn't get if I let you go backstage. So let's move, sweetheart."

Moxie had ordered this guy to prevent her from going backstage?

All the starch fled from Brynn's legs as she allowed herself to be led away. So this was how the pieces had fallen.

She wasn't wanted. Wasn't needed. While all the Norths she had seen today had been pleasant and polite, it was time for her to be on her way.

If not for the fact that she was in public, she never would have let the sound guy lead her anywhere. But for once she was glad of the years of faking a smile, of making people think she was in control when she was breaking into a hundred sharp, pointy pieces inside.

She was so focused on holding herself together

that she didn't notice the chair until she was almost on it. But there in the middle of the benches sat Old Faithful, adorned with ribbons. A foam crown decked out with stick-on stars and flowers hung from the top corner. It might as well have held a sign that said Millie Was Here.

"What is this?"

Sound Guy shrugged and pointed to the chair. "Dunno. My orders were to get you here and start the music, so that's what I'm doing."

With that he gave her a little push toward the chair, watched while she sat down—oh, but her legs were grateful for the familiar curves after a day of running—and took off toward the equipment at the back.

Maybe it was because of the chair, but all of a sudden, Brynn didn't feel quite as close to shattering as she had a few seconds earlier.

The door to the backstage tent parted. Moxie stepped out, took the stairs with the energy of a world-class sprinter and walked to the microphone. The fringe and sparkles on her twenties-style flapper dress made it seem she was moving even when she stilled and waited for the applause and whistles to die down.

"Evening!" She waved at the crowd filling the benches. "On behalf of all the folks at Northstar, I want to say thanks to everyone in Comeback Cove for one hundred years of support. We couldn't have done it without you."

A loud cheer and more applause met her words. She nodded, waved at a few more people, then raised her hands for quiet. "Speaking of thanks, there's someone we need to introduce to all of you. Her name's Brynn Catalano, and she's the one who whipped us into shape and made this festival happen. Brynn, stand up and take a bow!"

Slightly embarrassed, Brynn did as ordered. Moxie clapped in her direction, frowned and pointed to the crown still hanging from Old Faithful's upper post. Brynn's cheeks warmed but she plopped the crown on her head to much laughter and applause.

Movement at her side distracted her. She turned to see Sam, Libby and Casey being ushered to the bench at her side.

"Hi, guys!" She gestured to the chair. "Were you in on this?"

Libby shook her head, raised a finger to her lips and pointed to the stage, where Moxie still stood at the microphone, watching them get settled. Once everyone was seated, Moxie faced the crowd again. "Yes, folks, if we hadn't had Brynn riding herd on us, we'd still be sitting in a conference room talking about doing a festival instead of actually, you know, pulling it together. So, Brynn, we have a special little thanks for you. Sit back and enjoy."

The Norths filed onto the stage. Brynn couldn't keep from switching into manager mode, checking out each costume.

Her throat tightened as Millie moved into place, her smile shaky but her chin raised high. The jeans they had decorated together were topped by an equally glittery, if still slightly stained, shirt-turned-lab-coat.

Oh, Millie.

Brynn caught her eye and blew her a kiss. Millie responded with a smile that seemed to spread all the way from her face to her suddenly skipping feet. Janice and Robert rolled their eyes but still grinned in their tie-dyes and beads. Ian and Cash looked as dorky in their eighties tracksuits and parachute pants as predicted, but they had the confidence and grins to make it look good.

Her heart squeezed a little when Ian's arrival was met with both a jump in the applause and a buzz of whispers, and she sent up a quick prayer for his happiness. Taylor was right. He was a good guy who deserved someone who could appreciate him.

Then came Hank, bringing up the rear in spiked hair and overalls with one side left undone. He kept his gaze firmly on the steps. While the others took the stage and waved to her, he gazed into the distance, tension shimmering off of him. Because of the dance? Or because of her?

Sam's hand closed on her arm. "Sit down," he whispered, and it was only then that she realized she was half out of her chair. She started to protest but the first notes of the music started and she dropped into her chair in surprise. Because the

lineup in front of her was not one she had created.
And the song coming over the loudspeakers was
not "We Are Family."

Why were they playing "Time of My Life"?

Millie was the first to move, smiling and showing not a hint of nerves as her little hips rocked
back and forth beneath her lab coat. Brynn was
just catty enough to hope that Noelle and her min-
ions were present to see the smile on Millie's face.
The other Norths joined in a few beats later, arms
rising and falling in time with the slow intro. They
hit the line about "owing it all to" and in unison,
they pointed to Brynn.

Oh, my God.

Her hands flew to her mouth and she laughed
and cried at the same time as she realized what
was happening. She could read the understanding
and forgiveness in their faces, even Ian's. Hank
still wasn't looking at her, but this was good and it
filled some of her emptiness, and she sat back and
prepared to be amazed.

The tempo picked up. The Norths stepped and
kicked and turned, moving through actions she had
taught them but in a different sequence. Judging
from the number of catch-up steps she saw taking
place, this dance was a fairly new development.
The effort was all the sweeter for knowing that
they had most likely created this after Taylor, despite Carter, even with the way she had kept things
from them.

If only Hank would look at her....

Millie boogied forward, lab coat flapping as she tossed her ponytail and grinned for the crowd. She was going to be the queen of the school come Monday morning. Moxie moved beside her, high-fiving her for a couple of beats. The others stepped up and the volume increased and they hit the line that said this could be love—

And Hank looked at her at last. Smiling at her. Winking at her. Pointing at her.

"Brynn?" Sam spoke into her ear. "Something you haven't been telling me about you and the landlord?"

The other Norths turned and cha-cha'd as the chorus kicked in. At least she thought they did. She couldn't take her eyes off Hank. His smile, his joy were all she could see for the rest of the song—with the exception of the big jump moment, when Millie flew across the stage and into her father's arms.

The song ended. The Norths—almost all of whom finished in time with the last notes—stood grinning, chests heaving, applauding in Brynn's direction. She rose to her feet with the rest of the audience and wiped tears from her cheeks, crying and laughing and bouncing up and down in her shoes.

Moxie reclaimed the microphone and indicated that the crowd should sit. The rest of the family clustered around her, except Hank, who clattered down the rear stairs and ran to Brynn.

"Come on." He held out his hand.

Her hand was in his and she was on her feet before she realized she'd moved. With a last glance at the rest of the family and a fervent hope that someone was taping all of this, she let him lead her to the tent behind the stage.

"Hank, what—"

He silenced her with a kiss that was way too fast for her spinning heart. "I'll tell you everything later. Right now I have about four minutes before I have to be up there again, five or six if Moxie stretches out her welcome like I asked, so be quiet and listen. I'm an idiot." He kissed her right cheek. "I'm sorry I didn't believe in you." Left cheek. "And I was lying when I said 'just sex,' because I think I was already halfway in love with you then, and now I—"

Whatever he was going to say could wait. Brynn yanked him close and kissed him the way she'd longed to do since he came onstage, since she told him she wanted to stay, since she woke up on his sofa and knew she was in love. She wound her arms around him and molded herself to him, feeling his heart pound against her chest, and told him, with every bit of her being, that she never wanted to be apart from him again.

"I love you," she whispered when she came up for air, then rested her forehead against his and said it again because it sounded so right on her tongue. "I love you."

"I know," he said in such a dead-on Han Solo imitation that she burst into laughter until he placed one finger over her lips.

"Listen, okay? You interrupted me before I could finish."

She bit down lightly on his finger. "Complaining?"

"Not in the least. But you're making me forget—"

"Good."

"Not good. Not yet. Tonight you can drive every rational thought out of my brain. But right now I need to say this."

Her heart was pounding harder than his had been right after the dance, but she took a deep breath and mimicked Millie's zip-across-the-lip motions.

"Thank you. Now look. Like I said, I was an idiot. I was sure—no, I was *afraid*—that you didn't have it in you to stay with anyone or stick with anything. I think that had a lot more to do with me than it did with you. Then I finally got a clue and realized that everything you do, you do for your family."

"You weren't the only one who was afraid," she said, only to clamp her lips together again at his mock scowl.

"As I was saying, once I got the rocks knocked out of my head, it was easy to see the solution. The one thing you would never do is desert your family. So it's time to make sure that Millie and I are part of it."

The faint rise and fall of Moxie's voice came to a halt. Applause erupted. Hank grinned down at her.

"Time for the kickoff dance."

She nodded and stepped away, even though it was killing her. Whatever he was about to say would have to wait. Surely she could wait five more minutes.

He shook his head, laced his fingers through hers. "Uh-uh. You're coming, too. There's no way we can do a dance called 'We Are Family' without you."

"What?"

"Brynn." He cupped her face between his hands. "When you gave me the notebook, even before I figured out how wrong I had been, I kept looking at your lineup and thinking someone was missing. Then I drew it all over again and put a picture of you in there, and just like that, it was perfect."

Was he saying what she thought he was saying?

"You're part of us, Brynn. Part of me. You belong out there dancing with us, and back at the cabins with me and Millie, and in my bed every night. I want to be part of your family, and for you to be part of mine, and for us to make a whole new one together." He grinned. "Preferably one with a real wedding so Moxie doesn't give me hell."

Her chest was so full, so tight that she couldn't breathe in to say yes. She had to settle for a nod, a squeak and another kiss, this one slow and tender and salted with tears.

"Hank?" It was Cash, his silhouette visible through the tent. "You ready?"

"Yeah," he called, but his gaze never left Brynn's. "More than ready."

She slipped her fingers through his and walked out of the tent to mount the stairs at Hank's side. The Norths turned almost in unison. Ian nodded as if giving his blessing. Cash broke out in the biggest smile Brynn had ever seen from him. Janice and Robert smiled and reached for each other's hands. Moxie winked. Millie gave them a giant two thumbs-up.

Brynn took her place beside Hank, waving at the sea of smiling, applauding faces. Joyful laughter bubbled out of her. Hank grinned and pulled her to his side and she blew kisses to Millie, to Sam and Libby and Casey, to all the people sharing in this most perfect moment of her life.

And to Cupid, wherever he might be.

* * * * *

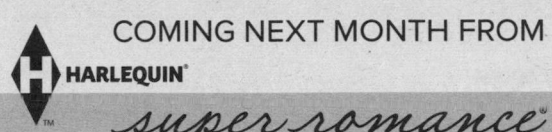

The Sweetest September

By **Liz Talley**

Shelby Mackey would have been happy
to *never* revisit the night she met
John Beauchamp. Well, that's not entirely true.
It was a good night...until the end. But now
avoiding him is no longer an option!

Read on for an exciting excerpt of the upcoming
book **THE SWEETEST SEPTEMBER**
by Liz Talley...

Shelby took a moment to take stock of the man she hadn't
seen since he'd slipped out that fateful night. John's boots
were streaked with mud and his dusty jeans had a hole in the
thigh. A kerchief hung from his back pocket. He looked like
a farmer.

She'd never thought a farmer could look, well, sexy. But
John Beauchamp had that going for him...not that she was
interested.

Been there. Done him. Got pregnant.

He looked down at her with cautious green eyes...like she
was a ticking bomb he had to disarm. "What are you doing
here?"

Shelby tried to calm the bats flapping in her stomach, but there was nothing to quiet them with. "Uh, it's complicated. We should talk privately."

He slid into the cart beside her, his thigh brushing hers. She scooted away. He noticed, but didn't say anything.

She glanced at him and then back at the workers still casting inquisitive looks their way.

John got the message and stepped on the accelerator.

Shelby yelped and grabbed the edge of the seat, nearly sliding across the cracked pleather seat and pitching onto the ground. John reached over and clasped her arm, saving her from that fate.

"You good?" he asked.

"Yeah," she said, finding her balance, her stomach pitching more at the thought of revealing why she sat beside him than at the actual bumpy ride.

So how did one do this?

Probably should just say it. Rip the bandage off. Pull the knife out. He probably already suspected why she'd come.

As they turned onto the adjacent path, Shelby took a deep breath and said, "I'm pregnant."

How will John react to the news? Find out what's in store for these two—and the baby—in THE SWEETEST SEPTEMBER by Liz Talley, available August 2014 from Harlequin® Superromance®.